FRIENDS WITHOUT
BENEFITS

Praise for Dena Blake

A Country Girl's Heart

"Dena Blake just goes from strength to strength."—*Les Reveur*

Unchained Memories

"There is a lot of angst and the book covers some difficult topics but it does that well. The writing is gripping and the plot flows."
—*Melina Bickard, Librarian, Waterloo Library (UK)*

"This story had me cycling between lovely romantic scenes to white-knuckle gripping, on the edge of the seat (or in my case, the bed) scenarios. This story had me rooting for a sequel and I can certainly place my stamp of approval on this novel as a must read book."—*The Lesbian Review*

Where the Light Glows

"From first time author Dena Blake, *Where the Light Glows* is a sure winner."—*A Bookworm's Loft*

"[T]he vivid descriptions of the Pacific Northwest will make readers hungry for food and travel. The chemistry between Mel and Izzy is palpable."—*RT Book Reviews*

"I'm still shocked this was Dena Blake's first novel...It was fantastic...It was written extremely well and more than once I wondered if this was a true account of someone close to the author because it was really raw and realistic. It seemed to flow very naturally and I am truly surprised that this is the author's first novel as it reads like a seasoned writer."—*Les Reveur*

By the Author

Where the Light Glows

Unchained Memories

A Country Girl's Heart

Racing Hearts

Friends Without Benefits

Visit us at www.boldstrokesbooks.com

FRIENDS WITHOUT BENEFITS

by

Dena Blake

2018

FRIENDS WITHOUT BENEFITS

ISBN 13: 978-1-63555-349-9

This Trade Paperback Original Is Published By
Bold Strokes Books, Inc.
P.O. Box 249
Valley Falls, NY 12185

First Edition: December 2018

CREDITS
Editor: Shelley Thrasher
Production Design: Stacia Seaman
Cover Design by Melody Pond

Acknowledgments

I cannot say enough about the awesomeness of the Bold Strokes Books team. You take care of all the details and make my job so much easier. My thanks, always, to Len Barot and Sandy Lowe. Without the two of you, my books would never reach the world.

To my editor extraordinaire, Shelley Thrasher. You are the best editor EVER. You tirelessly sift through my mistakes and repetitions while still making me feel as though I've created a masterpiece.

Thanks to the BSB family for taking me in and treating me like one of your own. I truly feel the love. You are all the best.

To Kate for loving me. You're my lobster. To Wes and Haley for saying "that's awesome, Mom" whenever I have a new idea. To my family, always know that each one of you is very special to me. I love you.

To my readers, thanks for being there to pick up this book and cheer me on when I'm writing the next. You'll never know just how much that makes my day.

To the girl next door who never knew…

CHAPTER ONE

Dex Putnam stood helplessly as the kiss of death spiraled toward her. The voices around her stilled and everything slowed. She was frozen, unable to move from its path. Faces blurred as people moved in slow motion toward her. The crowd gasped as the impact forced the breath from her chest. Flickers of red clouded her vision, and she fell backward to the floor. She raised her head, blinked, and stared at the crimson splattered across her chest. This was the end of life as she knew it.

She looked up at the stunned faces around her as they watched the lethal scene unfold. It was like a grisly scene in a horror movie, and Dex was in the middle of it. They seemed to all know her life was over too.

She closed her eyes and took in a deep breath, shrugging off the pain slashing through her heart. She'd made the wrong choice in getting out of bed this morning, the wrong choice in coming here, and so many wrong choices in her past. The look on her sister Juni's face reflected her pain as she dropped to the floor next to her and stared into her eyes.

"Dex. Dex!" Juni's voice echoed in her head as she watched the crowd close in around her. "It'll be all right." Juni wiped away the tear beginning to form in Dex's eye.

It wouldn't be all right. Nothing would ever be right again. Regrets swam in her mind as Juni stood and offered Dex her hand. She gripped it and hauled herself to her feet, staring into the bride's vibrant blue eyes as the roses from the crimson wedding bouquet that cursed her chest fell to the floor. Dex had just watched her soul mate promise herself to another. Now she'd been branded as the next in line to marry. Considering who held her heart, that was a long shot.

"Come on, love." Juni tugged Dex's arm. "Let's get you a drink."

She couldn't get to the bar fast enough. Twenty or more women rushed toward the bouquet left abandoned on the floor as she and Juni walked away. It was like a Black Friday mob scene, and all these women lived and breathed for those flowers. The bouquet indicated they would be the next to wed, but not Dex. She'd never intended to marry anyone other than Grace.

Juni leaned against the bar and shouted to the bartender, "Gin and tonic, and a shot of whiskey."

Dex smiled at her sister, who knew exactly what she needed. She glanced back at several women who seemed to be checking her out, then turned back to the bar and groaned. "Why does this shit always come my way?" She picked the remaining crumpled rose petals from her cleavage and then stared at her boobs for a moment. She did have a nice set to offer but didn't let them out in public often. She tugged on the semi-strapless gown—a ridiculous pink chiffon, eighties-throwback prom dress ten times too expensive for something she'd never wear again. If anyone dared to present such an atrocity on *Project Runway*, Heidi Klum would be running after this designer onstage screaming "You're out" at the top of her lungs.

"What? The bouquet?" Juni shook her head. "Grace nailed you on purpose. Now every girl at this wedding will be after you. I've written your number on a stack of napkins by the cake to make it easier for them to get in touch."

"I'll make sure to get a burner phone in the morning."

"Come on, Dex. Have a little fun tonight. It's the beginning of the rest of your life without Grace."

"Easier said than done." The bartender returned with their drinks, and Dex downed the shot. "This day started out crappy and has only gotten worse." She glanced back to the dance floor, where the remnants of the bouquet lay scattered about, taunting her. Then she caught a glimpse of Grace dancing with her new husband. "Another shot, please." She slid the glass back to the bartender, and he poured.

"Take it easy, little sister. It's gonna be a long night."

She nodded. "Just doing a little prep for it." She threw the next shot back and blew a breath out through her nose as the alcohol burned its way down her throat.

As of three hours ago, Grace would take on the name of Richardson, not Putnam, as Dex had hoped for all those years. She glanced at Grace and Brent, who'd moved to the dance floor. The two of them had met at the gym, where Grace worked the front desk, and Brent had been a customer. Dex had been forced to listen to all the details from the start of this fairy-tale romance. Grace seemed to be gloriously happy since she'd met Brent, and it crushed Dex to know she hadn't been the cause of that happiness. She was destined to be left on the sidelines of Grace's love life, as only a spectator while it played out.

She'd loved Grace Standish since childhood, and Grace was well aware of her feelings. Her life would've been perfect if only Grace had loved her the same way, but she didn't have the tiniest interest in women. Dex was the first one to admit that Grace had loved her more than any woman, other than her sister, but that was the extent of their relationship. Friends without benefits…forever. At least the kind of benefits Dex wanted.

The music had slowed, and suddenly Dex felt arms around her waist. She closed her eyes and took in the sultriness of Grace's voice as she whispered in her ear, "It's our song. Come dance with me."

The slow beat of James Taylor's "You've Got a Friend" pulsed in Dex's head. Of course their song couldn't have been a fast one.

The alcohol was beginning to take effect, and the song hit Dex square in the chest as she held Grace in her arms. Grace was more gorgeous tonight than she'd ever seen her. Thick black lines traced her eyelids, and Grace's indigo eyes danced with a sparkle she hadn't noticed before. Grace tugged her closer, and Dex melted into her and took in her essence. With their cheeks pressed together as they danced, the sweet smell of hyacinth filled her head and she warmed all over. She wanted to be part of Grace's happiness, just not in a spectator sort of way. This was too much. She pushed back and stared into Grace's eyes, the compassion she saw in them overwhelming. Grace knew exactly what she was feeling, and Dex thought she might be feeling a little of it herself.

The music morphed into Queen's "You're My Best Friend." Grace seemed as though she wanted to say something but didn't know what. Dex held her gaze for a moment before she smiled and kissed her lightly on the cheek. Then she immediately threw Grace out into a twirl and pulled her back against her. It should be clear to anyone watching that they'd danced together many times before, and they had. They moved in sync as Dex spun Grace around the dance floor, smiling and laughing while her heart was bleeding from within. Dex refused to ruin Grace's big day no matter how much it hurt.

"Happy Together" by the Turtles played next, and then Brent was there, pulling Grace away from her. The torment in Dex's heart raged as her hand slipped from Grace's and she danced away from her. The classic A-line, V-neck sleeveless Chantilly lace dress made her into the most perfect princess, only no lost glass slipper would be found tonight. Time to go back to the bar.

Juni sidled up next to her. "I saw you dancing out there. Showing off your stuff." She swiped the shot from in front of Dex and drank it. "Looking good."

"Since when do you drink whiskey?"

"Just taking one for the team." Juni grimaced as she dipped her head to get Dex's attention. "You okay?"

"Hanging in there."

"Awesome." Juni glanced at the table where she'd been sitting. A man there seemed to be keeping her attention. Dark hair, nicely trimmed beard, wearing a dark-gray suit and tie. At least he knew how to dress for a wedding. That was a plus.

"Who's that?" Dex asked.

"His name's Josh. He owns Crushed Beans, the coffee shop on the corner by the bookstore."

She glanced at the table where Juni had been sitting. She seemed to be keeping Josh's attention as well. "Learning all the ins and outs of coffee brewing?"

"And more," Juni said with a huge grin.

"Wouldn't that be awesome if the Bookworm merged with Crushed Beans?" Dex pulled her mouth in to a grin and widened her eyes. "Then you could call it Crushed Worms."

Juni slapped Dex's shoulder. "That's absolutely awful. I haven't put all my sweat into that business to destroy it with one shitty logo."

"I thought it was rather unique." She chuckled louder than the line probably deserved.

Juni had bought the bookstore years ago, when the place was on its last legs. The owner had been taking any profit he made and putting it into his lifestyle rather than the store. He'd let the inventory run down so much that by the time Juni bought it, the store was barely seeing ten customers a week. Dex had helped her clean, paint, and reshelve the space, and now Juni had turned it into a thriving business.

Dex eyed Josh for a few more minutes, and he waved. "Well then. You'd better get back to him."

"You sure you're okay?"

"Spectacular." She tapped her fingers on the bar.

"Okay. I'll be back in a bit." Juni sped off toward the table where Josh was waiting.

"How about Beans and Books?" she shouted after her.

Juni swung around, pulled her eyebrows together, and mouthed, "Stop."

When Dex caught sight of Grace again, she was absolutely stunning, glowing as the sunset rained through the plate-glass windows behind her. She remembered the night she'd realized Grace knew she was in love with her. They were on a girls-only skiing trip in New Mexico with some of their other friends. They'd reserved a vacation rental with only four rooms for eight of them. Dex had immediately regretted going when she found out she and Grace would be sharing a room with only one queen-size bed.

After dinner the first night, even though she was exhausted from skiing, Dex had fidgeted and talked endlessly in an attempt to prolong getting into bed with Grace. She'd thought once Grace fell asleep, she'd just sleep in the chair or lie on top of the blankets. Hazy eyed, Grace finally got out of bed, kissed her on the cheek, and said very sweetly that she knew how she felt about her. Then she took her by her hand and told her to come to bed. Grace snuggled up behind her and spooned her all night long. It was the closest she'd ever been to the woman she loved, a night filled with palpable pleasure and unrelenting pain. She shook the memory from her mind as she waved at the bartender and pointed to her empty glass.

CHAPTER TWO

Dex's head throbbed, and her mouth felt like someone had stuffed it with cotton. How much had she drunk last night? Things had become hazy, and she'd lost count after the fourth shot. She remembered Juni walking away from the bar and bringing her back a plate of food soon after that. *Or was that later?* Then a glass of water had appeared on the bar in front of her. A fuzzy image of a pair of light, silvery-blue eyes and curly black hair flashed through her mind. *Wait. Was that Juni?*

The sun was seeping through her eyelids. She rolled over, smashed her face into the pillow, and took a deep breath to settle her stomach. She immediately blew it out and took in another breath. The soothingly sensual scent of jasmine and orange blossom filled her head. *Not my pillow!* She snapped her eyes open and scanned the room. *Not my bed!* Bolting up, she squeezed her eyelids closed to force away the constant thumping behind them and fell back to the warm place she'd come from. Her stomach needed to settle before she moved again. *Open bars at weddings are never a good idea.*

Lying perfectly still, she let her sight stretch to the far edges of her peripheral vision. Muted beige and sage-green colors covered the walls, a nice combination with the white molding. Whose bed was she in? Not hers. Not Juni's. *Fuck!* Who had taken her home? Clearly she'd blacked out at some point last night.

Listening for sounds of someone in the house, she didn't move for what seemed like an eternity, until her bladder couldn't take it anymore. Noting her lack of clothing as she sprinted into the bathroom, she wondered if she'd had sex last night. She didn't feel like it, but it wouldn't be the first time she'd pleased another woman without gaining any gratification of her own. She really needed to stop drinking.

As she came out of the bathroom, she spotted her bridesmaid dress hanging from a hook on the wall. A stack of clothes sat on the chair next to it, a pair of flip-flops on the floor, and a note written on pink, rose-patterned paper lay neatly on top of the T-shirt.

In case you'd rather not be seen in public wearing this retro-piece-of-shit dress from the wedding.

The sentence was punctuated with a wink face at the end. "Oh my God." She shook her head. Obviously she'd spilled many of her thoughts to this woman last night, whoever she was. She pulled on the T-shirt and yoga pants, which were a bit snug, before she slipped through the doorway and crept down the hall. It led to a decent-sized living area with a breakfast bar that peered into the kitchen. She'd hoped to avoid an uncomfortable reunion with whomever she'd latched onto last night, and it seemed she'd been successful.

On the kitchen counter she found a bottle of water as well as half a loaf of bread next to the toaster, accompanied by a jar of what appeared to be homemade jam. *And* another note.

You'll find coffee in the pot. Drink the water, make some toast, and use plenty of the crystallized ginger jam. Trust me. It'll make you feel better. I'm going to work and won't be back until this afternoon, so no need for you to rush. Make yourself at home. There's a smoothie in the fridge to take with you. Oh, and you're more special than you realize. Don't let some spoiled straight girl make you think otherwise.

The words resonated in her head in a low, throaty voice, which sent an unexpected zap of excitement through her. Apparently she'd poured her heart out to a sweet, lovely stranger last night, and she had no idea who she was.

After pouring a cup of coffee, she sank down onto a barstool and scanned the room. A couch with a square, wood, apothecary-type coffee table in front of it anchored the room. A long console table against the wall centered a beautiful beach watercolor. The table was topped with a few candles and decorative items, but no pictures. Across from the couch stood a square entertainment center, which housed a medium-size flat-screen TV and several other items in each of its cubes. Again, no pictures. Apparently, she wasn't going to get a glimpse of her benefactor even from a photo. The whole place was modern but homey, somewhere Dex felt comfortable. This entire experience gnawed at her memory and comforted her all at once. Something must have gone right with the woman who lived here, but she had absolutely no recollection of her.

Her stomach grumbled, making it loud and clear that she needed to eat. She dropped a couple of pieces of bread into the toaster and picked up the small jar of jam from the counter. Even though Dex had noticed ginger jam in her local health-food store, she'd never tried it before. She usually took the safe route with peach or strawberry. She was actually looking forward to tasting it, even in the state she was in. It certainly couldn't make her feel worse.

She covered the toast with a light coating of jam and settled in on the couch. The ginger was surprisingly good—sweet with a hint of pear and a nice zing that snuck up on you. She took the blanket from the corner of the couch and covered her legs before she pulled open one of the coffee-table drawers in search of a remote to click on the TV. Oddly, she felt extremely comfortable here. She had no idea why she wasn't hauling ass out of this place right now. Someone could come home any minute and catch her happily snuggled up in their wonderfully warm fleece blanket just like it was her own home.

After finishing her toast, she watched two episodes of one of her favorite sitcoms that had been recorded on the DVR, another sign the woman was something special. She pulled open the refrigerator and noted the array of healthy foods—including yogurt, chicken breast, fresh vegetables, and cheese—on the shelves. It seemed as though the woman could cook. She found the smoothie front and center with another note.

Take the jam. I have more. Feel better.

A cute smiley face punctuated the end of the sentence. *Oh my God, this woman is a dream.* A flash of creamy white skin popped into her head, along with the subtle scents of jasmine and orange blossom. Dex couldn't help but think that if she'd met this woman under different circumstances, they would've at least been friends, possibly more. But no way could she live down last night's fiasco. She was sure she'd made a fool out of herself, crying over a woman she'd never have. *Love sucks.*

❖

Dex hustled off the train and walked the short distance to Juni's house. A plastic shopping bag swung from her hand as she paced. She'd rolled the chiffon bridesmaid dress up and stuffed it inside. Otherwise, carrying it on the L would've been embarrassing at best. The huge bow attached to the single shoulder strap had made it difficult, but she'd managed to get it all in the bag. Thankfully, she'd never have to wear the pink monstrosity again.

She knocked on Juni's door, and it swung open almost immediately.

"I've been worried about you. Your phone is going straight to voice mail."

She held up her phone. "Battery died sometime last night."

Juni didn't hide the once-over she gave her. "You look like shit."

She pushed through the door. "Thanks. I needed that."

"Whose clothes are those?" She'd apparently noticed the Northwestern University T-shirt.

"They're on loan." She dropped her bag on the couch and headed to the phone charger on the end table.

"From who?"

"The girl I went home with last night."

Juni's eyes went wide. "You went home with someone?"

"Can we postpone the interrogation until after you get me a cup of coffee?"

"Oh, sure. Be right back."

Dex settled in on the couch. She didn't have the slightest idea what she was going to tell her sister about the woman from last night, simply because she couldn't remember a thing about her...except her low, throaty voice and the wonderful scent of jasmine and orange blossom. She held her wrist to her nose and took in a breath. She'd found the fragrance on the bathroom vanity and sprayed a hint of it on herself. Even if she never saw her again, she really wanted to remember this woman.

Juni returned with a mug of coffee and set a plate of buttered toast in front of her. "This will help settle your stomach."

She tilted her head and smiled. "I don't really feel bad. I already had some toast and this awesome ginger jam this morning." She reached in her bag and took out the jar. "It settled my stomach instantly."

Juni took the jar from her hand. "She makes jam?"

"Apparently, and it's really good. She left it for me, along with a note, when she went to work." She purposely omitted the fact that the woman wasn't there at all this morning.

Juni raised her eyebrows. "Well, she's awfully trusting to leave you alone in her house." She sat down next to her and wiggled her fingers at her. "Let me see the note."

That was very true. Dex would never leave someone she'd met only once alone in her home. She pulled the notes from the bag, along with the crumpled bridesmaid dress, and handed them to Juni.

"Is that your dress?"

She nodded. "I'm going to donate it to the Glass Slipper Project." Thanks to her parents' constant volunteerism when she was a child, Dex had seen the good it had done in helping others and did a fair amount of volunteer work now as an adult, as did Juni. Her brother, Ranny, did more taking than giving. The Glass Slipper Project was one of her favorite organizations. She loved to watch young girls find the dress of their dreams for prom night each spring.

Juni set the notes on the table, jumped up, grabbed the dress, and hung it from the door. "Really?" Juni laughed as she pulled at the bottom. "Do you think anyone will wear it?"

Dex took a swallow of coffee before she answered. "Not with that huge fucking bow on it, but they can alter it. In any case, it'll be free to a girl who needs it. And, best of all, it'll be out of my hands."

Juni went back to the notes. "Wow. She left you three?" She passed them between her hands, examining the pink notepaper.

She nodded. "She's very sweet."

Juni unfolded the first one and read it. "She's a fucking miracle. Where is she?" Her eyes widened as she went through them. "*Who* is she? I want to meet her *now*."

She contemplated telling Juni a lie, but Dex wasn't very good at lying, and Juni could always see right through her. "I have no idea. She didn't sign her name, and if she told me what it was last night, I don't remember. That's all a big blur." Not that she'd ever see her again anyway.

"So you don't remember anything about her?" Juni's shoulders dropped.

She took in a deep breath and shook her head. "Except the wonderful way she smelled." She put her wrist beneath Juni's nose, and she inhaled the scent. "And I think she had curly black hair." She sighed. "And silvery-blue eyes."

"Damn it, Dex." Juni tossed the notes onto the coffee table. "You picked a hell of a night to get stinking drunk."

"Under the circumstances I think it was appropriate." She picked up the notes and stared at them. "And forgivable."

"Fuck."

"Did you see me with anyone in particular last night?" Someone had to have noticed her. Surely the mystery woman hadn't thrown a bag over Dex's head and sneaked her out the back door.

Juni shook her head. "No. After I left you at the bar, I danced a few times. When I came back you'd disappeared. I thought you'd gone home."

"I probably should have, after the fourth shot." She'd known she should be happy for Grace, but seeing her in such joy had only made Dex want to deaden the pain. So that was exactly what she'd done, and now the love gods were punishing her for doing it. Would a day ever come when she could bring someone new into her heart? She certainly hoped so, but not today. Her mystery woman was a complete blur.

"Humph. You were only on number two when I left you."

"So you didn't bring me any food?"

"Nope. I was busy rounding up my own entertainment for the night."

"You met someone, right?" She did remember that. Dark hair, dark beard, nice smile, and very attentive to Juni.

"Well, I didn't really *meet* someone. I already knew him. We just got friendlier."

"Who was it again?"

"Do you remember Josh? He owns Crushed Beans on the corner by the bookstore. I pointed him out to you last night."

"Oh yeah." She tilted her head. "Crushed Worms. That worked out for you?"

"Yes." Juni grinned. "And stop saying that. He heard you last night." A flush of pink took over Juni's face.

"Look at you? All flustered. He must be something special."

"I am not flustered."

"Uh, yes. You are. Your cheeks could rival the pink on this notepaper right now." She dipped her head toward the notes on the coffee table and grinned. "Does he know Brent and Grace?"

"Apparently he's good friends with Grace's brother. He doesn't get out much because of the business but had taken the day off. So, he dragged him along."

"Wow. That's certainly serendipitous."

A huge smile spread across Juni's face. "Right?"

"So it was a good night." Dex smiled. "*I poured my heart out to a complete stranger.*" The low, throaty voice resonated in her head again, and she shook it from her thoughts. "And *you* started something new with the coffee man."

Dex's phone chimed multiple times as it came to life. "What the hell? Was I that popular last night?"

Juni shrugged. "I may have called you once or twice…and texted a few times."

"Three calls and five texts."

"I was worried. You should be glad I didn't call the police." She tossed a couch pillow at her, and it hit Dex in the head. "Ooh. Maybe the mystery girl got your number and called."

The pillow shot to the head didn't faze her. "No such luck." Or maybe it was lucky that she hadn't called. Dex could only imagine what she'd thought of her last night.

As she scrolled farther she skipped over a message from her mother that she knew would be a couple of paragraphs long and found one from Grace that had come through after midnight. Her stomach churned. What could Grace have possibly wanted to tell her last night? She scrolled to it first, touched it with her finger, and read it.

I was disappointed that I didn't get to see you when I left tonight. We're on the plane, getting ready to take off. I'll see you in a couple of weeks. Ciao xoxo.

The expression on Dex's face must have given it away. Juni

snatched the phone from her and read the message. "That bitch. On the plane headed to Greece. On her *honeymoon*. Why can't she just leave you alone?" Juni shot to her feet and tossed the phone onto the couch.

"I'm her best friend. Who else is she going to text?" She spoke with a sad sort of irony.

"She shouldn't be texting *anyone*. She's with her new husband."

Dex picked up her coffee cup and stared into the blackness filling it. The color matched her mood as she remembered how just a week ago she'd reminded Grace how she felt about her, then asked her to reconsider her upcoming marriage to Brent. Dex had thought she might have a chance when Grace had pulled her into an embrace, held her tight, and whispered that she'd never been closer to any other soul besides Dex. They were indeed soul mates. But then she let go, and with shimmering, vibrant blue eyes, Grace told her she was sure about her decision to marry Brent.

That was that. No more hope. The decision had been made. Truthfully, she knew Grace had made it a long time ago. Dex had watched Grace fall in love with Brent and had wallowed in self-pity. She hadn't even thought about finding someone to fall in love with herself. She'd held out for a half-court bucket shot, and the ball hadn't even grazed the rim.

"You need to stay far away from that woman when she gets back." Juni nudged her shoulder with her hand. "Are you listening to me?"

"Yeah, sure. I will." She glanced at the time on her phone. "I need to get going," she said as she pushed off the couch.

Juni's expression went blank. "Oh, I rented the best *Star Wars* movies. I thought maybe we'd hang out here and have a movie marathon." She was clearly disappointed.

"Can't. I have to go draw out a design in Roscoe Village." She took her cup into the kitchen, rinsed it, and put it in the dishwasher. Working would keep her mind off yesterday, and Grace.

"But it's Sunday." Juni drew the word out slowly.

"Um, rich people have their own schedules."

"Since when do you conform to them?"

"That's how I make the big bucks." She swiped the notes from the coffee table, slipped them into the waistband of her yoga pants, and took off to the door. "And why aren't you minding the books at the store today?"

Juni followed her. "I left Grant in charge."

"Letting the new guy run the shop. That's a big step." Dex tugged open the door.

"He can handle it. It's been six months since he started, and he's picked up things extremely well. That brain of his absorbs everything." Juni leaned against the open doorjamb and watched Dex carefully. "I thought this might be a tough day for you."

Dex couldn't stand the sad puppy-dog face she gave her. "First three in the series?"

"Duh." Juni had definite opinions about *Star Wars*, and Dex happened to agree with her on this one.

"How about I go home and shower, take care of my appointment, then pick up a pizza and see you in a few hours."

The smile that spread across Juni's face melted her instantly. "Sausage and mushroom?"

"Heavy on the cheese."

"Yay!" Juni jumped up and down and clapped her hands wildly.

Dex fell against the door and laughed. "I love you, sis."

"I know." Juni smiled and pushed her out the door. "Now, hurry back."

CHAPTER THREE

Her knuckles had barely hit the door before Grace pulled it open. Dex stopped cold at the sight of the woman glowing in front of her. She was dressed in jeans and a coral V-neck sweater that brought out the color of her electric-blue eyes spectacularly. The deep, warm, bronze tone now blanketing her usually creamy, white skin made her eyes even more vibrant than usual. Grace was definitely even more beautiful than Dex remembered. This "absence makes the heart grow fonder" crap was for the birds.

Grace flew through the doorway and pulled Dex into a hug. "Oh my God. It's so good to see you."

"You too," Dex said as Grace took her hand and pulled her into the living room. The two weeks were up, and Dex's heart was finally beginning to feel normal again. Just the sight of Grace blew that out of the water. She'd made three new bids on landscapes and five on outdoor Christmas decorations while Grace was gone. The holiday season would soon be here, and she'd be too busy to listen to her heart pining away for Grace. The message had been clear, and Dex had promised herself to move on. She didn't see any sense in holding out for something that was never going to happen. But at this moment, with Grace holding her hand, everything she'd told herself seemed iffy. She needed to get ahold of her emotions, suck it up, and hear all about Grace's honeymoon.

"Have a seat, and I'll get you some coffee."

Dex did as she was told and slid into the oversized leather couch. The house seemed different somehow since Dex had been here last.

But nothing had really changed. She guessed she just hadn't noticed how Brent's furnishings were making a presence in the living room. The comforting man-cave and contemporary-modern styles mingled surprising well, with chocolate and cream colors filling the room. The modern end tables accented the furniture nicely. Dex was sure the whole mix was an agonizing sacrifice for Grace.

"What happened to your couch?"

She tilted her head toward the hallway. "In the office."

"Why?"

"Because this monstrosity couldn't fit through the doorway."

"Meant to be the center of attention, eh?" Dex ran her hand across the worn leather. "This is nice, though."

Grace rolled her eyes. "For now," she said, handing her a mug of coffee.

She sipped at the steaming brew that Grace had made especially for her. Grace was a tea drinker, always had been, but since Dex liked coffee, she'd learned to make it.

"Here," Grace said as she handed her a shopping bag and sat on the couch next to her. "I bought this for you at one of the galleries."

Dex set her coffee on the table before she reached into the bag. "Wow." She admired the small, white, kneeling female sculpture. "Grace, this is…"

"I know how much you love contemporary art." Grace dunked the teabag in her mug up and down a few times.

"Really, Grace. This must have cost a fortune. It's too much."

"No, it's not. You helped me a lot with the wedding." She searched her bag for something else and handed her a string of what looked like marbles. "Plus, you're my best friend."

Dex held it up to her neck and scrunched her nose. "A necklace?"

Grace laughed. "Definitely not. They're komboloi beads, made of amber. They're supposed to keep your hands busy."

Dex held up the colorful string and let the marbles slide from side to side. "Oh. Nice."

"Or you can just hang them on the wall." Grace stood and reached for her hand. "Leave that and come with me." She pulled her into the office, sat in the chair behind the desk, and motioned for Dex to get the one in the corner. "I've got so many pictures to show you." She put the camera card in the slot on the side of the laptop and fiddled with the mouse. "Do you know how to make these play?"

Dex stood up. "Here. Let me drive."

Grace switched seats with her, and Dex had the pictures pulled up in just a few clicks.

As Dex clicked through the massive number of pictures, her stomach started to twist. She saw pictures of Brent and Grace at the beach, Brent and Grace at dinner, Brent and Grace at the Acropolis.

"Can you help me make a slide show out of these?"

"Sure. Do you have some music you want to add to it?"

"Yes. We bought some in Greece that would be perfect." Grace ran out of the room and returned quickly with a CD.

While the pictures copied to the laptop, Dex opened iTunes, and they created a playlist with the songs that Grace chose from the CD, as well as a few other favorites. When they were done, Dex merged the music with the pictures and let the show run, watching the entire trip again. Dex tried to seem interested as the pictures slid slowly across the screen, but the first time had been enough for her, and she zoned out during the last ten minutes. When the slideshow ended, she found Grace sitting forward in her chair staring at her.

"What's the matter with you?" Grace said and pressed her lips together. "You don't seem interested in my trip at all."

Dex sat up and moved closer to the laptop. "What? Of course I am. I was just gauging the timing between pictures." In all honesty, it was hard enough to see Grace's spectacular honeymoon and all their happiness the first time, and she just couldn't take watching the love in them again.

"Are you sure that's all?" She pulled her eyebrows together. "I hope you're not mad about me leaving without saying good-bye. I tried to find you."

Dex shook her head as she saved the slideshow and shut down the laptop. Dex had made sure that didn't happen, and it was probably good that Grace hadn't found her, or she might have spilled her guts in front of Brent. It probably wouldn't have made the slightest bit of difference to Grace, but Dex would've regretted it for life.

"Did something happen while I was gone?"

"No. Everything's fine." But everything wasn't. She and Grace would never be fine again. Their relationship had changed significantly. Dex felt like an outsider now.

"Okay, then." Grace reached for her hand. "Come on. I'll show you some of the other things I bought." She led Dex into her bedroom.

Dex stopped and scanned the room. It looked like an F3 tornado had come into the room, swept everything up into the air, and let it crash to the floor again. Clothes and bags were strewn everywhere.

Grace seemed to notice her surprise. "Sorry. I haven't had a chance to do anything since we got back." She picked up a few stray pieces of clothing and tossed them into a pile on the floor next to the bed before she opened her unpacked suitcase perched on the upholstered bench at the bottom of the bed. She took out several bikini bathing suits, held them in her hand, and closed her eyes.

"The beach was covered in golden sand, and the water was such a clear blue, the ocean floor was visible as far as I could see." Her eyes sprang open. "I could see my feet the whole time I was in the water, and the snorkeling was perfection. One day we were surrounded by little yellow-finned fish. I have no idea what they were, but it was surreal, Dex." She smiled as though she were reliving every moment. "And the sunbathing was wonderful. We had our own umbrella and lounge chairs every day. I thought of you a lot. Two women were under the umbrella next to us the whole time we were there. They'd just gotten married too."

She was quiet for a moment, and Dex wondered what exactly she'd thought about her while she watched the women. She took in a breath. "We swam in the ocean at sunset every night and then had drinks on the beach. We even made love on the beach." She tossed the bathing suit into the pile. "But that's totally overrated." She lowered her voice and raised an eyebrow as though she was telling her the secret location of a sunken treasure ship. "Sand gets just about everywhere."

An image of Grace and Brent on the beach together flashed through Dex's head, and she shook it from her thoughts.

"And dinner was absolutely fabulous every night." The pile of clothes on the floor was growing as Grace tossed more onto it. Thong underwear, sexy lingerie, short shorts, tight tops, and bikini bathing suits with minimal cover-ups. Clearly Grace had hoped for a very intimate honeymoon.

"You did that every day?" Dex knew it was an unrealistic dream, but she'd love to find a woman she could share an adventure like that with someday. Not Greece. That was totally ruined for her now, but possibly Italy.

Grace slapped the empty Louis Vuitton suitcase closed and rolled her eyes. "Not really. Brent drank a little too much once or twice and had a pretty good hangover the next day." She dug through one of the beach bags that sat on the chair in the corner of the room. "But it was good most of the time." She scrunched up her face. "They have some crazy customs. You wouldn't believe what they did for us this one night. They brought grapes and flaming cheese before dinner. Then they danced around the table and gave me this beautiful necklace." She pulled it out of the bag and tossed it to Dex.

She caught it with one hand and let it swing from her fingers before she examined it. It was a pendant of Rhea, the goddess of fertility and motherhood. Dex had always been fascinated with mythology. She was sure Grace had no idea what the necklace represented.

"With roast lamb, baked pasta, champagne, and candlelight, it was the perfect dinner. I must have gained at least ten pounds on the trip." She glanced at her ass, at Dex, and then her ass again.

"Nah. You look great." Dex gave her the expected response. She might have gained a pound or two, but whether she had or not, the vacation would justify Grace's next few weeks of crazy workout sessions. The weight would be gone in a week. Grace had a great job at the gym and got her membership for free. She'd gotten Dex in free on her friends-and-family discount as well, but she didn't have time to go. Besides, she already did enough heavy lifting on the job.

Grace was fortunate, like Dex, in that way. They could pretty much eat whatever they wanted and still stay slim. She glanced at the medallion again and wondered if that would still be the same once she and Brent started having children.

"Are you and Brent going to have kids right away?" *Oh, shit. Did I really ask that?*

Grace snapped her gaze back to Dex and blinked rapidly. The question must have surprised her as well. "Who said anything about kids?"

"I just thought now that you're married, having a family would be the next step."

"I have a lot of things to do before *that* ever happens. I'm not done having fun yet." Grace was more like her mother than she liked to admit. Only her parents had created their family and then continued to do what they wanted while they left them in the care of relatives or babysitters while they went on their adventures.

Dex tossed the necklace back to Grace. "Then you'd better not wear that. Rhea is the goddess of fertility and motherhood."

The necklace slapped against Grace's chest as she moved her hands and let it fall to the ground. "Oh my God. No wonder they told me to always wear it." She picked it up between her thumb and index finger as though it were a dirty diaper and carried it to the trash.

Dex chuckled. "Since when are you so superstitious?" Dex swiped it from her fingers and hung it on the corner of a picture frame on the dresser.

"Since I don't want babies right now. Do you think it's easy keeping this figure? I can't imagine getting back into shape after pushing a little human out." She closed her eyes and shivered. "No. Absolutely not."

"Hang on to it. You may change your mind someday."

"Yeah, maybe." She shook her head. "But not right now."

Her expression made Dex think all wasn't perfect in the world of Grace and Brent. "You okay?"

"Yeah. I'm fine. I just didn't know I was going to be forced into such domestic bliss so quickly." She stared at the pile of dirty clothes on the floor from their honeymoon. Grace had always gotten an allowance from her parents and sent her clothes to the cleaners weekly.

"Do you need help with laundry?"

"Would you mind? I have no idea what to do with it. Brent says we need to rely on his salary now and put whatever money my parents give us into savings."

"Sounds like a good plan to me." Dex picked up the pile of laundry and started sorting through it. "You need four piles. Whites, lights, darks, and delicates." She pointed to a pair of Brent's boxers. "You're in charge of those."

❖

When Grace got back home, Brent was in his usual position slouched half-mast, relaxing on the couch in front of the TV with his feet on the table. She took a breath and calmed herself before proceeding into the house.

"Hey, babe. Where you been?" Brent said as he quickly removed his feet from the coffee table and replaced them with the bowl of salsa that had been sitting on his chest.

"I went to the grocery store. And I saw that." She hated it when he put his dirty shoes on the table.

He gave her a big grin. "I thought Dex was coming over today."

Grace melted. She loved it when he smiled at her that way. "She did, but then she had to get back to work." She forced herself not to run into the kitchen to grab a towel and cleaning spray to wipe down the table. It still irritated the fuck out of her when Brent put his feet on the table. He knew she hated it, yet he kept on doing it.

"I bet she's glad you're back?"

"I really don't know if she is." She tossed her purse onto the couch. "She acted totally uninterested when I was telling her about our honeymoon."

"She probably had enough of it from all the pictures you sent her. Looking at someone else's trip is kind of boring." He held up a bag of tortilla chips. "Want some?"

"It is not." She plucked a chip out of the bag and dipped it in the bowl of salsa. "And I didn't send her that many."

"You sent her a bunch." He glanced up from the TV for a minute. "Maybe she needs to go out and have some fun once in a while. She never really goes out with anyone, does she?"

"No. Not really." She went into the kitchen and set the bag of groceries on the counter. "I thought she was going to fall asleep halfway through the slideshow."

"You made a slideshow?" He popped up off the couch and followed her. "Like on the laptop?"

She pulled her eyebrows together. "Yeah." She took a couple of beers out of the six-pack before she put it in the refrigerator. Brent took them from her hand and screwed the tops off.

"That's awesome, babe. I want to see it." He handed her one of the bottles and sprinted to the office.

"Really?" She didn't think he'd be this excited. She put the milk and vegetables into the refrigerator and the rest of the groceries in the pantry. She wasn't in the mood for shopping today and had only picked up a few essentials. She'd go again later in the week.

"Of course." He came back out with the laptop. "I'll hook it up to the TV."

"You can do that?" Dex hadn't done that earlier. Another sign she wasn't interested.

"Yep. Where is it?" He plugged the cord into the laptop before he grabbed her by the waist, pulled her to him, and kissed her. "I can't wait to see my beautiful bride in our tropical paradise."

"Stop." Grace laughed and felt all warm inside. "She put it on the desktop."

"We need to go back next year," he said as he clicked the file and expanded the slideshow to full-screen. Grace sat on the couch, and Brent flopped down next to her and put his arm around her shoulder. "Showtime."

CHAPTER FOUR

Dex had finished her last bid for the day and had ended up at a bar that she frequented from time to time with her work crew. It was a locals' place that didn't have a lot of flair. Warm, medium-colored walls and dim accent lighting in the ceiling accompanied by flattering pendant lights gave the place a comfortable dusky atmosphere at all times. A couple of pool tables were in the back, a jukebox lined the wall, and close to a dozen wooden tables and chairs sat in the center of the bar.

The visit earlier with Grace had been a little too much for her to take. She sat down and ordered a beer and a shot of whiskey. Nothing was going to scrub all the honeymoon details Grace had shared from her mind. Specifically, the details of their lovemaking session on the beach, no matter how much sand was involved.

The bartender slid the drinks in front of her. She drank the shot and forced herself to concentrate on the burn as the alcohol went down her throat. It was a momentary distraction from the pain plaguing her heart.

Fuck! Why can't I get her out of my head? She took a pull on her beer. *Because she's gorgeous and you're in love with her, dumbass.* After knowing Grace preferred men for all these years, why was she *still* in love with her? The knot in her stomach reappeared as she remembered how she'd asked Grace to reconsider marrying Brent the week before the wedding. The understanding in Grace's eyes was clear when Dex had choked out her reasons, professing her love. Tears had immediately streamed down Grace's cheeks, and Dex hadn't been able to contain hers for much longer than Grace had. After capturing Dex in an embrace, they stood together through moments of silence and plenty of tears from both of them.

Then Grace had released her, regained her composure, and told Dex that, although she loved her and that she would be in her heart forever, she was *in love* with Brent. Her feelings for him outweighed her feelings for Dex. It had been a huge blow. Dex had been holding out for a miracle to sweep in and change her destiny, but it hadn't happened. Grace had made it perfectly clear that her feelings for Dex were purely platonic, and Dex had been forced to accept the reality of their situation. The day had been very emotional for both of them, but their conversation had been necessary to provide closure for her to move on, and now that was exactly what she intended to do.

The place was unusually full tonight, with a surprisingly mixed crowd of people. The sexy blonde that slid onto the barstool next to her was the last person she'd expected to appear. The place had the usuals, as well as a few newcomers, but hot, single women weren't usually among them.

"Can I buy you a drink?" the blonde asked.

"I'm good. But thanks." Dex turned and stared into her startling blue eyes. They were almost the same color as the royal-blue dress she was wearing, which fit her curves spectacularly.

"I hope you don't mind if I sit next to you. This is my first time here."

Dex smiled. "You're fine. So you've really never been here before?"

"No. Just had a late appointment over this way and stopped in for a drink afterward. It's been a rough day, and I'm not in the mood to get hit on."

Seemed reasonable enough. "I understand that." Dex lifted her beer in acknowledgment. "I think you're pretty safe here." She took a drink.

"I'm Candice," the woman said as she shifted sideways in her barstool and crossed her legs.

"Dex," she said, trying to keep her focus on her beer instead of the long, lean legs displayed next to her.

"Dex," Candice repeated. "That's an interesting name."

"You have no idea," she said, shaking her head.

Candice raised an eyebrow. "Care to elaborate?"

Dex explained to her about the unconventional way her parents came up with her name. They seemed to pull names out of a hat for their children, naming them after sports figures, movie titles, or the evergreen they'd seen or been planting during the timeframe each child had been conceived. Candice just happened to be from Canada and had actually heard of the obscure Canadian hockey player Dex had been named after. She also chuckled a bit about people getting it confused with the serial killer TV show. Dex hadn't gone into the torment she'd endured in her youth because of it. That would be too much information for a lovely stranger. With a brother named Ransom, after a crime-thriller movie, and an older sister named Juniper, her life could be pure hell at times. She'd been tempted more than once to take on a serial-killer persona just to get the kids off her back.

The one Candice really found funny was her sister's name, Juniper. From that point on, she began naming everyone who sat down at the bar after evergreens. The tall girl with the skinny legs and gobs of wild hair became Willow. The short, dark-haired guy with the flattop next to her became Hedge. The funniest was a tall, stocky, red-haired, bearded guy she named Redwood. He definitely fit the description. Dex had to admit it was kind of fun and had unexpectedly lightened her mood. The bartender smiled and shook his head. He'd overheard the whole conversation and seemed to be equally amused as he continued sliding drinks in front of them.

After a few more drinks, they left the bar, and Dex walked Candice to her car. At least that was her intent, but they ended up in the darkened parking lot with Candice pressed against her Ford Explorer, making out instead. She reached inside Dex's jacket and tugged her closer, indicating she was more than willing to go further. When Dex reached under Candice's dress and found no panties, only wetness between her legs, she took what was offered, sliding her fingers through the silky warmth and pushing them inside. Candice clutched her, pressed her face into Dex's shoulder, and moaned. Dex closed her eyes and found herself imagining Grace in her arms, under her hands, clenched around her fingers as they worked her arousal, and she went with it. Candice came hard against Dex's hand before she slumped into her, apparently satisfied.

"That certainly turned my day around." Candice smiled and glanced up into Dex's eyes. "Can I get your number?"

She was sweet and beautiful, but Dex found it hard to make eye contact with her. "I don't think that would be a good idea. I mean…" She swallowed hard. "This and earlier inside was really fun. There's just someone else I'm not quite finished with yet." *What an asshole I am.* Dex expected Candice to be upset. She couldn't believe what she'd just done. But Candice only smiled and seemed to understand, and she didn't press.

"Okay, then." Candice took out a piece of paper and pen, wrote her number down, and handed it to Dex. "In case you ever get over her…Or just need a distraction."

Dex smiled and nodded. But that wasn't going to happen. She'd just imagined making Grace come while she was actually touching Candice. She'd never be able to do that again with Candice without seeing Grace's face.

Candice kissed her on the cheek, climbed into her Explorer, and drove off. Dex went back inside the bar and called her sister. She was in no shape to drive.

❖

Dex picked up the pizza box from the seat as she slid into the car. "Sausage and mushroom?"

Juni nodded. "I thought you might need a little food chaser with that alcohol. Tough day?"

She nodded. "I just couldn't stand to listen to Grace go on about how wonderful her honeymoon was. Plus she showed me hundreds of pictures of her absolute bliss."

"So, you thought you'd go tie one on again?"

"No. I thought I'd have a drink. Maybe meet someone new."

"Did you?"

"Actually, I did."

"Then why am I picking you up?"

"She was really nice and all. I just wasn't in the mood to put on my sparkling personality." She didn't want to tell Juni the whole story. She wouldn't be judgmental, but she would be disappointed in her for having random sex in a parking lot. Dex was doing a good enough job of being disappointed in herself on her own. Thinking about Grace while she was fucking other women wouldn't get Grace out of her head any faster. It would just cement her further into it.

"Seriously? She probably could've helped you purge Grace from your heart. If not that, at least your mind for a night."

Definitely didn't help. "What if I'm not ready to do that?"

"Dex." Juni let out a heavy sigh, the kind she always gave Dex when she was about to tell her what she should be doing instead of what she was actually doing. "When are you going to stop pining after her? That ship has clearly sailed out of the harbor and into the deep, blue sea of Brent."

Fuck Brent. "I need you to be supportive, Juni. This is really hard for me."

"I'll support you in anything you want except your obsession with Grace." Juni pulled into the driveway and threw the car into park. "I'm not even sure what the hell you see in her. I get that she's pretty, but come on, Dex. She's way too self-absorbed." She shifted sideways in her seat. "She's back for just one day, and look at what she's done to you already."

She *was* a fucking mess, for sure. "She brought me a gift," she said softly as she stared at the pizza box in her lap. "A sculpture. She actually went to a gallery and bought it. She hates art, but she went there for me."

"Dex." Another sigh. Juni shook her head slowly. "Please don't make anything out of that." She took her hand. "She told you who she wants."

"Don't you think I fucking know that?" She yanked on the door handle and got out of the car. "I've relived it in my head a thousand times since that happened. I can't just cut her out of my life, Juni. She's always been a big part of it." She slammed the door and took off toward the house.

When she was a child, Dex had endured endless teasing about her name, thanks to her unconventional parents. She'd been branded by her cruel classmates after a show about a forensic pathologist turned good-natured serial killer. Then Grace had moved to town. Grace was cool, sweet, and beautiful. She remembered the spring day vividly, just as though it had happened only yesterday. Grace wore a pink-flowered dress covered by a white cardigan sweater. Dex had been instantly captivated by her, as were so many of the other kids at school. They listened when Grace talked. Grace had told them Dex was an awesome name, and no one, not even the popular kids, challenged her. From that day on, Dex and Grace had been best friends for life, even after Dex had discovered she loved Grace, and Grace had discovered she loved boys.

Juni killed the engine, jumped out of the car, and followed her. "You're not kids anymore, Dex. She's moved on, and you need to as well." Juni blocked the doorway to get her attention. "You need to start doing what you want instead of whatever the hell Grace thinks is important at the moment. You can't keep putting yourself on the back burner for her or anyone else. You need to be happy." They stood for a few minutes in silence until Juni reached over and squeezed Dex's arm. "Come on. Let's go inside and eat. I'm sure there's something on Netflix we can binge-watch."

In light of the late hour Dex and Juni had gone to bed last night, and with the science-fiction borderline horror show they'd been binge-watching, Dex had thought she might have nightmares. To the contrary, the dream she was wrapped up in this morning sent warm feelings through her, and it had nothing to do with Grace. It revolved around a beautiful woman with dark hair, beautiful silvery-blue eyes, and a deep, throaty voice. It seemed the girl she'd met at the wedding was playing a vivid role in her unconscious thoughts. She still couldn't make out her face clearly, but her eyes sparkled as she laughed and smiled at her like Dex was the most entertaining girl in the universe. For a short time during the dream, Dex had actually felt like she was that girl. She lay in bed with her eyes closed, trying to remember more about the mystery woman. Then Candice from the night before at the bar popped into her head, and she felt miserable again. The evening had all been good until the last part, when Dex had let her imagination get the best of her.

"Good morning, princess." Dex opened her eyes to see Juni coming into the room grinning. "How are you feeling today?" She flopped onto the edge of the bed.

"Like I've been thrown in front of a bullet train and then dragged a thousand feet under it." That was putting it lightly.

"Well, I guess the pizza wasn't enough to absorb all that alcohol." Juni chuckled and handed Dex the cup of coffee in her hand. "I made scrambled eggs and toast." She popped up and headed to the doorway. "Come on, before they get cold."

Dex pulled on her jeans and sweater, then went to the bathroom. She stared at herself in the mirror and threaded her fingers through her hair. *This is a shitty look for you, Dex. No more alcohol.* She splashed some water on her face before she went to the kitchen and slid into the chair adjacent to Juni.

"Thanks for this." She picked up her fork and dug into the eggs.

Juni slid a piece of paper in front of her.

She flipped it around. "What's this?"

"It's a pros and cons list."

"About Grace?"

Juni nodded. "I thought it might be helpful."

It was a pretty extensive list. She read the first couple of lines and noticed the disparity in lengths between the two columns. "Well, if I didn't already, I certainly know how you feel about her now."

"Yep." Juni gathered her backpack and headed toward the door. "I'm not going to lie. She's not good for you, Dex." She opened the front door before she said, "You want to have coffee later this week? You can meet Josh."

"Sure." There was nothing she'd love more than watching her sister's blooming romance when Dex knew she'd never have the one she wanted.

"We can go over your additions to the list then."

"That's assuming there are any."

Juni pulled her eyebrows together. "I'm sure I missed at least one or two."

"Okay. That means you're buying."

"Whatever. I'll call you." Juni walked out the door.

Dex glanced at the list.

Cons
Self-centered
Shallow
Controlling
Manipulative

Pros
Protective

"Just one pro? Seriously?"

She couldn't argue with most of the cons, but she had some things to add to the pro column that Juni probably wouldn't agree with. She took a pen from the jar on the counter and started writing. Juni would find that out soon enough.

CHAPTER FIVE

B rent carried in what was left of the groceries from the car as Grace began putting everything away. She'd picked up only a few things to get them by yesterday and needed to get more in order to start being domestic during the week. She didn't really mind doing that, but she just had no idea where to begin cooking on a daily basis. Her skills in the kitchen were severely limited. She'd become really good at one or two dishes because Brent liked them. Other than that, she'd never prepared much beyond grilled cheese and tomato soup. Maybe a baked chicken breast to put on salad here and there. But that was it. She'd definitely have to call Dex for reinforcement.

"When did food start costing so much?" Brent said as he emptied the bags.

"It always has. You've just never gone to the store with me before."

He held up the small bottle of truffle oil and studied it. "What the hell is this stuff? Gold?"

"I use it to make that mushroom pasta you like." It was one of her favorites, too, and one of the dishes she knew how to make.

"Jesus. I thought pasta was cheap." His voice rose. He obviously thought the truffle oil was a waste of money.

"Not that kind of pasta."

"We need to start watching what we buy since we'll be surviving on our salaries." He turned to Grace and nonchalantly said, "Maybe you should find a different job."

"Why would I do that?" Grace still did the books at the gym as well as manning the counter a few times a week, and Brent was on the fast track at a prominent advertising firm in Chicago. They'd never discussed her changing jobs before.

"You've already found the man of your dreams." He spread his arms out in front of himself.

She rolled her eyes. "I'm not leaving the gym. I get to work out for free, and so do you now. Besides, you know I have plenty of money in savings."

"That's money your parents gave you, not ours. It needs to stay in savings."

"What difference does it make where it came from?"

"It makes a difference to me." He was tossing groceries into the pantry now.

"You're just being ridiculous." She grabbed the package of spaghetti from his hand. "And stop throwing the food around unless you want to use a spoon to eat your pasta."

"Just being practical. We need to live on what we make. That money is only for an emergency."

What the fuck? "So you're telling me I can't buy truffle oil anymore?" That kind of thing was not going to fly with her. No one told her what she could and couldn't do. Not even Brent.

He immediately stopped putting groceries away and took her in his arms. "Of course you can, baby. We just need to keep better track of our money, especially if we're going to renovate this place."

Instead of buying a new place to live, Brent had moved into Grace's house just before the wedding. It was comfortable and also located in Wicker Park, a booming neighborhood known for its live music, restaurants that had become prevalent in the James Beard award-winning dining scene, and countless art galleries. The way real estate was skyrocketing in the area, they both thought it was a good idea to keep the house and refinance to put it in both their names.

"And go back to Greece, or Spain, or Italy." The excitement in his eyes was clear, and Grace found it hard to stay irritated.

Every day was new and interesting with Brent. He made her want to do things she'd never dreamed of before. She never had to worry that everything they did would go perfectly, just as he said they would. Brent was definitely a planner, and Grace loved that about him.

He gave her a quick kiss on the lips and went back to the groceries. "So, I was thinking about what you said about Dex yesterday."

"What'd I say about Dex?" She had no idea what he was talking about.

"That she might be lonely."

"That wasn't me. I think you said that."

"Either way. I think Dex needs someone," Brent said as he put the cereal in the pantry.

"You mean someone other than me?"

"Unless you're sleeping with her. Yes." He leaned up against the counter. "Do you think she's on Tinder or Plenty of Fish?"

"Hell, no. Dex would never sign up for something like that. At least not without telling me." She couldn't remember Dex mentioning anything about dating anyone in particular over the past year or so. Dex seemed to have had the sporadic hookup here and there, but nothing serious. She'd always had to pry those tidbits of information out of her. It all made sense after their heart-to-heart the week before the wedding.

She wasn't surprised, but she hurt realizing how deeply Dex felt and knowing she couldn't return those feelings. Since Grace had first realized, when they were younger, how much Dex cared for her, she'd done her best not to encourage any thoughts that they could be together in any other manner than as friends. She'd grown up with Dex, and they'd had so many awesome adventures together, experiences that were happy, sad, and sometimes strangely fun. She truly loved Dex, but not with the same sexual intimacy she needed from Brent.

"We should help her find someone." He glanced over his shoulder as he slid the milk into the refrigerator.

"Dex can find her own dates."

"You want her to be happy, don't you?" He raised his eyebrows and stared at her.

She hung the reusable grocery bags on the peg by the door in the garage. "Of course I do." But it had to be with someone just as special as Dex. Was there anyone else out there like that? "I guess I could probably round up one or two women to set her up with." She had no idea who to call. Dex was pretty much her only gay friend.

He turned and swept Grace into his arms again. "You don't sound so sure about that."

"Oh, no. I've got this." She said it like it would be the easiest thing in the world to achieve.

"Great. I can't wait to meet her."

She closed her eyes and melted into him. Brent wasn't the guy who simply nodded and agreed with everything Grace said. She liked the fact that he pushed her like no other person ever had, but he had no idea how huge the task was that he'd just put on her to-do list.

❖

Grace flipped through her phone as she sat behind the front desk at the gym. She'd spotted one of the part-timers who'd had to go on break. She waved at one or two regulars as they came through the door, but it was early in the afternoon, and the gym wasn't super busy yet. The fake profile she'd set up for Dex on Tinder had been hot and sweet. She'd been surprised at the number of responses she'd received. Single tall, dark, and beautiful women must be rare on the site because Dex was in big demand.

She swiped to the left multiple times. "Too cute. Too sexy. Too hot." She halted the automatic motion taking over her thumb when she came upon the first candidate. "Okay, Ms. Elena Edwards." She stared at a picture of the woman with blond hair highlighted with magenta and read through the profile. Twenty-five, hates sports, loves reality TV, and doesn't eat anything but red meat. "Bingo." She swiped the profile right, and the message page popped up. She quickly typed.

Hey, would love to meet you for drinks this week if you're up for it.
A message immediately returned with, *Def, where and when?*
Byron's, 8pm Tonight.
See you then, gorgeous.

Grace hit the End button and continued with her search. *Ugh.* This was going to be easier than she thought.

All the women seemed to be conveniently available on short notice, which might have been telling. But availability was the reason they were on the dating app in the first place. After scheduling the last one, she slipped her phone back into her bag, completely satisfied with her choices. If these didn't work out, she'd introduce her to her friend Ruby as a last resort.

The part-timer came back from break, and Grace headed back to the office to wrap up a few last-minute things before heading home to change for her dates. She hadn't told any of the women what she was doing. If they had a problem with it, they'd definitely be out of the running.

❖

Grace slid into a barstool at the end of the bar she and Brent frequented often, said hello to the bartender, and ordered a club soda with lime. She wanted to be perfectly coherent while talking to these women tonight. Dex was her best friend, and she didn't want anyone to hurt her. She planned to be extra careful to make sure that didn't happen.

She'd set up three meetings, total, over the span of four hours. She'd given herself time to have a conversation with each of the women to see how they would fit with Dex as well as to weed out any catfish crazies or possible serial killers. None of them would be a perfect fit. In fact, she was sure Dex would absolutely hate them all, since she wasn't a fan of blind dates. But she'd told Brent she'd try, and that's exactly what she was doing.

Grace tapped impatiently on the bar as she waited on the barstool for Suzanne, the first woman, to show up. She was late, which wouldn't be acceptable on a date with Dex. She was always punctual and expected others to be as well. When she finally appeared, Grace noticed she was prettier than her profile picture, which might present a problem. But after watching her at the bar, she knew it wouldn't. Suzanne was skeptical at first, but when Grace held up two one-hundred-dollar bills and offered to pay for the meal, she'd agreed.

As soon as Elena, the second woman, saw the two hundred dollars, she was all in. She was weirdly happy to be in on the surprise and thought it would be an awesome adventure.

The third had bailed before she'd gotten halfway through her explanation. So, she was left with only two, quirky and desperate. That would have to do for the first two dates. The third would be Ruby, who Grace knew would turn out to be nothing more than a good time if Dex would let it happen.

CHAPTER SIX

It was almost seven when Dex left her car with the valet at Mastro's Steakhouse. She'd made it with a few minutes to spare. She would've liked to be early, but Grace had FaceTimed her while she was getting ready and objected to her first outfit of slacks and a sweater, stating it was too casual. They'd gone through half a dozen more before she'd approved the off-the-shoulder, wide-leg black jumpsuit with minimal accessories. Grace had suggested a drop necklace and earrings as well, but Dex wasn't a fan of jewelry unless it meant something. Plus, she'd been on the cusp of being late and had been forced to drive like a madwoman to keep from giving Suzanne a bad impression. Nothing was worse than sitting in a bar alone waiting for someone.

The place was super classy with a sort of old-school, club charm, and as Dex stood waiting at the hostess stand, she noticed diners coming and going. She definitely would've been underdressed in the first outfit she'd chosen. The maître d' directed her to the bar where she and Suzanne were to meet. As she entered, she'd found that her clothing choice had been somewhere in the middle of most of the diners'.

She spotted Suzanne sitting at the end of the bar. Her red coat was slung over the back of her chair, just like Grace had said it would be. As Dex moved closer, her legs came into view, and she immediately thought the night might be promising. The woman was wearing a black slip dress accented with a long silver drop necklace fashioned with a large turquoise stone at the bottom.

"Hi. Suzanne?" Dex asked as she approached.

"And you must be Dex," Suzanne said as she gave her an obvious once-over and smiled. "Would you like a drink?" She held up her tumbler filled with a small amount of amber liquid.

"Sure." Dex slid into the barstool next to her. "What do you have there?"

"Scotch old-fashioned." Suzanne glanced around the bar. "It seemed to be fitting."

"Agreed." The bar was decorated with dark walls and leather bar stools and chairs.

Suzanne smiled and nodded. "Would you like another?" She waved down the bartender. "Another old-fashioned for the lady, and I'll have the same."

They talked mostly about the restaurant and its history while they drank in the bar. It wasn't long before the maître d' came to get them and led them to their table. Dex settled up with the bartender for the second round of drinks. Suzanne had already taken care of the first.

After they were seated, the three-piece ensemble playing in the bar resonated faintly through the restaurant as the waiter brought them menus and recited the specials. Suzanne ordered a nice bottle of Cabernet and asked for sauce recommendations for her bone-in rib eye. The waiter spouted a number of choices that included Gorgonzola sauce, peppercorn, and Oscar, which included asparagus and lump crab meat. She opted for plain, while Dex went with the Gorgonzola and was glad she had. It was like liquid blue cheese dripping from the steak.

The evening went smoothly, and they had sporadic bouts of conversation about art, current events, and even politics during the meal. The conversation was engaging, but Dex would've probably enjoyed Suzanne's company much more if she hadn't been looking at her reflection in the mirrors mounted on the wall behind Dex the entire time. Dex felt like the most concealed player in a game of hide-and-seek as Suzanne kept a steady gaze on herself. Dex found herself staring out the window to avoid the discomfort of watching the woman watching herself or whomever else she'd been keeping an eye on all throughout dinner. Reminder, never have a first date at this place again.

The waiter brought the check, and Suzanne quickly snatched it away from Dex. "I've got this."

"But—"

"No. I've really enjoyed your company tonight. Maybe we can do it again."

The most common words spoken after a date and never followed through. Oddly, Dex felt good about receiving them this time. Suzanne was way more interested in her own reflection all night than she had been in Dex.

❖

Eager to hear how Dex's date went the night before, Grace raced into the diner. She spotted her sitting in a booth near the window and hurried right to her. She took off her coat and tossed it into the booth before she flopped down onto the seat. "God, it's getting cold outside," she said as she crossed her arms and rubbed her shoulders.

A waitress followed her to the table. "What can I get you to drink?"

Grace glanced up at her. "Just water, please." And then she gave her attention to Dex. "So, how was it?"

Dex bobbed her head from side to side. "The food was spectacular. The girl, not so much."

"What do you mean, not so much? Suzanne has an awesome personality, she's well-read, beautiful, and a great conversationalist." Out of all the women Grace had interviewed, she'd thought Suzanne would be the best fit for Dex, which was the exact reason she'd set her up as the first date. If they'd hit it off, Grace had planned to cancel the other two.

"That may be the case, but—"

"Ready to order?" The waitress set a glass of water in front of Grace.

Dex peered up and smiled. "I'll have the special."

"What's the special?" Grace asked.

"Meatloaf, mashed potatoes, and green beans," the waitress said.

Grace grimaced. She needed something lighter. "Do you have any salads?"

"On the back." She flipped the menu in front of Grace to the other side and pointed to the salad section. "Chef, Cobb, spinach, all the usuals."

"I'll have the chef salad."

"Blue cheese, thousand island, balsamic, or ranch?" She spouted the words out quickly, as though she said them a hundred times a day.

"Is the ranch homemade?"

The waitress nodded. "Fresh daily."

"On the side, please."

"You got it." The waitress went back behind the counter and shouted the order to the cook.

Grace took a drink of water and let her attention veer back to Dex. "Now what were you saying about Suzanne?"

"She may be beautiful, have an awesome personality, and be spectacularly well-read, but she was a whole lot more interested in herself than me. Probably where the well-read factor comes into play."

"What? That's ridiculous." She hadn't come off like that to Grace at all. She'd found her interesting and downright engaging. "I know she has a strong personality, but she never seems to run out of things to talk about."

"Strong isn't the word I'd use. She was intriguing but, like I said, much more interested in herself than me." Dex shifted forward. "Did you know they have mirrors on the walls behind the tables there?" She pointed to the wall above her. "Like right up above them."

"Honestly, I don't remember." It was possible, but it had been a while since Grace had been there. The place was pricey, and she'd stopped doing pricey when she'd started seeing Brent steadily.

"Well, they do. I thought she was going to end up with food all down the front of her a couple of times because of them. I don't know how someone can manage to eat while watching their reflection. You'd think that would be difficult, it being backward and all."

"Nooooo," Grace's voice rumbled. "She didn't."

"Yep. She kept a pretty good eye on herself all through dinner. I'm pretty sure she didn't absorb anything I said into that self-absorbed brain of hers."

The waitress came back with their food, slid their plates in front of them, and asked if they needed anything else. They both declined and she went on her way.

"Dex, I'm so sorry."

"It's okay. The night wasn't all bad. We had a couple of drinks in the bar first. There weren't any mirrors in there." She let out a laugh and grinned.

"I promise the next one will be better. She's an artist." She forked a piece of turkey along with some lettuce and ate it.

"Oh? What kind of artist?"

"Paint. Oils, watercolors, abstracts, portraits. You name it, she paints it." At least that's what Elena had told her. She hadn't asked to see any of her work. "I think she has some things hanging in one of the galleries in Wicker Park."

"Cool. They have a lot of contemporary there. Do you know which gallery?"

Grace shook her head while she chewed another bite and swallowed. "You know me and art. In one ear and out the other." It was true. Grace had no interest in art whatsoever. Taking her to a gallery anywhere was the worst kind of punishment.

"Hopefully, this one will be better company than Suzanne." Dex took a bite of meatloaf and washed it down with a drink of water.

"She will be. I promise."

"How's married life?"

"Not much different than before, except now I have to save all my money."

"Really?" Dex raised her eyebrows. "What's up with that?"

She rolled her eyes. "Brent wants to keep the money I get from my parents for trips and special occasions." She pushed what he'd said about unnecessary spending from her thoughts.

"Sounds reasonable."

Grace pursed her lips. "But I like shopping and going to lunch."

Dex's forehead creased. "Did he say you couldn't do that?"

"No, not directly, but I know that's what he meant."

Dex scooped a forkful of mashed potatoes and held it up in front of her. "Maybe you should have a conversation with him to clarify that point."

"I'm not ready for that yet. If he says he wants me to stop shopping and I disagree, we're going to fight." She let out a sigh. "We just got married, and I don't want to do that."

"Hiding it from him isn't good either, Grace. He'll find out sooner or later. Just have a conversation with him and work it out before it gets too big."

Grace tilted her head back and forth. "You're probably right. I'll talk to him about it."

They finished eating and fought over the check, and as usual, Grace won out. She didn't care what Brent said about saving the money she got from her parents. It was her money, and she was going to spend it on what she wanted. Today she wanted to spend it on Dex.

CHAPTER SEVEN

Dex cursed the heels she'd worn tonight, although they were the perfect height for her flowing black pants and form-fitting coral blouse. It had been a while since she'd worn them, and she'd forgotten how they squished her toes. Every step she took from the parking lot to the restaurant reminded her with a short shot of pain. She couldn't wait to get seated.

As soon as she was inside, she spotted Elena pacing in front of the hostess stand and glanced at her watch. Fifteen till—she was early. She took in the view as she moved closer. Elena had worn a chic black dress with a rounded neckline and long fitted sleeves. When she paced away, Dex noted the full skater skirt that had been hidden by the long emerald coat hanging over her arm. She followed the line of her lean legs to see a pair of single-strap, open-toed stiletto heels. She winced. It was a little cold for them, but they certainly increased the hotness of the outfit. She'd also met a fair amount of artists in her day, and the style didn't fit the majority of them.

Elena swung around just as she approached, and Dex was met with a dazzling white smile and caramel-brown eyes. She was quite a bit younger than Dex had expected.

"Hi, I'm Dex." She smiled and offered Elena her hand. "Sorry if I kept you waiting long."

"Elena," she said as she took her hand and gave it a soft squeeze.

After a moment or two of chitchat, Dex caught the bar in her peripheral vision. "Do you want to get a drink first?" The bar was crowded and they'd have a hard time hearing each other, but she felt she needed to offer.

"The table is ready. How about we get a bottle of wine?"

"Sounds wonderful." Dex let the maître d' know they were ready to be seated, and after a few moments he led them to their table. Maple & Ash was a sort of contemporary steakhouse that spawned sheer, forest-like, silk dividers from the ceiling to accent the leather decor, which created an elegant dining experience. The menu included traditional dishes that were morphed into modern cuisine using a wood-fired oven.

As they made their way through the tables, most of them were already full, as usual. They were seated quickly in a quiet little corner in the back. Dex would've preferred to be in the middle of the restaurant where there was more light and distraction, but Grace had set up the reservation, and Dex knew changing tables would mean close to an hour wait.

When the waiter came to take their drink orders, they decided to skip the cocktails, and Dex ordered a nice mid-range bottle of merlot on which they'd both agreed.

Once the waiter left them alone, Elena started the conversation. "What do you do for a living, Dex?"

"Custom landscaping."

"That sounds interesting. Do you create your own designs?"

"Most of the time. Sometimes people come to me knowing what they want already."

"Seems to me either way would be expensive. That must be challenging. I mean creating something affordable and eye-pleasing."

"It can be, depending on the greenery they choose. Some trees can cost thousands of dollars. The ones who can afford those kinds of trees usually want irrigation as well." Elena's brows came together, creating a tiny crease between them, so Dex continued. "You know, underground sprinklers, soaker hoses, drip irrigation for the flower beds."

"Sounds messy."

"Yes. It's definitely messy, but it's the best way to go for people with time constraints."

"And you do that yourself?"

"With my crew. We have a ditchdigger that creates the path for the PVC pipe. After we lay that and connect it all together, we put on the sprinkler heads." Dex stopped when she noticed Elena's attention swerve to the couple at the next table. "But you don't really want to hear about that."

Elena's gaze snapped back to Dex. "Do you take the winter months off? I wouldn't think you'd have much business then."

"Starting in mid-October through December, I create and install holiday displays for homeowners."

Elena's eyes lit up. "Like those beautiful decorations in Oak Park?"

She nodded. "I have a pretty good clientele in that area. I do most of those."

"Wow. You're an artist in your own right."

Dex had always thought her art skills showed up more in landscaping than in Christmas lighting.

"How do you come up with your ideas? I'd love to use those vibrant colors to bring more vision into my art."

"I can't really explain it. There's no formula. They just show up in my head." Dex took the opportunity to steer the conversation to Elena. "So, tell me about your art?" Grace had mentioned a few things about it already, but Dex had been waiting for the right moment to move the conversation from herself.

"I dabble in paint here and there. Mostly abstracts." She picked up her fork and set it on the inside of the rest of the silverware and then seemed to absently continue moving each piece in a repetitive pattern.

Dex hoped she wasn't making her nervous. Most artists enjoyed talking about their work. "Modern art is my favorite. Are you being shown anywhere currently? I'd love to see your work."

"I'm kind of in a slump right now. Nothing's really selling."

"Oh. Grace told me you had art in a gallery in Wicker Park."

"That's been sold." She glanced away. "I need to replace it with something new." She sipped her water. "I'm actually on the hunt for a new studio. You know, one of those lofts where I can paint and sleep all in the same space. Do you know of any place like that?"

"Not off the top of my head, but I can keep an eye out for you."

"That'd be great. Even a guesthouse in Oak Park or anywhere close would work."

The waiter approached the table, and Elena relaxed into her chair. "Welcome to Maple & Ash," he said as he handed them the dinner menus. He then proceeded to recite the dinner specials before leaving them to read over their choices.

Elena focused on the menu as she opened it. "Everything here looks so yummy."

"You've never been?"

Elena shook her head. "My first time."

"Oh, well, you're in for a treat. I've only been here a few times myself, but I've never had anything that wasn't absolutely wonderful." Dex had been here exactly twice before with Grace.

When the waiter reappeared to deliver the bottle of wine and take their order, Elena went first. "I'll start with the Maple and Ash Wedge, then the Twenty-Eight Day Dry-aged Bone-in Rib Eye with the Roasted Autumn Vegetables and the Whipped & Buttered Potatoes." She handed the waiter her menu. "Oh, and can we start with a Prawn Fire Roasted Seafood Tower?" She glanced at Dex.

The amount of food she'd ordered had just settled into Dex's head. "Sure," she said. *What the hell?* She'd ordered enough food to feed them plus the tables on each side of them. Why not top it off with seafood?

"And for you, miss?" the waiter asked.

She closed her menu and said, "I'll have the I Don't Give a F*@k." That was a completely appropriate menu item for the way Dex felt right now.

They didn't mention landscaping or art again, and the discussion eventually drifted to idle chitchat about the weather, the Cubs, the impending holidays. Those subjects seemed to keep the dialogue going smoothly. Dex hadn't wanted to go further with the housing situation or she might end up with an unwanted houseguest.

By the time Dex had finished the last of her meal, Elena had barely touched half of hers. Not a surprise. Who could actually eat that much food? The waiter had boxed up the remainder to go and packed it neatly in a bag. Dex was quite sure this would be Elena's dinner for the rest of the week.

When the waiter returned to ask about dessert, Dex quickly waved him off. She refused to throw another dime into Elena's take-home feast. She'd been there before, unemployed and too broke to even afford a loaf of bread, let alone groceries. Dex hadn't held it against her until the bill came and Elena had disappeared into the bathroom for a full fifteen minutes—a clear sign she wasn't kicking in on the check. Dex was sure that if Elena hadn't had to leave the food at the table to go to the restroom, she probably wouldn't have even come back to the table. Dex had planned to pay but didn't like to be pushed into it. It made up for the free dinner she'd received from Suzanne on her last date.

Neither one of them indicated they would do this again. Clearly Elena had done this before and had merely suffered through the night with Dex for the free meal. Dex was going to kill Grace for this one.

❖

Grace couldn't wait to hear about Dex's date last night. She'd told her on the phone that it hadn't been all bad, that Elena had shown some interest in Dex's landscaping business and light-stringing work as well. But when Dex had reversed the conversation posing the same questions to Elena, she'd talked only briefly about her art and the galleries in Wicker Park and nothing specifically about pieces she was showing anywhere else, which was strange for an artist. She mentioned that Elena had described a couple of her pieces, but when Dex had asked her where she could view them personally, she'd given vague answers. A huge red flag had gone up for Grace when she'd heard that. What artist didn't like to talk about her art? Dex had said that Elena seemed to skirt around each one of her questions and would then point the conversation back to Dex.

When Grace pushed through the front door, she spotted Dex waving at her from the back. She could feel the cool air whoosh through the small, hole-in-the-wall Mexican restaurant as the door closed behind her. They'd decided to meet there because it was a gem frequented by mostly locals.

She shrugged off her jacket as she strode through the small aisle and tossed it into the booth before she slid in. "Okay. Give me the full story." She sure hoped there was more than Dex had already told her. At least better than the last date. Even though she didn't see a perfect fit for Dex in Elena, she'd thought they'd at least have something in common.

"The night started well. We had some good conversation."

Oh no. This didn't sound good. "I see a *but* coming."

Dex smiled and held up a finger. "As I said on the phone, Elena peppered me with questions about my job most of the night."

Okay. That was a good sign. "She was interested in what you do. That was nice, right?"

"It was." Dex nodded. "She genuinely seemed interested as I told her about the different kinds of plants, trees, and shrubs that work well in the area. And she seemed to have some horticultural knowledge as well. I think she said she'd taken a class in college. But when I went into irrigation, her eyes glazed over."

"You didn't. Dex, I told you just minimal information about your job. Women don't want to hear about digging in the dirt."

"She asked." Dex raised her eyebrows. "When I mentioned that I also do Christmas-light decorating in the off season, she perked right up. Said that she loves Christmas lights and that's one of the places she gets her inspiration." She threw her arms in the air. "The vivid colors bring vision to her art." Dex's tone lilted up and turned playfully sarcastic.

"She really said that?"

"Yep." Dex flattened her lips into a cocky grin.

"Christmas lights? That's what inspires her?" Grace stared blankly at her, trying to visualize the whole scene. She hadn't seen that coming. Her conversation with Elena had been perfectly normal, and she seemed very knowledgeable about art.

"Remember when we used to lie under the Christmas tree for hours staring up through the branches?" Dex asked. "They were mesmerizing."

"Yeah, but I never once thought about them as art."

Dex blurted out a laugh. "She showed me some of her art." Dex picked up her phone and pointed at it. "On the big screen, no less. From what I saw, the wildly abstract paintings seemed to already have plenty of vibrancy. I doubt she has anything hanging in Wicker Park, and I think I may have paid her food bill for the rest of the week."

What the…I gave her money for dinner. "Oh my God, Dex. I'm so sorry."

"It's okay. I got off free on the last date."

"But Maple and Ash is pricey. This one probably cost you enough for both."

"It did. But that's fine. She can be my pay-it-forward for the week. My parents would be proud."

Grace chuckled. "They would be, indeed."

Date number three had been up for discussion, but Grace had convinced Dex that she'd have a great time with Ruby. It would be an adventure for Dex if she'd just let it play out. Ruby and Grace had met at the gym years ago. She was the best personal trainer they had and the only woman she felt comfortable with coaching Brent during their budding romance period. Ruby strictly dated women and was also fun and spontaneous. She wasn't opposed to becoming intimate on the first date and leaving it at just that, fun.

Chapter Eight

Gibsons Bar & Steakhouse was one of Dex's favorite restaurants in Chicago. It had a comfortable atmosphere and burgers to rave about. As she got out of her car she glanced down at her black skinny jeans and riding boots, wondering if she'd dressed too casually for the night. Her leather jacket covered the scoop-neck goldenrod T-shirt she wore. She'd chosen the color because Grace had told her more than once that it brought out the sunbursts in her eyes.

Ruby had said in her text that she was familiar with Gibsons, so Dex had hoped she'd worn jeans as well. She wasn't disappointed when she spotted Ruby sitting at the bar dressed in the leather jacket they'd both agreed to wear as an identifier, a powder-blue V-neck underneath, and skinny maroon pants that led to black stiletto-heeled boots. Her auburn hair swayed across the middle of her jacket as she turned to survey the bar.

As soon as Ruby spotted Dex over her glass, she set it on the bar and charged her way. Dex was taken off guard by the strength of the hug she was swept into.

"It's so great to meet you. Grace has told me so much about you," Ruby said with a huge smile.

That was a first. Neither one of the other dates had mentioned anything about Grace. "It's nice to meet you too." Grace had given her minimal information on Ruby other than she was fun.

"The table should be ready shortly." Ruby took Dex's hand, led her to the place at the bar where she'd been sitting, and pulled out a barstool. "I saved you a spot. Do you want a drink?"

The woman was like a whirlwind as she waved the bartender over and then slid onto the stool next to Dex.

"What can I get you?" the bartender asked.

She noted the copper mug in front of Ruby. "I'll have a Moscow Mule."

Ruby smiled. "Good choice. They're excellent here."

They'd finished their drinks and ordered a second round before they were seated. Dex had learned a lot in their short time at the bar. Ruby and Grace had been friends for a little over a year. They'd met at the gym where she and Grace both worked. Ruby had fully admitted that she'd hit on Grace a number of times. They both agreed Grace was sizzling hot and it was a shame that she was straight. It was funny how a little alcohol made that reality hurt less, or maybe Dex was just finally getting over her.

They both ordered burgers and, at Ruby's suggestion, a side of French fries and mushrooms to share. As the conversation progressed, Dex found Ruby to be completely laid-back and engaging. This date might actually be promising.

"How's your dinner?" Ruby asked.

"It's good. The mushrooms are really awesome."

Ruby reached across the table with her fork and speared a mushroom from Dex's plate. The way Ruby was staring at her, she suddenly felt like she was on the menu. "Grace was right. You are delicious."

Dex's cheeks warmed, and she veered her eyes to her plate.

"Dessert?"

Dex nodded. "Sure." She was full but not quite ready for this night to end yet. "Do you want to share something?"

That got an adorable grin from Ruby. "I like that idea."

They looked over the menu, and Dex thought the chocolate-mousse cake sounded good until Ruby suggested the Meaning of Life cake that Gibsons served only on Saturday nights. It was a five-layer chocolate cake made up of cake, chocolate mousse, sliced ripe bananas, and raspberry preserves that sounded absolutely divine. Somehow, during all her visits to Gibsons, this treat had remained a secret to Dex. She was all in.

A different waitress appeared at their table. "Would you like the usual for dessert?"

The usual? Something pinged in the back of Dex's head. Apparently, Ruby dined here often.

"Yes." Ruby glanced up at the waitress and then across the table to Dex. "My date has never had it before."

"Ooh, then you're in for a treat tonight."

Dessert was delivered by the same waitress, a tall, blond bundle of hotness that seemed to have a clear connection with Ruby.

She smiled as she set two fresh forks on the table, slid the dessert between them, and winked. "I'll see you later."

Ruby nodded, and Dex was confused. Apparently, Ruby saw Dex's expression because she immediately said, "My girlfriend, Sarah."

A cold shiver rushed over Dex as she processed the information. "Oh, wow. Grace didn't mention you had a girlfriend." She glanced at Sarah, who was now walking toward the back of the restaurant. Dex hadn't expected that.

"No worries. We have an open relationship."

Seriously? There went her evening.

Ruby handed Dex a fork, then picked up another and dove right into the colossal slice of cake. She seemed perfectly happy to share, in more ways than one. But Dex wasn't. She took a few bites before relaxing into her chair. She'd thought maybe she'd get something more from tonight, at least another date. But that was off the table now. She had absolutely no luck with women.

The whole night became awkward from that point forward, and Dex couldn't get out of there quick enough. Dex could tell Ruby was disappointed when she'd told her she'd had a really good time, but opted not to go back to Ruby's place afterward. Ruby apologized and explained that she wasn't aware that Grace hadn't shared her current relationship status with Dex. Of course Grace hadn't mentioned the girlfriend. Dex would never have gone on the date if she had.

It was perfectly clear that she should never have agreed to go out on another one of Grace's blind dates. But Grace had begged her, said she'd have a lot of fun with Ruby. Little did Dex know she meant *group* fun. This would be the last date she would let Grace set up for her.

As soon as Dex got to her car, she took out her phone and hit Grace's number. No answer. She hung up and called again.

"Hey, Dex. Hang on a minute," Grace whispered.

Dex heard her say something, and then there was silence for a few minutes.

"What's up? We're at the movies."

"I can't believe you set me up with a woman who's in a relationship."

"I didn't know that." She seemed surprised. "I thought they were just dating."

"That's a big *no*."

"I'm sorry, Dex. I guess I've gotten them all wrong," Grace said. "Why don't we get together tomorrow, and you can tell me what you want in a woman, and we'll try again."

"No. No more blind dates. I'll find my own women from now on, thank you." She hit the End button and tossed her phone into the console. "Holy fuck." She let out a chuckle. This one would go down in the books.

It was a frigid morning in Chicago. Dex and her crew had been hanging Christmas lights since sunup, and they all needed a break. She'd given them each twenty bucks, told them to go get something warm to eat and to be back by one sharp. Working in this weather was ridiculous.

As she rounded the corner of Crushed Beans, Dex saw Juni sitting at the corner table near the end of the counter talking to Josh. She plucked off her gloves as she dodged the people in line to warm up their days with coffee and threw Juni a wave. She'd taken her jacket off before she arrived at the table, and she laid it across the seat of the plastic chair for extra insulation before sliding down onto it.

Juni pushed a large chocolate mocha in front of her with a leaf design in the foam. "I knew you'd be cold, so I ordered for you."

She observed the cup in front of Juni, which featured an intricately designed Christmas tree drawn in the foam. Josh had probably made it for her personally. "What'd you get?"

"Vanilla latte."

"Should've tried a mocha." She lifted the oversized cup to her lips and took a sip. "Um. Thank you for this. I was fucking freezing."

"Josh will have our lunches out soon. Sleeping with the owner has its perks."

Dex choked on her drink. "Wow. Already?"

Juni giggled and turned beet red.

"This must be serious. Do I need to give him the talk, or do we need to get Ranny involved?" She turned around and spotted him at the espresso machine. "Maybe I should do it now."

"Stop." Juni took in a deep breath and gazed at Josh behind the counter. He turned, smiled, and winked. "He gets me, Dex. It's like we're living in the same head."

"That must be crowded." She laughed, but, in truth, Dex wished she had someone to smile at her that way, to beam the radiance that Juni glowed with when he walked into the room. If the past few dates had been any indication, that would never happen for Dex, and it made her feel hollow inside.

"I heard from Mom today."

"Checking on Ranny?" Their brother had turned out just like their parents, flitting from country to country helping people in need.

"No, you. She found out about the wedding."

"Damn it, Juni. I asked you not to tell her."

"I didn't. She saw it on some society page online somewhere." She winked. "Besides, you know I never listen."

"What'd you tell her?"

"I told her you're fine and dating."

"Which I am." She took in a deep breath. "Even if they were total disasters."

"Only because Grace set you up." Juni tapped the table. "Now let me see the list."

"What list?" Dex hesitated.

"Don't tell me you forgot it."

She hadn't forgotten the pros and cons list they'd started last week, but she'd been hoping Juni had. "No. I didn't forget. I have it." She pulled it out of her pocket and slid it across the table.

Juni rolled her eyes as she unfolded the piece of paper. "Sweet, helpful, and compassionate? You've got to be out of your mind if you see these things in Grace."

"She just doesn't show them to everyone."

"That's a fucking understatement. She doesn't show them to anyone. I've never considered any of these qualities to be in the same zip code as Grace."

"I see them," Dex said calmly.

Juni pressed her lips together and blew a breath out through her nose. "Even if you have noticed these qualities in her, she's married now, and they're probably going to disappear soon." She pushed the list back to Dex. "You need to back out of that cozy picture and find someone else to put your energy into."

Dex raised her eyebrows. "Like one of the crazy women I just went out with?"

"Oh, I forgot. How was your date last night?" The excitement in Juni's voice was ridiculous.

"I never want to go to another restaurant, bar, or coffee shop to meet a woman."

Juni tilted her head. "You're here meeting me now."

"You know what I mean. I feel like I've been on a blind-dating roller coaster and haven't even had time to strap in." She took a sip of her mocha. "Isn't meeting women supposed to be at least a little bit fun?"

"Maybe if you'd stop letting Grace set you up on them, they'd be more enjoyable." Juni reached across, picked up Dex's cup, and took a sip. "Ooh, this *is* good."

"Told you."

"So what was wrong with this girl?"

"Besides the fact that she has a girlfriend?"

"Oh my God." Juni covered her mouth to smother a laugh. "Seriously?"

Dex nodded, then leaned in and whispered, "Apparently she's in an open relationship." She leaned back long enough to let the waiter slide the food in front of her. "Her girlfriend actually showed up for dessert. She works at Gibsons and delivered it personally."

"Nooooo way." Juni's voice rumbled.

"Yes way." Dex picked up half of her sandwich and took a bite.

"Unfuckingbelievable." Juni shook her head. "That's it. No more blind dates set up by Grace. She's a miserable matchmaker." She blew on a spoonful of her potato soup before she slipped it into her mouth. "It's like she's setting you up with losers on purpose."

"She wouldn't do that." Dex glanced at her food, then back at Juni. "Would she?"

"I bet she would. She doesn't really want you to find anyone. If you do, you won't have time for her."

"That's not true. I wouldn't ignore her just because I have a girlfriend."

"Why not? Now that she's married, she ignores you."

"She does not. She calls me a couple of times a week. More since the blind dating started."

Juni tilted her head. "But how often does she respond when you call her?"

Dex thought about it for a minute and realized Juni had a point. "Not very often."

"See? It's on her timetable."

"She's just busy getting used to her new life. That's all."

"With her new *husband*. The *center* of her world." Juni enunciated each word slowly.

"What do you propose I do?"

"Stop jumping when she calls." Juni took Dex's hand. "My God, Dex. You are so strong in every other aspect of your life. Stop waiting in the wings for something that's never going to happen."

Dex pulled her hand away. "I'm not doing that."

"Yes, you are." Juni dropped her spoon into her soup. "Listen, Dex. I love you. I'll support you in whatever you do, whatever relationship you choose. But I'm not going to lie to you." She glanced up at the counter. "Even Josh sees it."

"What? Don't you two have better things to talk about than me?" She glanced over her shoulder. "If I'm what you talk about in bed, you clearly have a problem."

"That would be a problem." Juni chuckled. "Don't change the subject."

"But really, is it good with him?" She wanted this subject changed. She'd heard enough about Grace's faults for one day.

"Okay. I'll lay off for now, but think about what I said. And no more blind dates set up by Grace."

"Gotcha." She took a few last bites of her sandwich and pushed her chair back. "I gotta get back to work. It doesn't look good if the boss is late."

Josh brought a jug of to-go coffee and a stack of cups to the table. "This should keep your crew warm for a while this afternoon."

Dex stared at Juni and let her mouth drop open. "That's so sweet, Josh."

"Gotta keep my girl happy. That means keeping you happy too." He winked at Juni before walking back behind the counter.

She hooked a thumb over her shoulder at Josh and whispered, "Fucking gold mine."

"I know." Juni stood up and gave Dex a hug. "Be careful out there, little sister."

"Always." She put on her jacket before she swiped up the coffee and cups and headed out the door. It was becoming perfectly clear that Dex was going to have to find the perfect woman on her own. But that would mean making time in her schedule to do it, and she didn't have any of that right now.

CHAPTER NINE

G race took all the ingredients for the chicken piccata from the refrigerator and laid them on the counter before she checked the recipe on her phone. It seemed like a crazy jumble of complication that Grace had a hard time wrapping her head around.

She wasn't used to being domestic, but since she and Brent had gotten married, Brent seemed to expect dinner when he got home. It had been a fun adventure at first, but now it was just frustrating. She'd gone through all her standard easy recipes when they'd returned from their honeymoon. She really should've given the living-together thing a trial run before the wedding. Dex was the only reason she was surviving this domestic whirlwind now. Thank God she was always there to help when Grace needed her.

When the call screen popped up and Grace saw that it was Dex calling, she immediately answered. "Hey. I'm so sorry about last night."

"That's the last blind date I let you set up for me."

"I really had no idea she had a girlfriend."

Grace made sure she sounded distinctly surprised as she reached into the lower cabinet and took out a skillet. Ruby saw several women on a regular basis, but Grace actually hadn't known she had a specific girlfriend now. "Hang on a minute. I'm going to put you on speaker." She set the phone on the counter and hit the button. "Can you hear me?"

"Loud and clear."

"Did you two at least have a good time? I mean, until the girlfriend showed up?"

"Yeah. We had a great time. We had some things in common, but I'm not into sharing."

"Well, I *am* sorry about that. I knew she'd been dating a few women, but I really didn't know she was involved with anyone specific." She reached inside the refrigerator and took out a bottle of chardonnay. "Hey. I'm trying to make your chicken piccata for Brent before he gets back from his parents' house. Can you help me?"

"Um, sure. Do you have chicken, capers, and a lemon?"

"I do." She let her voice lilt up. She was proud of herself for remembering the ingredients. She'd watched Dex make it for her hundreds of times but had never really paid attention to how she did it.

"First you need to pound the chicken flat."

"The butcher did that for me."

Dex laughed. "Taking the easy way, eh?"

"Is that bad?" The thought of actually touching the chicken made her shiver.

"Not gonna lie. I've always done that myself, but I'm all for process improvement."

"Okay, what's next?"

"You're going to need a couple of eggs and some flour."

Ingredients she had on hand but hadn't considered. She took a carton of eggs from the fridge and the flour from the pantry. "Got it."

"Now Google *chicken piccata*."

"Dex." She sang the name in a sweet melody.

"You know I'm working now, right?"

"Please, please, pretty please?" Again with the sweet melody.

"All right, but I have to make it quick."

"Yay." She squealed into the phone.

"Hang on a sec." Dex's voice was muffled, "Mike, take over for me for a few minutes. I'll be right back." Grace heard what sounded like a car door slam. "Okay, you ready?"

"As I'll ever be." Grace said. She wasn't much of a cook but was willing to try anything to please Brent.

Grace followed all Dex's instructions and managed to somehow get flour all over herself in the process. She'd just finished cleaning up when she heard the front door close.

"Hold on a minute. Brent's home." She met him at the entrance to the kitchen and fell into his arms as he kissed her. "Say hi to Dex, honey. She's been on the phone with me while I've been fixing dinner."

"Hey, Dex."

"Hey, Brent. It sounds like you're in for a treat tonight. Grace has been slaving away at this chicken piccata."

"Yeah? It smells awesome." He lifted the lid and scooped out a spoonful of sauce. "Tastes awesome too." He leaned in and kissed Grace again. "What have you two been talking about besides piccata?"

"My disastrous date last night."

"Isn't that the third in a row?"

"Wow. Grace has been keeping you up to date on her matchmaking."

"Who'd you set her up with this time?" Brent asked as he ate another spoonful of sauce.

"Ruby."

"Ruby?" He clanged the lid back onto the pan. "Ruby has a girlfriend."

"I found that out last night when she showed up for dessert." Dex laughed.

He chuckled. "Did you get extra whipped cream?"

"Brent." Grace's tone sharpened.

Brent pulled his brows together. "Just stating the obvious."

"I didn't know they were exclusive," Grace said softly.

"Apparently, they're not." He went to the refrigerator and pulled it open. "She's not the kind of girl you want to set Dex up with."

"Thank you, Brent!" Dex's voice came through the phone loudly.

He took a beer out of the fridge and twisted off the cap. "Listen, Dex. I have a friend at work who I think you might like."

"No, thanks. I've had enough blind dates for the time being."

"Who are you talking about?" Grace asked. This was a new development.

"Emma. She's single, smart, and cute. Perfect for Dex."

"I thought she was involved." Grace knew she wasn't.

"Nope, not since last year." He set his beer on the table and slipped off his jacket. "How about we have a little get-together here at the house, Dex. You come, she comes. If you don't like her, no harm done." He raised his eyebrows at Grace. "We can do that, right, baby?"

"Uh, sure. I guess it's about time we had a housewarming party." She was stuck. She couldn't very well tell him no. She picked up her phone from the counter and took it off speaker. "I'll make all the arrangements and let you know the date, okay?" She turned away so Brent couldn't hear the rest of the conversation. "You're going to have to help me with the food."

"You just made chicken piccata. You're a champ now."

"I'm serious, Dex." Grace's voice was low and demanding as she whispered into the phone.

"Okay, sure. Just let me know when."

"I will. You can count on that. Oh, and thank you for your help tonight." She wasn't quite sure how she'd gotten herself roped into this one.

"No worries. I have to get back to work."

"Bye, Dex." Grace hit the End button on her phone and slid it onto the counter before she spun around to Brent and planted her hand on her hip. "Emma? Really?" Emma was probably the last person Grace would pick for Dex. She was arrogant and mouthy. The woman had no filter.

"Yeah." He shrugged. "They both like sports, they're both alone. Perfect for each other."

"Women need more in common than sports to date, Brent."

"It's a start. What happened to opposites attract? That's how we got together." He tugged her to him. "You hate sports, but you watch them with me anyway. Because you love me."

She took in a deep breath. "I do, on both counts."

"And I definitely didn't marry you for your cooking." He kissed her again before he smiled and slapped her on the butt. "But that tastes awesome." He pointed to the pan on the stove. "When's dinner? I'm starving."

"Go change. I'll plate it." Grace wasn't sure about the match between Emma and Dex. Emma was strong, smart, and passionate about her opinions and the things she loved. Not unlike herself. She was the kind of girl who could fill Dex's world with tumultuous happiness, but also fill it with pain if it didn't work out. Her passion for life rivaled Grace's, and she'd clashed with Emma on more than one occasion over the years. The woman was as blunt as they come, and Grace wasn't used to being called on her shit. She might very well throw a huge monkey wrench into her friendship with Dex.

❖

When Emma got to the office that morning, she was actually glad to see Brent. She hated to admit it, but she'd missed him while he was on his honeymoon. She'd kept an eye on his accounts while he was gone, and he'd taken an extra week off to move in with Grace. He'd logged in a few times over the past week, but he'd checked in with Emma only via email and text a few times when she'd had questions. It had been three weeks since she'd actually seen him. He could be a big pain in her ass at times, but the sight of him, gloriously tanned, standing in the break room in his usual I'm-Mr.-Wonderful manner, made her surprisingly happy.

"Aren't you going to welcome me back?" he said as he picked up the coffee decanter.

"Were you gone?" she said as she took a mug from the cabinet and let him fill it with coffee.

"Ha ha." He bumped her with his shoulder. "I know you missed me. I have tons of pictures to show you."

"How about you help me out with some of these new clients first, Mr. Three-weeks-off?" She headed to her office and he followed.

"Two weeks in Greece and it was awesome! Sex and wine every day." He waggled his eyebrows.

She slipped in behind her desk and sat in the chair. "Seriously? Sex every day?"

"Sometimes twice. Grace is a savage in bed." Brent slid into the chair across from her.

Emma scrunched her brows together. "I would've never thought that. She seems so uptight."

"It's how she works out her aggression." He winked.

Emma threw her hand up for a high five. "Sweet!"

Brent bolted out of his chair, slapped her hand, and sat again. "How are things going with you? I saw that you brought someone with you to the wedding."

"She's just a friend." She sighed. "She actually met someone there and ended up leaving early."

"Well, then, I want you to meet someone."

She shook her head. "Oh, no. No setups." Those never work out well.

"Come on, Em. I know you'll like her. What could it hurt?"

She raised an eyebrow. "Do I need to remind you of the last time?"

"She was a little crazy." He gave her a huge smile. "But she was a freak in bed, right?"

"Definitely not worth the aggravation, though. Do you know she showed up at my parents' house and made a huge scene? I thought my mother was going to have a heart attack."

"What an awesome way to come out."

She scrunched up her face. "Ha ha. Thank God they already knew."

"Dex isn't anything like that, I promise. If she is, I'll do all your copy for a month."

"Grace's best friend, Dex?"

"Yeah. That's her."

Dex…That could be a handful. Emma remembered how drunk she was at the wedding. She also remembered how absolutely stunning she was. Huge green eyes with vibrant yellow sunbursts in the middle. Even as drunk as she was, Dex was absolutely dreamy.

Brent tossed a wadded-up sticky note at her and pulled Emma out of her thought. "Well? What do you say? Deal?"

Emma raised her eyebrows. "A whole month? That's a big promise, Mr. Vacation."

He nodded. "Yep, but I'm not worried. You'll like her."

Emma knew she'd like her, just didn't know if she was up to the challenge. "Okay, then. Where and when? You have to be there or it's a no-go."

"We're having a little housewarming party next weekend. I'm going to invite some other people from here, and Grace is planning to invite some of her friends."

"Ugh. Grace's friends are ridiculously spoiled." *Just like her.*

"Most of them are, but Dex is actually pretty cool."

She surveyed him carefully to make sure he wasn't bullshitting her. "Does she know I'll be there to meet her?" She trusted Brent, and it had been a long time since she'd been out with anyone.

"Of course not. You'll just be two people that I randomly introduce."

"Sounds doable." Stunning green eyes with rays of yellow flashed in her head. Dex was definitely doable. One-nighters weren't Emma's style, but sometimes they were worth it.

His lips curved into a big smile. "Believe me, she's definitely doable."

"You're such a dude." And apparently so was Emma.

"To the core." He gave her a fist bump and headed to his office.

Emma had gone out with friends a few times since her breakup last year with Amy, but it had been a long time since she'd been on an actual date. She took in a deep breath, took a gulp of coffee, got up and took the same path to her office door, and closed it. They'd been friends since the day he started five years ago. She'd shown him the ropes of marketing and public relations, and he'd become an awesome buddy. She trusted him, even if the last chick he'd set her up with had been a total freak in more ways than one.

CHAPTER TEN

The party appeared to be in full swing when Emma took her first pass by the house. There were so many cars on the street, she'd have to park halfway down the block. She should've worn more comfortable shoes, but her flats didn't go with this particular pair of skinny jeans she'd chosen tonight. As it was, she hadn't had any time to do anything to her hair. She'd just twisted it up and pinned it to the back of her head. She probably should've put more effort into the whole thing, but her day hadn't gone as she'd planned. She parked and retrieved the housewarming gift from the back seat before heading up the sidewalk and then the pathway to the house.

She knocked on the door and then fidgeted as she waited for someone to answer. She wouldn't have even come if Brent hadn't called her this morning and begged her. But that wasn't totally true. The prospect of starting something new had pushed her to make an appearance as well. After the miserable day she'd had at her parents' house, a nice hot bath and a movie sounded so much better tonight. They were in the process of downsizing, and she'd been there most of the day, which meant they were pawning off their unneeded crap on Emma and her brothers.

She had enough crap of her own she hadn't dealt with since last year when she'd moved out of the house she'd shared with Amy. The move had been her choice, to a certain degree. The other woman had just made it happen sooner than she'd expected.

When the door swung open, she was met with scowling blue eyes. "You're *late*." Grace planted her hands on her hips.

She shoved the gift into Grace's stomach. "Brent said any time after seven."

"Within reason." Grace twisted her wrist to check her watch. "It's almost nine."

"Listen, Grace. I've had a tough day, so can you save your satire for later?" It would be nice if the woman could cut her a break once in a while.

"Fine." Grace slammed the door behind her. "Brent's out back."

"Thanks...for nothing," Emma said under her breath as she moved toward the crowded living room. The doorbell rang immediately, and Emma glanced over her shoulder to observe a man at the door. Grace gave him the half-grin and trademark two-beat laugh that flew from her lips when she was flirting. *Ugh.* It was clearly only Emma who spiked Grace's anger.

She hated going to these things without a date, but if she'd brought someone along, she'd be attached to them by the hip all night. That was a pain in the ass at a work party as well. She'd promised Brent she would meet Dex, and if they didn't click, she'd just leave. As it was, unless this girl was able to keep her from falling asleep on her feet, Emma was already planning to put in the minimal courtesy hour and then bolt. She definitely wasn't in the mood for Grace's shit. She'd never understood what Brent saw in her. She was a spoiled princess who always seemed to get what she wanted, including Brent. They *must* have really hot sex.

She pushed open the sliding glass door and stepped out onto the deck. She spotted Brent across the way leaning back casually against the railing talking to a tall, muscular woman wearing jeans and a pale-green cable-knit sweater. As she moved closer, a smile broke onto Brent's face.

"Hey, Em. I'm glad you made it."

The woman whom he'd been talking to turned her head, and Emma was caught by gorgeous green eyes centered with vivid yellow sunbursts. *Dex.* She couldn't help but stare for just a moment before she forced herself to swerve her gaze to Brent.

"Sorry I'm late. It's been a long day."

As he pulled her into a hug, Dex created some distance between them and started to turn. "Hang on a minute," he said, and swung Emma around, tucking her under his arm. "Have you guys met?" He pointed from Emma to Dex and back again. "This is my best bud, Emma." He looked at Emma and pointed to Dex. "This is Grace's best bud, Dex."

"Well, that must be hell." Emma couldn't interpret Dex's expression, so she quickly held out her hand. "Sorry. Inside joke."

"She does have her moments," Dex said with a laugh and took her hand. "Nice to meet you."

Passed round one. Emma was already intrigued.

Brent removed himself from between the two of them. "Can I get you two something to drink?"

"A beer would be great," Emma said.

Dex lifted hers to the light, checking the level. "Make that two."

"I'll be right back." He took off toward the cooler in the corner of the deck.

Emma tried to let Dex start the conversation, but she seemed to be floundering, so she took the lead. "You were the maid of honor at their wedding, right?" She probably should've stayed away from the subject, but she had to know if Dex remembered what had happened. "How long have you known Grace?"

"It seems like forever." She chuckled. "I think I was twelve when she first rescued me from the mean-girl firing range."

"Wow, that's a long time. The two of you must be really close."

"Here you are, ladies." Brent handed them each a beer and immediately left the conversation.

They watched Brent walk across the deck to a group of guys. "Not as close as we used to be since Brent came into the picture, but close enough."

"I've known him for a while. On the scale of pain in the asses, he's about a four." She turned to Dex and winked.

"It's always good to know the rankings." Dex smiled and lifted her beer. "To new friends."

Emma clinked hers against it and smiled. "To new friends." The two of them were going to get along just fine.

By the time Emma finished her beer, the conversation had been nonstop, and her stomach actually ached from laughing so much. Dex had a unique way of choosing a person from the crowd and creating a personality for them. Oddly enough, she was spot-on with most of the people Emma knew at the party. She had a wickedly odd sense of humor that Emma thoroughly appreciated.

"You want another beer?" Dex asked.

"No. I'd better not. I've already had a long day, and I'm afraid another one might put me under." Damn, she shouldn't have said that. Dex's smile seemed to falter. She didn't want her to think she'd been boring. In fact, Dex had been the total opposite. Emma hadn't had this much fun in a long time and, surprisingly, wasn't quite ready to leave her company yet. "A cup of coffee would be nice."

Dex's eyes seemed to brighten. "I brought them a French press as a housewarming gift tonight, so I can make you one with it."

"Awesome." She followed Dex inside. "Their house is beautiful."

"It is. Have you seen the whole thing?"

She shook her head. "No. I came straight to the deck when I got here."

"Well, let me get you fixed up with that coffee, and then I'll give you a tour."

"Sounds wonderful. That is, if you don't mind." She followed Dex to the door and couldn't help notice the way her hips swung ever so slightly as she walked. So much sexiness to go with those gorgeous eyes.

"No, not at all," Dex said, glancing over her shoulder, and with that, Emma had been caught checking out the very nice ass in front of her.

Emma's cheeks warmed when Dex smiled at her as she opened the door and motioned her in front of her. She wasn't usually so dude-like. Checking out women's body parts wasn't something she made a habit of doing, but there it was right in front of her, packaged nicely in olive-green skinny jeans and looking perfectly touchable. She'd had no control at that point. Her eyes had hijacked her mind and led the way to the glorious sight.

When they zigzagged through several people to the kitchen, they found Grace at the counter scraping spanakopita triangles from a pan she'd just removed from the oven onto a tray. "Can you help me with these?" She motioned to another tray of wings in the open oven.

"Uh, sure." Dex swiped the hot pad from the counter and took out the tray. "Can you grab me that bowl," she said to Emma and pointed to a bright orange, fiesta-style serving dish by the sink. "Where are your paper plates?"

"In the pantry." She squealed. "I'm so overwhelmed here, Dex. I don't know what to do."

"I'll get them," Emma said as she set the serving dish for the wings where Dex could get to it and then went in search of plates. She found the paper plates, plastic ware, and napkins in the pantry and set them all out on the counter with easy access for the guests.

The three of them had the rest of the food plated and on the dining-room table within fifteen minutes. Emma hadn't realized how useless Brent was at home. If Grace had been her wife, she would've been right in here helping her get everything ready, which seemed to be what Dex had done. She watched the two of them interact as Dex handed Grace a glass of wine and then poured two cups of coffee from the press. Dex seemed to be a helluva prize in every way.

Dex turned and caught her staring. "Sorry about that. Ready for that tour now?" She handed her a cup before taking a sip from her own.

"Sounds wonderful. If you're still up for it."

"Absolutely." Dex rounded the kitchen counter and led her through the living room and into the hallway. "This is the…I forget… what do they call it? Oh yes, the hallway." She pointed at the crystal chandelier hanging from the ceiling. "The most elegant hallway I've ever frequented." Her voice took on a British accent, and Emma let out a burst of laughter.

She led her to the guest bathroom next. "Here we have the loo." She continued in the upper-crust dialect. "The elegant charm of the beveled mirrored vanity finished with crystal knobs centers the oversized room. But the pièce de résistance is the decorative handmade Italian mirror." Dex lightly tugged her in front of the mirror and captured her gaze in the reflection. "Where you can view the most beautiful of faces."

Emma's body sizzled in all the right places. *Gorgeous and charming.*

After going through a couple of other rooms listening to Dex's *Lifestyles of the Rich and Famous* descriptions, Dex balked as they entered the master bedroom, and Emma walked right into her. Standing there alone, this close to Dex, made her body heat soar. She was feeling things she hadn't in a very long time. The dark look in Dex's eyes made an image of the two of them naked under the down comforter fly through her head. If she'd known her for just a few weeks longer, Emma would've locked the door and taken advantage of their proximity. A new gift-set of sheets would've definitely been in order. She forced the image from her mind and stepped back.

Dex cleared her throat. "And this would be the boudoir." She moved her hand in a typical Vanna White motion, showing her the room. "Spacious yet cozy enough for the most intimate of trysts." She seemed to purposely finish this part of the tour quickly. Perhaps she was feeling the same heat as Emma.

When they returned to the living room, most of the guests had left, and it was almost eleven o'clock. Emma hadn't realized they'd been away from the actual party for so long. She glanced around at the few people standing in scattered circles and suddenly felt sad that the night was about to end. Grace was out on the deck with Brent talking to another couple and, from the motion of her arms, seemed to be explaining something vividly.

She took her empty cup into the kitchen. "I guess I'd better get going."

"Oh, so soon?" Dex twisted her wrist to check her watch. "Wow. I didn't realize it was that late. Can I walk you to your car?"

"I'd love that." Emma was surprised at just *how much* she'd love that.

"Give me just a minute." She rushed outside to Grace and told her she was leaving. From what Emma could hear, Grace wasn't happy. She was complaining about cleaning up, but Brent put his arm around her and shooed Dex with his hand. He looked over at Emma and waved. "We got this. I'll see you Monday."

She smiled and was surprised at the dip her stomach took when Dex came back her way. *Slow down, Em.*

"Did you bring a coat?"

"No. I didn't think it was going to get this cold."

"No worries. You can wear mine." Dex reached into the closet, pulled out a down jacket, and held it up for her to slide an arm inside. "I'll just wear one of Grace's."

Giving up her coat for me? Could she get any sweeter?

They were both quiet as they walked to Emma's car. She pushed the remote and the car chirped. "This is me." Emma glanced around at the lack of cars left on the street. "Did you drive?"

"Nah, I took the L. It's just a couple of blocks away."

"You can't be out walking at this time of night. That's dangerous."

Dex opened the door for her. "I'll be fine."

She hit the unlock button for the passenger seat. "Get in. I'll give you a ride home."

Dex shook her head. "That's completely unnecessary."

Emma tilted her head and smiled. "I'd like to."

Still hesitant, Dex gripped the top of the door with her hand. Emma covered it with hers. "Really. I would."

"In that case, I'd hate to disappoint a beautiful woman."

Again, surprised by the bounce in her stomach, Emma smiled.

Their conversation was sporadic as they traveled across town to Dex's house in Oak Park, a place Emma was quite familiar with, having grown up in the area. Even in the dark, she couldn't help but notice the beautifully landscaped front yard when they pulled up in front of the house.

She noted the stenciled logo on the side of the SUV parked in the driveway. *Scenic Landscaping and Design.* Emma had seen a few yard signs on her parents' street with the same logo.

"Wow. Did you design this?"

"Designed and installed," she said with a subtle sense of pride.

"It's so intricate, and it all flows together perfectly."

She shrugged. "It's what I do."

Emma got out of the car and wandered up the pathway to the door before she turned around to take it all in. "You're very talented."

As they stood at the front door, surrounded by sweet aromatic roses in the beds by the house, Emma could see the blush rising in Dex's cheeks. It was as though the moon had created the perfect ambience just for them. Emma stopped resisting and leaned in for a kiss. Dex's lips were soft and sweet, with just a taste of coffee still left on them. When Dex's hands went to Emma's cheeks, she thought maybe it was too much, too soon. She was pleasantly surprised by the warmth of Dex's tongue as it passed through her lips. She slipped her arms around Dex's waist and pulled her closer, desperately wanting more contact. She fought to keep her hands from inching up Dex's shirt as the kiss deepened, their tongues mingling gently. All of Emma's senses were heightened to an intense level, ready to uncoil into a blissful pool of satisfaction with just the right touch. When they finally broke the kiss, they were both hot and breathing hard.

Emma buzzed all over, and she sucked in a deep breath. "I had…" She had no words to explain just how she felt about the night, that kiss, and what this woman did to her.

"Me too." Dex smiled. "Can I see you again?"

"Yes," she blurted. "I mean, of course." She put her hand out. "Let me see your phone, and I'll put my number in it."

Dex handed her the phone, and she typed in her number and handed it back. Dex quickly typed in something.

"I sent you a text so you'll have mine too." This was a clear sign that they'd made a connection. Dex opened the door and stood in the threshold. "I'll call you tomorrow, okay?"

She moved closer and brushed a stray strand of hair from Dex's face. She needed to go now, or else she was going to push Dex through that door, take her to the closest piece of furniture, and make her scream with pleasure.

"Sure. That'd be great." She swung around and walked to her car. At least she thought she was walking, though at this moment, she felt like she was floating. She would definitely thank Brent for this one.

❖

Dex watched Emma drive away before she closed the door and dropped against it. Her legs were as pliable as the spandex covering them. The mega earth-shattering kiss had rattled her so much she'd had a hard time unlocking the door. She took in a deep breath and went into the kitchen, picking up her cat and scratching her belly on the way. "This one's promising, Panda." Her black-and-white face held its usual indifference to the attention. She kissed her on the nose and then let her jump to the floor. Dex had been totally prepared for this evening to be a disaster, just like all the previous dates Grace had set up for her over the past week.

But the chemistry with Emma was unreal. They'd talked about everything from books to food to basketball. And the banter was ridiculously fun. With every witty line of dialogue she fired at her, Emma returned something wittier. The girl was not only beautiful, but she also had smarts. Emma had received her MBA at Northwestern University, and even though Dex had received hers from the University of Chicago, she wouldn't hold it against her. They'd found they both liked unique and sometimes quirky modern art and agreed to go to the Museum of Contemporary Art sometime in the future. Even when Grace had dragged her away to help in the kitchen, Emma had pitched right in without complaining. Dex hadn't had that much fun with another woman in a long time. And the kiss was off-the-charts sizzling. Had Emma felt it too?

Her phone chimed and she glanced at the screen. A text from Emma.

Me too. It was an incredible night. I hope we can do it again soon.

The sentence was punctuated with a smiley face at the end. Dex's stomach fluttered. Question answered.

CHAPTER ELEVEN

Dex's phone chimed on her bedside table. She picked it up and read the message from Grace.

Hey, sleepyhead. Wake up. I'm about to be at your front door.

Dex moved Panda from her legs to her side and slid out of bed. "I know. It's not even eight yet," she said in response to the cat's protest. She tugged on her sweatpants and trotted down the steps. She wasn't expecting to see Grace today, and definitely not this early. She checked her reflection in the mirror hanging in the front entryway and finger-combed her hair before she opened the door.

"Hey. What are you doing here so early?"

"Are you alone?" Grace peered around her after she entered.

"Technically, no. Panda is still in bed and not very happy that you woke us up."

"I thought maybe you and Emma…"

"Sadly, no." Dex sighed. "I slept alone. Just like every other night."

"Didn't you two have a good time last night?"

"Actually, yes, but she only dropped me off. She didn't stay." She closed the door and followed Grace into the kitchen, where she perched on one of the breakfast-bar stools. "Did you expect her to spend the night?" Maybe there was something more she needed to know about Emma.

"No. Just checking." Grace held up the McDonald's bag she'd had clutched in her fingers. "I brought breakfast."

"No coffee?"

"I knew you'd want your own. You always say it's better." Grace scrunched up her nose. "So, you really had a good time last night?"

Dex pulled her eyebrows together. "Shouldn't I have?"

"Oh, yeah. Sure. It's just that Emma doesn't really seem like your type. She brought a box of freaking cigars as a gift. Can you believe that?"

"I didn't realize I had a type, and what's wrong with cigars?" She filled the kettle and put it on the burner before lighting the gas stove.

"It wasn't a bachelor party, for God's sake." Grace rolled her eyes as she took two breakfast biscuits from the bag. She pushed one over to Dex and kept the other for herself. "I thought you liked girlie girls." She smiled her amazing smile.

Dex's heart squeezed a little, and she ignored the giddy feelings it provoked. "You mean girlie girls like you?" Grace used how Dex felt about her to her full advantage.

"Yeah, I guess so." She shrugged and took a bite of her biscuit.

"Thus the reason none of the girls you set me up with worked out. They were all super high maintenance." The pot whistled. Dex flipped off the burner, dumped a couple of scoops of coffee into the French press, and then added the boiling water. Then she took out a tin of tea, fished out a teabag, put it in a cup, and added water.

Grace raised an eyebrow. "Are you saying I'm high maintenance?" She broke off a small piece of biscuit and slid it into her mouth.

Dex shifted her eyes wildly from side to side. "High is an understatement. I'd say more like skyscrapingly so. No, Jack-and-the-beanstalk high." She took a bite of breakfast sandwich.

Grace blew out a short breath. "I *am* not. And that's not very nice of you to say."

Dex raised her eyebrows and tilted her head "*Yes*. You are. Have been since we were kids." She waited a beat before attempting to soothe the statement that seemed to shock Grace. "I'm just being truthful." She smiled at the scowl dampening Grace's beautiful smile, picked up the fancy tea tin, and pointed to the label. "The tea that comes in sachets. The only kind you drink." She opened the cabinet and tossed it back onto the shelf. "And, honestly, I love you for it." She pushed the plunger on the coffee and poured herself a cup. "I've learned a lot of things I never would have if it weren't for you."

Grace's scowl morphed into the smile that Dex adored. "Really?"

"Uh-huh." She nodded, planted her elbows on the counter, and stared into Grace's startling blue eyes. "Plus, you can be super sweet when I've done something for you. It kind of makes me all gooey inside."

Grace smiled softly. "Do you have any cream?"

"Just for you." Her voice ended with a soft lilt as she took it out of the refrigerator and added a splash to Grace's tea. She took a spoon from the drawer and dropped it into the cup.

"Do you think you'll be that way with Emma?" Grace mixed the cream slowly with the spoon as she stared into the cup.

"I don't know, but man, that girl can kiss."

"You kissed her?" Grace's voice rose, and her cup tipped slightly, sending small droplets of tea across the counter.

Dex spun a couple of paper towels from the roll and wiped up the mess. "She insisted on driving me home so I didn't have to take the L."

"Well, that was presumptuous of her." Grace sat back in the stool, seemingly not at all interested in her breakfast anymore.

"Presumptuous? Really?" She took a drink of coffee. "I thought it was kind of sweet."

Grace's raised an eyebrow. "So, she didn't spend the night, and you didn't sleep with her, right?"

"No. She's not here, is she?" She shook her head and laughed.

"For all I know, she could've left after you—"

"Stop. You know I don't do that anymore." The thought had crossed her mind more than once last night, but she wanted to see Emma again, and that wasn't the way she wanted to start whatever it was they were starting.

"Not even with blind date number three?" Grace asked.

"Especially *not* with blind date number three. Thank God I didn't give *her* my number."

"But you gave it to Emma."

"I did." She pulled her eyebrows together. "What's going on with you? You're acting like you don't want me to like her. You set the whole thing up, remember?"

"Well, technically, Brent set it up. She's his friend. I don't know her all that well."

"Don't worry. I'll go slowly with this one." She smiled, thinking about the evening. "I like her."

"Well, okay then." Grace straightened her stance. "Mission accomplished. Need any pointers on how to keep her interested?" She broke off another piece of biscuit and put it into her mouth.

"Thanks, but no. I got this." Emma was nothing like Grace. Her help would probably make her run far, far away with lightning speed. Dex really did like Emma and wanted to get to know her better. Much better.

Once Dex got Grace out the door, she picked up her phone and looked at the text she'd received from Emma the night before. She read the message again, and her stomach swirled. Panda jumped on the chair and stared at her in her usual manner. "I should really wait a few hours, right?" She set the phone on the counter and fished a scoop of cat food from the bag. "I don't want to appear too needy, right?" The cat hopped off the stool and followed her to the dish. The cat food clinked as she dumped it into the bowl. Panda glanced up momentarily before chowing down. "You're right. I'll text her. Who cares if she thinks I'm needy. It appears I am." She picked up her phone and typed.

I know it's early, but I was wondering if you might be free to get together today.

She set the phone down and tried not to freak out when she didn't get a response right away. Fifteen minutes later when the phone chimed, she sprinted across the room and picked it up.

Sorry! I was in the shower. I'm absolutely free today and would love to see you again.

Her heartbeat doubled as she typed.

Awesome! There's a jazz festival in Hyde Park, or if you don't like jazz, we can hit the Taco Festival on Southport Avenue.

The phone chimed again before she could set it down.

I'd love both.

Okay, then, first the tacos, then the jazz.

Sounds wonderful.

Pick you up at 11?

I have to be over your way this morning, so I'll pick you up, okay?

She typed in *Okay. See you then*, and debated whether to add a smiley face. She added it, hit the Send button, and was immediately rewarded with a smiley face in return.

Panda snaked between her legs. "Good call, buddy." She scratched under her chin before rushing up the stairs to take a shower.

❖

Emma pulled up in front of Dex's house and sat for a minute admiring the modern landscape. The design was crazy intricate, with colored gravel defining small pathways. Everything was arranged in symmetry. Flower beds were contained within crisp lined areas near the house, and giant pots filled with pencil hollies flanked the porch. Dex had an undeniable talent. How had she come about her profession? She picked up her phone, clicked on Dex's name, and smiled at the text she'd received from her last night.

I had an unexpectedly awesome time tonight, thanks to you.

She let the quick jolt buzz through her and then quickly scrolled down and typed in a message letting Dex know she was here. Within a minute or two, Dex sprinted out the door. She couldn't help but notice the beautiful smile on her face when she slid into the passenger seat.

"Hey, you," Emma said, trying not to give away the ridiculously crazy excitement she felt to see her again. Her stomach vaulted like she was on the downside of a roller-coaster ride.

"Hey," Dex said with a huge grin.

Emma lost the battle and grinned in return. She took in a breath to settle herself. "Your landscaping is even more beautiful in the daylight."

"Thanks." Dex's cheeks reddened. "I've been so busy lately. I don't always have time to work on my own yard."

Emma's stomach flip-flopped. She hadn't thought Dex could get more beautiful, but the blush had done it. She cleared her throat and focused back on the bushes. "Maybe you could give me some ideas on how to landscape my parents' lawn. My dad tries, but he just doesn't have the knack for it."

"Sure. What area do they live in?"

"They actually live not far from here. That was my stop on the way. I'd be happy to pay you," she blurted as an afterthought. She didn't want Dex to think she would take advantage of her.

"Oh, awesome. I love Oak Park. This is a great neighborhood." Her eyes sparkled as she spoke. "Let me take a look at it first and see what it'll take."

"Okay." She smiled and held Dex's stare for a moment longer than necessary.

Dex broke the stare and took out her phone. "Hungry?"

"Starving."

"Great. I programmed the address into my phone, and Siri says, 'Let's go! People are beating us there, and the tacos may soon be all gone!'"

"On it." Emma laughed as she put the car into gear and pulled away from the curb. "We don't want them to run out of tacos. That would be tragic."

"A colossal disaster."

Emma took in a deep breath and kept her eyes on the road. *Tacos and jazz.* This woman knew all the right buttons to push, and she did it well.

The taco festival was already packed when they got there. It didn't surprise Emma that it was close to seventy-six degrees, which was unusual for October. Chicago was known to have average temperatures between fifty-nine and sixty-five degrees, and today was an exception, with minimal wind and spectacular sunshine. It was as though Emma's fairy godmother had conjured up the weather just for her date with Dex.

The taco choices were imaginative. Some were made with traditional ingredients such as chicken, steak, chorizo, and beef, as well as unusual ingredients such as mushrooms, shrimp, cod, goat, and duck. Emma opted for a trio that included shrimp, mushrooms, and chicken. Dex went for steak, cod, and duck. After they picked up a couple of seasonal beers, they sat on a concrete barrier and shared them like they'd been a couple for years. The whole situation was surreal. Emma had never thought she'd meet anyone she clicked with so perfectly.

"Oh my God, this mushroom taco is divine." It was like an explosion of flavors in her mouth. She hadn't ever tasted anything quite like it, the blend of ingredients staggering.

"What's in it?" Dex asked.

Emma peeled the corn tortilla back. "One, two, three different types of mushrooms, kale, pickled carrots, and…" She pushed the mushrooms around with her fork. "Um, I think thyme." She took another bite and then held the taco up to Dex. "You want to try?" she mumbled, still chewing her last bite.

When Dex widened her eyes, tilted her head sideways, and opened her mouth, Emma couldn't hold her laughter and had to cover her mouth to prevent the food from bursting out. She fed her a bite, and Dex groaned.

"You're not kidding." Dex pointed at what was left of the taco remaining in Emma's hand. "That, right there, is the star of the festival. We should get ten more."

"Just ten? Not twenty?" She raised her eyebrows.

"At least twenty." Dex glanced around. "But what if they're sold out?" She held up her plate of tacos. "I'll trade you this tasty tempura-battered fish taco *and* this appetizing coffee-rubbed steak taco for the last bite of your magnificent mushroom taco."

"Sold." Emma laughed hysterically as she fed Dex the rest of the taco. "You're adorable."

Dex sat up straight, twisted to peek behind her, and shifted her eyes back and forth. "Me?" She pushed a finger into her own chest.

"Yes, you." Emma chuckled at her unpretentiousness. This gorgeous, funny woman apparently had no idea what kind of an effect she was having on her.

Dex lifted an eyebrow. "Seriously?"

"Absolutely." She instinctively reached over and wiped a drop of sauce from the corner of Dex's mouth with her thumb and then leaned forward and kissed her softly. She held the kiss for just a moment while every nerve ending in her body came to attention. How could this woman ignite every part of her with just a slight touch of her lips? Emma broke away and took in a deep breath.

"Wow," Dex said. "And I'm not talking about the taco."

Total understatement. Emma smiled softly, and before Dex could protest, she swiped one of the tacos from Dex's plate and took a bite. She couldn't help but notice the pink taking over Dex's cheeks, and judging by the heat in her own, Emma was sure hers were just as pink. Dex truly was adorable.

They shared the rest of the tacos and drank their beers before they went back to the mushroom-taco stand. Dex bought more tacos to go for the jazz festival later, and Emma grabbed a card from the booth with the restaurant's name. They'd definitely have to try these again.

Strolling around, they just happened upon the Mexican wrestling. Emma was surprised at how entertaining it was. The colorful masks alone made it worth watching. The rapid sequences of holds and maneuvers the wrestlers performed enthralled Dex, as did the high-flying tactics they used on each other. At one point the wrestlers ended up outside the ring, chasing each other through the crowd.

After that show, they picked up an apple strudel and found the music stage where they settled into a few open chairs close to the front. Dex laid her arm across the top of Emma's chair, and Emma settled into her. Emma tingled when Dex curled her hand around her shoulder and pulled her closer.

They never made it to the jazz festival, which was fine. Emma was comfortable right where she was, barely touching Dex in the chair next to her and enjoying her company. At one point, Dex ran to the beverage stand to get a couple more beers, and they ate the mushroom tacos she'd bought while watching the band play.

The sun had faded over an hour earlier, and it had begun to get chilly. They'd listened to a few sets before the wind picked up, but then Emma shivered as a gust came across her shoulders. Dex must have felt it because she pulled Emma closer and pressed her head against Emma's.

"It's getting kinda cold. You ready to go?"

Emma hesitated before she leaned back and stared into Dex's eyes. "I guess we should." She didn't want the day to end, but if they didn't leave now they'd get caught in the hordes of people leaving and would probably get stuck sitting in traffic for hours. Yet that honestly didn't sound so bad as long as she was stuck with Dex.

Emma walked Dex to her door, which was probably a bad move if she wanted to keep the pace slow. What she did want was another one of those heart-stopping kisses. When Dex invited her in for coffee, she wasn't sure she should accept. The night could turn out very differently than she'd planned, and she really needed to stay on course with this one. She didn't want things to happen too quickly, or she might just get her heart broken. There was always the risk of that happening anyway, but she'd been through that before and wanted to shield herself from heartache as much as possible.

As soon as they were in the door, all her restraint flew from her mind when Dex pulled her into a steaming kiss. Their tongues moved in motion as though they were made for the same mouth. Her hands went to Dex's waist and pulled her closer. She wanted, no, she needed more contact. She tugged the shirt from the waistband of Dex's pants, only to find a tank top underneath. She growled and pulled the cotton fabric loose, then swept her hands across the smooth, warm skin. She popped the buttons on Dex's shirt to gain more access, and her hand went immediately to her breast, which fit perfectly in her palm. Dex let out a soft moan and Emma was instantly wet.

Somehow they made it to the couch and Dex fell backward onto it, pulling Emma on top of her. Dex's leg was between Emma's, and she pressed into it as she pushed up Dex's shirt and reclaimed her breast in her palm. She was trailing her mouth down Dex's neck on her way to it when she felt a thud on her back.

Emma immediately stopped and widened her eyes. "Uh. What's on my back?"

"Damn it." Dex reached around her and plucked something from her back. A cat. A big black-and-white cat. "Sorry. She likes to be involved." She set her on the floor beside them.

Emma chuckled. "In everything?"

Dex flattened her lips and pulled her eyebrows together. "You have no idea."

Emma sat up and ran her hand down the cat's back. "She's cute."

"And annoying," Dex added.

"What's your name, little girl?" Emma rubbed her behind the ears.

"Panda. Because, well, you know."

"I can see the resemblance." Panda jumped into Emma's lap and settled. "I think she wants me to go, so you can give her some attention."

"Way to be a terrible wingman, buddy." Dex bent to eye level with the cat. "You really don't have to go."

Dex glanced up, and Emma was caught by the startling yellow clusters radiating within Dex's emerald-green eyes. She shifted and tried to ignore the desire the sight provoked within her. "Yeah, I think I do. I have an early day tomorrow, and if I stay, I don't think I'll get much sleep." True statement. Neither of them would. It would be a Monday from hell, but Emma had a feeling it would be totally worth it.

Panda jumped to Dex's lap as Emma stood and searched for her coat. Her cheeks warmed when Dex pointed to it on the floor.

"Oh, my. How did that happen?" Once they'd made it inside,

she'd been totally focused on the earth-shattering kiss that came next. Clearly, the momentum was intense. They'd made it to the couch at light speed, memories erased on the way. Both of their coats had come off, as well as Dex's flannel button-down, which she picked up and slid across her shoulders.

Dex shook her head and smiled. "I honestly don't remember."

Emma curled the edges of Dex's shirt into her palms and pulled her closer. "You're a really fun date. You know that?"

"It could get a lot funner." Dex let out a low groan and kissed her.

Emma let the tingle consume her from head to toe before she broke away. "I don't doubt that in the least." She chewed on her bottom lip. "But I need to go." She spun around to pick up her coat, but Dex beat her to it and held it up while she slipped her arms inside.

"Can I see you this week?"

"Plan on it." Emma gave her a quick kiss on the lips and sped out the door before she changed her mind. The way she was feeling right now, that could easily happen with just one more kiss.

Dex closed the door and leaned against it, trying to regain her footing. Emma had left her in the same state she had the night before—a hot, steaming puddle of desire. It wasn't an entirely new experience for her. She'd felt something similar before, but that was a long time ago when she'd first met Grace. She'd never felt like this since or with anyone else, and was truly afraid to run with it. The outcome with Grace had been painful, plus Emma had balked. She'd left in the middle of something that was definitely going to happen if Panda hadn't interrupted them.

What if Emma didn't have the same feelings? What if she ended up in the same "friends" place with Emma that she had with Grace? She took in a deep breath and blew it out slowly. There was one big difference between the two. Grace had *never* kissed her like that. She could still feel the kiss vibrating through her, with the sensation now settled uncomfortably between her legs. *Wow!*

The whole day had gone so perfectly. No complaints about the length of the walk from the parking lot to the festival. No off-the-cuff remarks about the lack of taco variety, or how they should always have a different type of food at any festival. Grace would've insisted on having a burger or something totally different than tacos, and Dex would've had to hunt down something for her.

The festival had been so much more enjoyable with Emma than it had ever been with Grace. Come to think of it, Emma hadn't asked Dex to do one single thing for her. She hadn't expected anything of Dex, and she'd even shared her tacos with her. The kiss they'd shared, right there sitting on the concrete, had been spectacular. She'd been so wrapped up in Emma, Dex had almost forgotten they were in public, surrounded by hundreds of people. The thought of it made Dex's knees go weak again. Emma was breathing life into her suffocating heart.

The comfortable easiness between them had been there from the beginning. Emma had even let Dex drive her car on the way home. She was so different from Grace, who always insisted on driving and was a constant backseat driver when she didn't. Total control freak. Emma was relaxed and let Dex make the choices all day, and Dex liked it. The whole day had been so much more fun without the pressure of someone scrutinizing her actions as well as the event.

When she'd stared into Emma's silvery blue eyes, she'd been mesmerized by the way the light scattered in them. Dex had also thought she'd seen a glimmer of want. Yes, that was definitely what it was. Emma had slowed down for some reason, and that meant Dex needed to be patient. Had she been through a recent breakup? Was it a surprise? Was it heart-destroyingly horrible? The thought of someone hurting Emma made her heart squeeze. She needed more details. Maybe she should get more background on her from Grace…or maybe she shouldn't.

CHAPTER TWELVE

Emma sat at her desk gazing out her office window at the city. Today seemed like the longest day in history. She had another date with Dex tonight, and time was literally crawling slower than a snail going up on the down escalator. Dex had sent her a text early this morning before she'd even gotten out of bed. The soft ting of the chime had gently pulled her from her sleepy haze into the surprisingly vivid dream she seemed to be living. She hadn't gotten much sleep after leaving Dex last night and had kinda hoped she'd had the same problem. It was ridiculous how giddy she'd felt when she read the message.

Do you know the ceiling fan above my bed rotates sixty-eight times per minute?

No, but I found out the Home Shopping Network has great deals on jewelry during the wee hours of the morning.

That's the best news I've heard all year. Can I see you tonight?

I think that would be wise or I may be making five small monthly payments for the rest of my life.

Dinner, my place @ 6?

Can I bring something?

Just you.

The tingle buzzed through her again as she thought about the text exchange that went on until they'd both, reluctantly, had to get up and dress. She would've never made it to work on time if she'd spent the night with Dex last night. She brought out the best of Emma, and she liked giving it to her.

Her boring weekend had quickly morphed into a wonderful whirlwind of fun and adventure. The sparkle of Dex's green eyes burned vividly in her memory. She'd have to remember to thank Brent for the introduction. She hadn't seen him yet today. In fact, she hadn't looked up from her desk all morning. The advertising copy she'd scheduled to work on at home yesterday had to be done early this morning instead. She'd arrived at the office after eight this morning, and it had been past midnight when she'd gotten home from Dex's house last night. She smiled. Yesterday was well worth the punishment this morning.

Brent poked his head into her office. "You have time for lunch?"

"Yes. I'm starving." She'd been so focused, she hadn't had anything but coffee this morning. Food would've put her into a coma.

"Downstairs okay?" Brent asked.

"Perfect."

He motioned her in front of him as they headed to the elevator. "So the party was good, eh?"

"It was okay."

"What? I saw you with Dex. You two were having a great time."

"She's nice, not pretentious like most of the woman I meet." Totally different from the rest of Grace's friends.

"Thanks for the cigars, by the way."

Emma chuckled. "I bet Grace was happy with those."

"You don't want to hear exactly what she said, do you?"

"Actually I do."

"Something to the effect of, 'What the fuck? It wasn't a bachelor party.'" His voice rose as he mimicked Grace.

Emma laughed loudly. "Awesome. I wish I'd been there."

"Troublemaker."

"You love me anyway."

He winked and moved her in front of him in line. They ordered their sandwiches, took a number from the cashier, and found a table in the corner of the deli. Brent picked up their drink cups and got them each a glass of water, hers with lemon.

"Did you get lucky?" he asked as he sat down across from her.

"No. It took all my resistance to walk away when I dropped her off at her house." She was sure it would've been a night to remember if she hadn't.

"What? Why'd you do that?"

"Because she's nice and I like her. Besides, she didn't invite me in."

"Oh, playing the sweet-girl game, are you?"

"It's not a game, Brent." She glared at him playfully. "I am sweet."

He chuckled. "You've forgotten who you're talking to." He raised his eyebrows. "You guys were together all night. I thought for sure something was going to happen. You at least had a good time, right?"

A young, floppy-haired waiter brought over their sandwiches and swiped the number from the table. Emma took hers and pushed Brent's in front of him.

She nodded. "We spent the day together yesterday too."

"Doubleheader." He threw his hand up for a high five, and she slapped it with hers. "And you still didn't get lucky?"

She shook her head. "She was even harder to resist last night, but I had work due by noon today, so I needed to get some rest."

He laughed. "You actually *are* a good girl. I would've blown it off and asked you to help me with it this morning."

"I'll remember that next time."

"I got your back," he said, then bit off a huge chunk of his sandwich. "When will that be?"

"Sometime this week. I haven't heard from her yet today." She didn't want to tell him she was seeing Dex again for dinner tonight. He'd run with it, and she'd never live it down.

"Yet." He bounced his eyebrows at her. "That sounds promising."

She let a big smile spread across her face. "In more ways than one."

He licked his finger and swiped it down in the air. "Chalk one up for the Brentster for setting up the party."

"I owe you one." She took a bite of her sandwich. "What was with Grace?"

He gave her a strange look. "What do you mean?"

"At the party? She pulled Dex into the kitchen to help her with the food. I thought you said she could cook."

"She can. There was probably just too much food for one person to handle."

"And *you* couldn't help her?"

He seemed surprised by the comment. "She didn't ask me."

"My point exactly. She seems to depend a lot on Dex instead of you." He needed to start taking care of Grace so Dex didn't have to.

"You depend on me, don't you?" He shrugged. "Who helped you move last year? Who got you a date with someone perfect for you?"

"Yeah, she is kind of perfect for me." She took in a deep breath and wondered if Dex was too good to be true.

"I told you, I got your back, Em. Now let me have the rest of your sandwich if you're not gonna eat it."

She kept the half she'd been eating and pushed her plate his way. "It's all yours."

She hadn't thought about it that way. It just seemed that Grace took a little more advantage of Dex than Emma ever had of Brent. She would never have hosted a party with her significant other and expected Brent to help her with the food. She'd probably put him in charge of the beer cooler, but never the food. Maybe she was making too much of it. Either way, she wasn't sure if Grace was in her court on this one. She'd seemed to like having Dex at her beck and call at the party and clearly didn't like the competition.

❖

When Emma pulled up in front of Dex's house, she flipped down the visor and assessed herself in the vanity mirror. Why was she so nervous? She'd had an awesome time with Dex yesterday. Who would've thought that tacos and Mexican wrestling could make for such a delightful date?

She adjusted the V-neck on her sweater, which seemed a little low right at the moment. It was the highest cut of the three she'd tried on, so she'd had to go with it. She didn't want to worry about her cleavage spilling out all night. She'd worn her loosest pair of jeggings, if there even was such a thing, because Dex was cooking and she actually wanted to eat whatever she made. She closed her eyes. She hoped it wasn't fish. She could handle shrimp, but she wasn't a big fish eater. She probably should've warned Dex of that little nugget of information, but she didn't want her to know she had flaws just yet.

She didn't know how long she'd been sitting in her car when she glanced up to see Dex sprinting out her front door. It was a magnificent sight. Beautiful dark hair flowed dreamily on her shoulders, creating the perfect contrast against the electric-green sweater she wore. That sweater fit her well, and everything slowed as Dex ran like Wonder Woman down the pathway, her arms moving effortlessly and the well-defined muscles in them appearing so incredibly touchable. And the flawless athletic legs wrapped in dark-blue skinny jeans were entirely too much for Emma. She needed something cold to drink. Now. She couldn't take her eyes off Dex as she rounded the car and opened the door for her.

"Hey, you."

"Hey," she said as she killed the engine and slid out of the car.

Dex seemed to take in the whole of her. "You look fantastic."

"Thanks. You look pretty awesome yourself." Her cheeks warmed, and she turned to grab the bottles of wine from the front seat. She handed the bag to Dex. "I didn't know what you were making for dinner, so I brought one of each."

"Perfect." She tucked the bag to her chest with one hand and took Emma's hand with the other. "I made roast chicken."

The house smelled amazing. Emma hadn't realized how hungry she was until her stomach let out a loud growl as soon as she took in the scent of food when they stepped through the door.

Emma grabbed her stomach. "Oh my God. Was that me?"

Dex laughed. "Well, I'm glad you came hungry." She took her coat and hung it on the hall tree. "There's some cheese and crackers in the kitchen."

She felt something against her legs and glanced down to see a black-and-white fur ball slipping through them.

"Sorry. I don't think you two have been properly introduced." Dex picked up the cat and held her out to face Emma. "This is Panda. She likes attention, as you saw last night. And her timing is ridiculously bad."

Emma took her into her arms and rubbed her behind the ears, and Panda purred softly.

"She likes you already," Dex said with a smile.

She followed Dex into the kitchen. The words *cheese and crackers* didn't do the spread on the counter justice. Three small round bowls with different spreads in them were surrounded by an assortment of crackers, and another plate was filled with a variety of black and green olives.

"This looks wonderful." She dropped Panda to the floor before she picked up a cracker, spread one of the cheese mixtures across it, and took a bite. "Oh, my. This is heavenly." She closed her eyes and let the flavors of rosemary and something sweet fill her mouth. "I could live on this alone." She popped the other half into her mouth, prepared another cracker, and handed it to Dex. "What is that sweetness? Dates?"

"Figs." Dex took a bite of the cracker. "They're not as sweet. It gives the cheese just the right balance with the rosemary."

Dex fixed the next cracker for Emma with a different spread. "Can you tell me what's in this one?"

Emma took a bite and widened her eyes. "Feta, dill, and maybe... garlic?"

"Close. Ginger."

"Wow, that's really good." Emma dipped the knife into the last bowl, spread the cheese onto the cracker, and took a bite before she fed the remaining half to Dex. "This one's easy. Blue cheese and green onions."

Dex shook her head. "Shallots. They're a little milder."

Emma smiled. "I think I may keep you." She regretted the words as soon as they left her lips. It was too soon. Dex wasn't really hers to keep...yet.

Dex stared into her eyes, and suddenly the air between them seemed charged. Maybe it wasn't too soon after all.

She broke contact and reached for a bottle of wine. "Chardonnay with the chicken?"

"Sounds fabulous."

Thirty minutes later they were sitting at the dining-room table with full plates of roast chicken, potatoes, and vegetables.

"I hope you saved room," Dex said as she refilled their glasses with wine.

"I reserved a hollow leg just for this."

"Really?" Dex glanced under the table and then squeezed Emma's thigh lightly. "Yes. I do feel a little extra room there."

The electricity of Dex's touch almost jolted Emma from her chair. She could still feel the heat when Dex removed her hand from her leg, and when the warmth faded, she missed it.

During dinner, the silence was clear but not awkward. They simply glanced at each other several times as they ate. The atmosphere was comfortable yet not entirely relaxed. Every time Emma caught Dex watching her, she actually had to think about breathing, an act she'd never questioned before.

"I don't think I've ever had such delicious chicken." She caught Dex staring again, and suddenly the candlelight seemed very intimate. Possibly too intimate. Even though they'd seen each other several times over the weekend, officially it was only their second date.

"It's one of my favorite meals." Dex must have felt the closeness too. She got up, gathered their empty plates, and took them into the kitchen.

"One of mine now as well." She picked up the remaining items from the table, followed her in, and slid onto the same barstool she'd claimed before.

Keeping the barrier between them, Dex slid a plate of brownies across the granite countertop. "Dessert?"

"You're going to kill me with all this decadence."

"Kill? No. Spoil? Maybe."

Emma took a brownie from the plate and bit off a corner. "Oh my God. This is delicious. What is that I taste? Cayenne?"

"Wow. I can't fool you. If you could tell that, you *must* be a foodie."

"Definitely a foodie." She nodded, took another bite, closed her eyes, and let out a groan. "It seems like I found the right woman to satisfy my addiction." When she opened her eyes, the expression on Dex's face was different. Her eyes were glued to Emma's lips as she slipped her tongue out slightly to catch the crumbs from them.

Her stare veered to Emma's eyes, and her cheeks reddened slightly. "They pair really nicely with a cabernet." Dex pushed away from the counter. "I'll open another bottle."

"I'll get it." Emma smiled, popped up, and headed around the counter into the kitchen. "You've been working like a madwoman since I—"

Her words were lost as Dex pulled her into her arms and covered Emma's mouth with hers. A red-hot bolt of erotic electricity threw her into an inescapable surge of desire. She'd been waiting for this all night, and it was so much better than she remembered. The first kiss had been sweet, slow, and tentative, like a slow sunrise tempered by a soft trickling rain on a summer morning. The second was borderline scorching, something that the most torrential downpour couldn't douse.

Each sensual spot on her body was completely and thoroughly awake now. It was becoming agonizingly clear that she was about to explode at any moment. She couldn't go back from this.

Dex lifted her onto the counter and wedged herself up against her. This position, with Dex nestled firmly between her thighs, had her wet beyond measure, and there hadn't even been any friction. Dex's mouth, soft and warm, trailed slowly down Emma's neck to the sensitive spot where her neck met her shoulders, where she stopped and kissed her skin lightly. Emma had to force herself not to squirm closer. When Dex's hands slipped under her sweater, Emma let out a growl and felt Dex smile against her neck. Dex slid her hands up Emma's sides, taking the sweater with them, and slipped it over her head, leaving her wearing only a black lace bra. She felt terrifyingly exposed until she saw the steamy glimmer in Dex's eyes.

"God, you're beautiful." Dex stood back slightly and stared as though she were memorizing every part of her before she captured her mouth again, harder, more urgent this time. Suddenly tongues and hands were battling for control, and Dex pulled her closer, creating the much-needed friction she craved, and Emma couldn't stand it anymore.

She ripped her mouth from Dex's. "We need to move somewhere else, or you're going to have me right here on this counter."

Dex pulled her lip up into a grin before she ran her hands down Emma's thighs to her calves and moved them behind her. Emma took her cue and wrapped them around Dex's waist, and then Dex slid her off the counter into her arms. She carried her effortlessly across the living room, and when they reached the bottom of the stairs, Emma attempted to release her legs to stand.

Dex held her tight. "Don't worry. I've got you."

Emma kissed her urgently and then clung to Dex as she carried her up the stairs. She'd never been with a woman so strong, so confident in every way, the total opposite of herself.

When they reached the bedroom, Emma dropped her feet to the floor and began trailing her tongue down Dex's neck to the sweet space between her breasts. She pulled at the neckline of her sweater. "This has to come off."

Dex grasped the hem of the sweater and tugged it off. Without delay, Emma started kissing the skin just above the top of Dex's bra line again. When Dex let out a tiny whimper, confidence surged through

Emma, and she unfastened Dex's jeans and pushed them to the floor. She dragged her hands up her legs and stopped to kiss the sculpted belly before her as she moved up Dex's body to her mouth. The sparks zapping through her were unreal, and they'd barely touched each other. How could a woman do so much to her so quickly?

Dex reached around and popped the hook on Emma's bra before she backed her up to the edge of the bed, and they both tumbled onto it. She'd never been more grateful for buttonless pants as she was when Dex went to her knees, slid her fingers under the waistband of her jeggings, and tugged them off, taking her panties along with them. Movement stopped, and Emma glanced down to see Dex staring up at her as though she were taking in every inch of her again. God, this woman could melt her with one look.

Emma sat up, took Dex's face in her hands, and kissed her hard, sending another steaming shot of arousal through her.

Dex kneaded Emma's breast in one hand as the other made its way between her legs. As soon as she felt Dex's fingers skim the wet heat of her center and then push into her, they both groaned.

"I have to taste you."

Emma fell back onto the bed as Dex slipped her arms under her knees and pulled her forward. The first touch of her tongue had Emma on the verge of combustion. Not wanting it to happen too quickly, she grabbed a fistful of sheet. She wanted to savor every moment of pleasure in all its intensity as it happened. Emma pressed herself into the mattress, and Dex came in stronger. *Oh my God.* This was happening… Now. She let go of her control and tugged a handful of Dex's hair as she spiraled into a blissful pool of ecstasy. Tremors rolled through her, again and again. Dex's tongue was the most magical experience Emma had ever felt. She twitched with every stroke. When the aftershocks finally subsided, she reached for Dex and urged her up next to her.

"I have to say this dessert was so much better than the brownies." Emma covered her eyes with her arm and laughed. "I can't believe I just said that." She'd never had a woman enjoy her so completely, and the feeling both excited and embarrassed her.

Dex moved Emma's arm from her eyes. "I'm glad you did. We'll skip the brownies next time." She kissed her softly and then gathered her into the crook of her shoulder.

This woman was incredible. She didn't even seem to want anything in return. If she was feeling any of the same things Emma was, she needed release. Emma skimmed her hand across Dex's belly and under the waistband of her boxer briefs. Her breath hitched, and she closed her eyes when she felt the silky wetness between Dex's legs. This night wasn't close to being over yet. Emma knew a thing or two about delivering dessert.

She captured one of Dex's breasts in her mouth and flicked the nipple with her tongue while kneading the other between her fingers. Dex let out a moan and squirmed beneath her.

It became clear she needed better access. The briefs had to come off. She tugged at the waistband, and Dex swiftly slid them down her legs and kicked them to the floor.

The shudder beneath her lips as she trailed them across Dex's stomach made all kinds of senses come to life in Emma. This was absolute paradise. She continued farther and glided her hand over the soft patch of hair, letting it tickle her palm. She glanced up to catch Dex watching her with scorching desire in her eyes. God, she was beautiful. Emma nestled herself between Dex's legs for more contact, just skimming Dex's center with her lips. Dex opened her legs wider, allowing more access. One swipe, then another. She watched Dex's stomach ripple with each subtle touch she made. It fascinated Emma that she could make Dex react so intensely. She swiped at Dex's center, just barely gliding her tongue through the slickness, and let out a growl. She tasted incredible.

"You're not being fair," Dex said, grabbing a fistful of sheet.

She laughed and Dex squirmed. "What would be fair right now?"

"I need more."

"Like this?" Emma pushed two fingers into Dex.

"Oh my God. Yes." She reached down and held Emma's head in her hands, arching into her.

With that, Emma sank her mouth into Dex's center, and in no time, Dex's fingers pulled at Emma's hair and her thighs came together against her cheeks with surprising strength. Emma took in everything about her. The way her body shook with each pass of Emma's tongue, her tangy taste, and how tense her muscles became when Emma finally sent her over the edge.

The whole glorious scene cemented in Emma's mind just how breathtakingly gorgeous the woman beneath her was and how she was seeping her way into her heart.

Emma crawled up Dex's body and kissed her before she settled into the crook of Dex's shoulder again. This, right here, was something Emma could do forever.

CHAPTER THIRTEEN

Dex was still asleep when Emma came out of the bathroom. She hadn't wanted to leave the warmth of Dex's arms. They'd spent every night this week together, and she'd woken up in Dex's bed every morning. Her body was screaming "slow down" loud and clear, but what was happening with Dex just felt so right. She didn't want to leave at all, but everything between them was happening with lightning speed, and Emma wasn't quite sure how to handle her intense feelings for Dex.

She glanced around the room like she had once or twice before and, for some reason, was still surprised at the decor. She'd expected dark colors to accent the maple hardwood floors she'd stepped out of bed onto this morning. Even though the muted purple walls went perfectly with the flooring as well as the turquoise-and-white comforter that lay halfway across the bed, the color scheme still puzzled her.

She crossed the room, sat on the side of the bed, and watched Dex sleep. Her face was calm, without a single crease stressing it, just the tiny laugh lines around her eyes, which Emma was coming to adore. Tracing a circle on the back of Dex's hand, she shuddered at how they'd made her feel when she'd touched her last night.

Dex's eyes fluttered open, she stared up at Emma and immediately smiled. "What time is it?"

"Time for me to go."

She threaded her fingers with Emma's and kissed the back of her hand. "You don't have to. I'd love to fix you breakfast?"

"That sounds wonderful, but I have a date with the woman who tries to run my life." *And very often succeeds.*

Dex appeared confused as she propped herself up on her elbows.

"My mother. I promised to take her shopping today." She grinned. "Sorry. I meant to tell you last night." She glanced at the ceiling. "But somehow you made me forget." Dex propped herself up and Emma kissed her.

"Oh, sure. Blame it on me." Dex moved a swatch of hair from Emma's eyes. "I totally understand. The most important woman in your world." Dex seemed relieved, which made Emma happy. "For now anyway." She raised an eyebrow and hopped out of bed. "At least let me walk you out."

Emma watched the naked, sculpted, muscular body cross the room, and her heartbeat doubled. Dex was stunning. She pulled on a long-sleeved Henley and sweats that were slung across the chair in the corner. Emma's stomach dipped as Dex's mussed hair sprang through the neck opening of the Henley. She had to look away, or she'd end up across the room kissing her and find herself right back in bed ravishing every bit of her again. Emma was thoroughly amazed at Dex's body and her confidence. Emma would've taken the sheet with her and headed straight into the bathroom to change. She'd even attempted to do just that earlier, but Dex had been so wrapped up in it she couldn't get it free, so she'd made sure Dex was still asleep, grabbed her clothes, and raced across the room instead.

On the way out to the car, Dex took Emma's hand in hers, and the gesture felt totally natural and wonderful all in the same moment.

When Emma reached for the car door handle, Dex frowned. "I got it." She pulled open the door and motioned for Emma to get in.

"Thank you," Emma said softly. She wasn't at all used to having someone take such care with her. Her previous girlfriend, Amy, had never opened doors for her. Emma had been the chivalrous one in that relationship.

"You're very welcome," she said as she leaned in and gave Emma a scorching kiss that made Emma immediately want to call her mom and cancel.

"You're really making it hard for me to leave."

"My secret plan." Dex's lips tugged into a half-grin before she captured Emma's mouth again.

Emma took out her phone. Dex swiped it away from her and threw it back into her purse. "No. You should go. Mom time is important." She smiled softly. "Come back later, and we'll have breakfast for dinner?" Her lips spread into a sexy grin.

"Deal." Emma gave her a quick kiss, and Dex closed the door. She couldn't take her eyes off the beautiful woman watching her drive away and couldn't wait to get this day of shopping done so she could come back to her.

❖

Emma parked in front of her parents' house and grabbed the box from the passenger seat before she hustled up the driveway to the open garage. The floor was covered with sawdust, and her dad stood at his workbench building something, as usual. The small flat-screen TV mounted above the bench had one of the Sunday football games blaring through it.

"There's my girl," Bill said as he spun around on the stool, stood up, and hauled her into a bear hug. She was surprised he'd heard her in the midst of the crowd and commentators from the football game.

"I brought doughnuts." She opened the box she'd been carrying.

"I knew you were my favorite daughter for a reason." He slipped a hand in and took out a glazed doughnut. Glazed was his favorite, and bread and sugar were all he needed. Well, maybe a little jelly once in a while, but he was an easy dad to satisfy.

She snapped the box shut and rolled her eyes. "I'm your only daughter."

The doughnut was in his mouth immediately. "That too," he mumbled as he chewed.

Various sizes of wood lay strewn across the bench, and Emma couldn't imagine what her dad was creating. "What are you building there?"

He pushed a piece of paper toward her with a design scribbled across it. "A charging station for my cordless tools."

"Oh, wow. That looks awesome, Dad." Her dad was crazy good at woodworking, even without plans.

Another bite of doughnut went into his mouth, and he grinned.

"Is there coffee left?" Emma asked.

"Brewed a new pot just for you." He'd known she was coming. Emma and her mother had set up the shopping date weeks ago. Her mother was a planner and intended to get all her Christmas shopping done early, just as she did every year.

"Awesome." She headed into the house. Her mother was settled in her chair in the living room, feet up on the ottoman, relaxed with her nose in a book. "Whatcha reading, Mom?"

Glo glanced up and smiled. "The new Lisa Gardner."

"Suspense?"

The chair creaked as she got up. "Her stories fascinate me. From what I've learned in her books, I could've plotted to kill your father hundreds of times."

She let her mouth drop open. "*Mom.* Do I need to keep an eye on you?"

"I would never." She waved her hand as she crossed the room. "He's too handy. Do you know he's building me a bird feeder for the backyard?"

"Is that what that was?" The image of the plan for the tool-charging station popped into Emma's head. She guessed the bird feeder would be her father's next project. "Are you hungry?" She lifted the doughnut box slightly.

Her mother kissed Emma on the cheek and took the box from her as she trotted into the kitchen. "I knew you were my favorite daughter for a reason."

Emma chuckled and shook her head. Her parents couldn't be more alike if they tried. She guessed that was from being married thirty-plus years.

The cabinet stuck halfway when Emma opened it to get a mug. "Hasn't Dad fixed this yet?" The hinge had been broken for months, but her dad had jerry-rigged it to work until he got around to fixing it.

"It's on his list after the bird feeder." That could be a few months down the road. Apparently, her mother hadn't seen the real list.

Emma poured herself a mug of coffee and refilled her mother's cup before she sat on the stool at the counter next to her. "So where are we going?" She hoped it was just a few specialty shops. The mall would be packed today.

"I need to get your father a pair of these jeans he likes from J.C.

Penney." She picked up the pair from the chair and handed them to Emma. "Can you read the label on these?"

Yay! It appeared Emma had dodged the mall bullet today. "Where's your phone?"

Her mother reached across the counter, picked it up, and handed it to her. Emma found the label of the pants and took a picture of it.

"Ooh, that's a good idea." And then her mother said, "And I need to pick up some makeup at Macy's. They have a gift this month."

Ugh. She knew it was too good to be true. Her mother lived and breathed to mall-shop.

"We can grab lunch at the food court there."

Even better. Emma smiled. She couldn't change her mother's love for shopping at this point. She just hoped she'd be worn out by midafternoon so Emma could get back to Dex. She took a deep breath, closed her eyes, and let the tingle wash over her. *Dex.*

The door swung open and Bill walked through it. He stopped at the coffeepot and filled his insulated mug. "Any doughnuts left?" he asked, heading for the box on the counter.

Glo put her hand on the box. "How many is that?"

"Just one."

She glanced at Emma to confirm, and Emma nodded. It wasn't true, but she'd learned to keep quiet about some things. If one more doughnut on occasion made her dad happy, Emma wouldn't spoil the enjoyment for him.

Bill gave her a sly wink. "I thought you two would be out the door by now. All the good stuff will be gone if you don't get moving." He laughed.

Emma rolled her eyes. "Stop feeding her addiction, Dad." Emma had thought they'd be long gone by now too, but her sleep last night had been interrupted in the best possible way, which had pushed her morning to start much later than usual.

"Okay, okay. Let me get my purse." She trotted through the living room. "I'll be right back."

"So Mom thinks the thing you're building out there is a bird feeder." She flattened her lips and tilted her head.

"It's next on the list." He took a bite of the doughnut. "She'll get it for Christmas."

Emma smiled. Her dad always came through with anything her mom wanted. Someday she hoped to have a relationship as solid as theirs.

❖

They'd been at the mall for almost two hours and had hit at least twenty different stores when Glo decided she needed energy to continue. If it were up to Emma, she would've just powered through to get out of there sooner. But her mother liked to enjoy the whole mall experience, which meant starting at one end, getting to the other, rounding the turn at the anchor store, and then making her way back to the middle to eat at the food court. Thankfully she didn't care for one or two stores, and they'd skipped them entirely. Emma hated the mall, but she tolerated it to spend time with her mother.

Emma stood in line to get the sandwiches, turkey for herself and ham for Glo, while her mother staked out a table. She was good at hovering until someone finished their food, and then she'd swoop in to grab the table as soon as they left. She'd been known to try to steal a table prematurely when someone had gotten up to get something more to eat. Glo had rules about mall eating: you got all the food you wanted all at once. Then you ate quickly. You didn't linger, holding a table when others had their food and needed to sit.

"So what happened this morning?"

She immediately thought about her dad's woodworking project. "What? With Dad?"

"You were late. You're never late on shopping days." She took a bite of her sandwich. "You like to get here early and get it over with."

"That's not true. I love spending time with you."

"But you hate the mall."

"Yeah." Emma nodded. "I do." She couldn't argue with that.

"So why were you late?"

"I had a date last night."

Glo dropped her sandwich to her plate and took a drink to wash down the last bite she'd taken. "And you're just now telling me this? What's her name? Did you have fun? Are you going to see her again?" Glo fired the questions at Emma without giving her a chance to get a word in.

"Her name is Dex. Yes, we had fun, and I'm having dinner with her again tonight."

Her mother leaned in with rapt attention. "You had dinner, not just drinks last night?"

"Appetizers, dinner, and dessert." Her body warmed at the thought of dessert. "The whole nine yards, Mom."

Glo smiled softly and tilted her head the way she always did when she read Emma. "You're blushing."

She put her hands to her cheeks and smiled. "I really like her, Mom."

"Tell me about her." Glo picked up her sandwich and continued to eat.

"She's smart, funny, and very creative. She does landscaping for a living." She took a bite of her sandwich.

"Outdoorsy, huh?"

Emma nodded as she chewed. "Has her own company."

"Maybe she can give your father a few tips on how to keep the grass alive."

"I'm sure she can. Her yard is gorgeous."

"So when do I get to meet this wonderful landscaper, Dex?"

"I'm gonna hold off on that for now. I'm just getting to know her, Mom." All she needed was for her mother to get in the middle and scare Dex away.

"You're not embarrassed to bring her home, are you?"

"Of course not. I just want to see where this is going first. Okay?" She finished the last bite of her sandwich, wadded up the paper wrapper, and tossed it onto the tray.

"Okay, but when you're ready to rein her in, I'm on board to help." Glo continued to eat what was left of her sandwich, as she'd been doing more talking than eating.

Emma chuckled. Her mom was totally serious. "Thanks, Mom. I'll keep you in the loop." That was so not happening.

After Glo finished her sandwich, Emma cleared the table, and then they headed to the next store on her mom's list.

CHAPTER FOURTEEN

The doorbell rang three times in a row, and then the knocking began. Dex knew it would ring several more times before she could get downstairs and answer the door. It had to be Grace, given the fifteen texts she'd sent her already this morning. She'd been in too good a mood to talk to her, but now she was going to have to do it whether she wanted to or not.

Panda hopped up onto the bed, and Dex rubbed her behind the ears. She'd interrupted them only once during the night with a loud meow, which, thankfully, Emma found hysterical. Except for that little incident, both last night and this morning had been perfect. Well, until Grace showed up.

She got out of bed, pulled on her hoodie, and went downstairs. She still hadn't showered. She'd put it off to keep Emma's essence with her for just a little while longer. She could still smell Emma on herself, and it did something wonderful to her—calmed her and made her feel content. Dex's outlook on relationships was changing. Maybe life *would* have a happy ending in store for her after all.

As soon as she opened the door, Grace barreled through it. "Where have you been? I haven't heard from you in days." She dropped her purse on the couch.

"I've been busy estimating jobs and taking orders. Light season's about to hit."

"You've called me every day for as long as I can remember."

"Well, um…I thought maybe I should cool that since Brent moved in." It was a plausible excuse.

"Is this your sweater?" Grace plucked the sweater from the counter with her thumb and index finger. "Oh, I see. This is why." She held it up and scrutinized it. "You found somebody to fuck, and you don't need your old friend Grace anymore."

"Jesus, Grace." Dex swiped it out of her hand and took it to the laundry room. Emma must have put Dex's on upstairs by mistake. "I can have a life too, you know."

Grace closed her eyes and took in a deep breath. "I'm sorry. That was uncalled for. I just miss talking to you. You get me. Remember? We go perfectly together. Dex and Grace like Dolce and Gabbana." Grace used to say that often, but had rarely mentioned the phrase in recent years since she'd met Brent.

"There is no more D and G, Grace. That's done. You have Brent. You're GB...Gianni Bini now."

Grace scrunched her face. "That's not fair. You can't just throw me out of the fun like that."

Dex shrugged. "I didn't throw you out, Grace. You left the party."

"But you're the only person who truly knows me. Even Brent doesn't know me as well as you do. We've always been each other's person."

"Things have changed, Grace. You're married now. I need that person to be someone else."

"And you think that's Emma?" Grace's voice rose again.

"Maybe. I don't know yet."

"She is so wrong for you." Grace strutted across the room.

"Why?" Dex followed her, took her arm, and swung her around. "Why is she so wrong for me, Grace?"

"She just is."

"Because she's not you?"

"You're damn right she's not me. No one can be *me*." The anger in Grace's voice spiked.

"You made your choice, and it wasn't me." She shook her head and blew out a breath. "It was never going to be me."

Whenever Dex would take the slightest interest in another woman, Grace would show up full force in her life and shatter any chance the other girl had at finding a place in Dex's heart. Purposely or not, she did it *every* time. Dex wanted it to be different this time. She really liked Emma.

Grace took in a deep breath. "Okay. Clearly you haven't had

enough sleep." She spun around and snatched her purse from the couch and sped to the door. "Call me when you've gotten some rest. We can talk again then." She yanked open the door. The house rattled when she closed it behind her.

"Clearly, I wasn't saying what you wanted to hear." She mimicked Grace. "Right, Panda?" She gave the cat a quick scratch before she filled her food dish. Then she went to the laundry room, picked up Emma's sweater, and smashed her face into it. Her head filled with comforting thoughts of Emma, and her world was good again.

❖

Dex's stomach fluttered when the doorbell rang. She'd been antsy since she'd received Emma's text letting her know she'd just dropped off her mom and was on her way. She'd been looking forward to seeing her again since the moment she'd left this morning.

When she opened the door, Emma stepped inside and kissed her until her knees wobbled.

"I take it shopping went well?"

"It did, but I couldn't wait to get back here." Emma tugged off her coat, and Dex hung it on the hall tree.

The somersaults in Dex's stomach continued. "Really?"

"Yes, really." Emma went immediately back to kissing Dex. "You haven't started dinner yet, have you?" she asked, breaking away for a moment.

The spark in Emma's eyes was unmistakable. "Dinner can wait." She took Emma's hand, and they hurried up the stairs. This woman was unbelievably sexy and had her turned on as soon as she walked through the door. Just the thought that Emma wanted her sent a surge of heat through Dex.

Clothes came off without delay, and as Dex took in the gorgeous woman before her she wanted to take her time and explore every inch of her. But when Emma pushed her onto the bed and trailed her tongue up Dex's neck to meet her mouth and kissed her with such urgency and power, it was clear who was in control tonight. Emma pulled back and heaved out a breath as she stared. Dex was mesmerized by shimmering silvery-blue eyes, heavy with desire, staring down at her. She was immediately ready for this woman and bit back the surge of arousal threatening to consume her.

"You're so beautiful," Emma whispered as she ran her fingertips across the swell of Dex's breast to her stomach and back again, grazing her nipple with her palm. Dex's breathing increased and her heart pounded wildly. She thought she might explode right then. Emma seemed to notice, and she immediately moved her hips between Dex's legs and pressed up against her. Dex let out a gasp at the contact and wrapped her legs around Emma's, urging her closer. The friction was delicious, and just when Dex was on the verge of spiraling into pure pleasure, Emma slowed and kissed her so deeply Dex thought she would implode. She reached to touch Emma, to feel her wetness, but Emma broke the kiss and stayed just out of reach before she slid down Dex's body. She slowly ran her fingers across Dex's thighs and around to the backs of her knees before she kissed the soft skin of her lower belly. Dex quivered at the contact, and Emma glanced up and smiled before she trailed her tongue farther, parting her folds and sending Dex spiraling upward again.

"Oh my God, yes."

With that, Emma pushed her fingers inside, and Dex couldn't help the cry that ripped from her throat as she sailed over the edge into a surging orgasm. Emma had watched her throughout the whole thing, and Dex had thoroughly enjoyed taking in Emma's heated desire as she came. When her muscles relaxed and the spasms began to slow, Emma slid her fingers free, moved up next to Dex, and kissed her softly.

"I like having you for dinner." Emma slapped her hand to her mouth. "Oh my God, I'm getting really bad about saying what's on my mind."

Dex laughed and pulled one side of her mouth up into a grin. She liked flustered Emma, who was extremely beautiful. "You are." She kissed her softly. "But I like it too." Dex enjoyed Emma's warmth as she nestled on her shoulder, her hand across Dex's stomach and their legs entangled. Her satisfaction and contentment were revealing. She'd been keeping her heart locked down for so long, she hadn't realized how good it felt to let someone in—someone other than Grace. What she had, right here, with Emma was so much better.

❖

Dex settled into the seat across from Juni in their now-usual booth at Crushed Beans. Josh had already delivered their coffees before she'd arrived: a vanilla latte that included a special heart design in the foam for Juni and a mocha with a reindeer, which resembled a dog, for Dex.

"Wow. You certainly are glowing for this time of year." Juni reached across the table and felt her forehead. "You're not sick, are you?"

"Lovesick maybe." She pulled her lips into a grin.

Juni's eyes widened. "Spill."

"I've spent every night this week with someone. Her name's Emma."

"Every morning too?"

She nodded. "I'm telling you, Juni. It's like we're made for each other. I've never been with anyone who's so aggressive, yet so sweet and gentle."

Juni leaned forward and whispered, "Wow. *Every night.* You really like her."

"Like her? I think I'm falling in love with her." Dex grinned as she raised her cup to her lips and slurped down a sip of warmth.

Juni clapped her hands like a little kid. "Oh my God. It's finally happened." She took Dex's hands and squeezed them. "I'm so happy for you."

"Stop. It's not like I just lost my virginity."

The grin on Juni's face was ridiculous. "No, but your heart is moving forward, and that makes me really happy."

Dex sighed. "I think so." Every bit of what Juni had said was absolutely true. Her heart knew it too.

"Have you told Grace about her yet? Or how you feel?" Juni took a drink of her latte and licked the foam mustache it left from her lips.

"Yeah. She came over yesterday while Emma was shopping with her mother."

"And?"

"And she freaked out a little when I told her things were different now."

Juni flopped back into the booth cushion. "Fuck her."

"Don't act like that. I knew it wasn't going to be easy."

The table rattled when she popped forward again. "She's freaking married." Juni's voice squealed, and they got a couple of stares from a few of the other people at tables surrounding them.

"That's what I told her." She spun the knife on the table in front of her.

Juni slapped her palm to it, sending it flying to the floor. "She wants the best of both worlds, and you have to tell her she can't have it."

"I'm working on that. It's just not easy." Dex smiled at the people at the table next to her as she picked up the knife and set it on a napkin near the corner of the table. "You know how long she's been in my life."

"I do, and I know how she treats you." Juni flopped against the booth cushion again.

"Stop." The booth was going to fall apart if Juni kept that up. "Can we move off the Grace subject for now? I was having such a great day."

The muscle in Juni's cheek jerked as she swung her gaze from Dex and stared at the ceiling. "Okay. Tell me more about Emma," she said, returning her attention to Dex.

"She got her marketing degree at Northwestern and works in advertising at the same firm as Brent."

"With Brent? Really? That's quite a coincidence."

"No coincidence. Brent thought Emma and I might get along, so he set it up. We met at their housewarming party."

"Wow, that must be chafing Grace's—"

"We're not talking about Grace anymore, right?"

"Right." Juni crossed her arms across her chest. "Well, I'm just glad he didn't let her stop him from doing it." She snarled her nose and flattened her lips.

The irritation on Juni's face was clear. Dex knew she was keeping a lot of choice words about Grace inside at this moment, and she was grateful for her restraint. While Emma occupied her mind, she wanted Grace as completely out of it as possible. Emma was taking over her thoughts in a colossal way, and the feelings of contentment Dex was experiencing astonished her.

CHAPTER FIFTEEN

Emma ran to the car and hopped into the passenger seat almost before Dex could put it into park. She'd been waiting on the porch dressed in a cute, above-the-knee-length royal-blue dress, flats, and a pastel-pink wool coat when Dex pulled up in front of her house. Apparently she was just as eager to see Dex as she was to see Emma. They'd spent a couple of nights away from each other, and Dex missed her warmth. The scorching kiss Emma gave her was worth the wait.

She glanced up at the house, noticing the lack of Christmas lights. She'd have to remedy that. She couldn't have her girlfriend living in a house with no holiday spirit. *Girlfriend? Is she my girlfriend?* She pushed the thought from her head. *One step at a time, Dex.*

"Which theater?" They had planned to go to a movie, a new factual drama that Emma really wanted to see.

"Let's go to the Cineplex. They have those cushy recliner seats." She fastened her seat belt and settled in. "And the popcorn's the best."

"I guess that means we'll need to get a large." Dex took her hand, lacing their fingers together, then placed it on her own thigh. Emma squeezed it slightly, and Dex smiled.

They were almost to the movie theater when Emma pointed frantically out the window. "Ooh!" she squealed. "Let's go bowling."

"But I thought you wanted to go to the movies?"

Emma dipped her chin. "Is that where *you* want to go today?"

"No, but you seemed excited about it. And now I want popcorn. And you're wearing a dress." Dex took in the legs slipping out from beneath the hem of the dress. Beautiful, shapely legs.

Emma smiled, seeming to catch Dex's assessment. "I'll be fine, but will you?"

The heat in her cheeks rose. "Oh yeah. I'd much rather watch you bowl." Dex flipped the SUV around and headed back to the bowling alley.

It was fairly empty when Dex and Emma arrived, just a few groups of people scattered across the place. They stopped at the desk to get a lane and shoes and then headed to number eighteen, a little over halfway across the alley. A few young teenage girls were bowling on the set of lanes next to them, as well as a group of rowdy teenage boys a couple of lanes over from the girls.

Emma started entering their names into the scoring system, and Dex went straight to the ball return to see if any of the weights would work for her. Several alley balls were left from the previous bowlers, so she hefted a few and then set them back down.

"These are all too small. I'm gonna go look for another one." She held one of the lighter ones up. "Do you want to try these, or should I find one for you as well?"

"Trying to sabotage my game already?" On the way inside, Emma had mentioned more than once that she was a pretty good bowler.

"Nope. I'm looking forward to the competition."

Emma grinned and raised an eyebrow. "Care to make a wager?"

This was getting interesting. "I would." Dex smiled, slid into the chair next to Emma, and slung her arm behind her. "What do you have in mind?"

Emma stared into her eyes for a few moments before she cleared her throat and glanced at the keyboard in front of her. "If I win, you put up the Christmas lights at my house?"

Dex nodded. "And if I win?"

Emma smiled at her as though she knew it wasn't going to happen. "I'll make dinner."

"Deal." Dex held out her hand, and they shook on it.

The ball return had stolen Dex's ball early in the first game, and Emma had beaten Dex by twenty-plus pins. Dex obnoxiously blamed the loss on the missing bowling ball, even though Emma had definite bowling skills.

They were in the middle of their second game when Dex caught Emma watching the teenage boys a couple of lanes down. She followed

Emma's stare to the phone in one boy's hand, which was discreetly pointed at the girls bowling next to them. When Dex glanced back to Emma, her eyes had narrowed, and she launched out of her seat like a missile. She was charging their way, and Dex scrambled to follow.

The first thing she heard out of Emma's mouth was, "What are you, *ten*?" She plucked the phone from the boy's hand. "It's *not* okay to film someone without their permission."

That got the girls' attention. They stopped bowling and came closer. The tallest of them took the phone from Emma and played the video. "If you dare post any of this on Facebook, Kyle MacGregor, I'll hate you forever."

"I won't. I promise." The boy's face went white as he bolted up from his seat. He even looked a little terrified. "I was going to show it to you later."

"Really? Why?" the girl asked.

"You're really good at bowling."

Dex and Emma both stared up at the scoreboard, wondering if what he'd said was true. One-thirty-five in the sixth frame. She was good.

The boy said, "I thought maybe you could help me."

In the midst of Kyle's embarrassment, each of the other girls had slipped in beside one of the other boys.

Emma shook her head, rolled her eyes, and turned to Dex. "Ugh."

Dex chuckled. "Seems like the morals police aren't needed here anymore." She put her hand on the small of Emma's back and motioned her to lead the way back to their lane. "Looks like they're friends," Dex said as she sat down next to Emma.

Emma shrugged. "Seems so now. I wasn't sure earlier. The girls hadn't even acknowledged them since we got here." She watched them intently. The girls had moved to the lanes where the boys were, and they were all laughing and bowling together now.

"Playing hard to get, you think?"

"Seems that way." Emma stared across the lanes at them as the girls leaned into the boys while they laughed and flirted. She glanced up at the scoreboard. "Is it my turn?"

"Mine." Dex shook her head. "Too many fucking games in high school. Someday they'll realize how useless it all was."

Emma's gaze moved to Dex. "Sounds like you may have a history with that."

The ball return clanked as it spit up the missing ball. "Too much history," Dex said and got up to bowl, avoiding the subject. Talking about it only made it all rush back, and that made her heart hurt.

❖

Darkness was just beginning to take hold when Dex plugged in the lights. She ran to the curb, stood next to Emma, and grabbed her hand, lacing their fingers together. She watched Emma's face as she stared at the lights. It hadn't been a difficult job. The house was medium-sized, not too large, as were the rest of the homes in the Forest Park neighborhood. It was a nice little suburb with somewhat of a city feel to it that included lots of small independent shops and restaurants. Plus it wasn't too far from where Dex lived in Oak Park.

Emma hadn't wanted to be the attraction of the block or create a competition with her neighbors who decorated every year. Turning the street into a traffic circus wasn't one of her goals either. She'd simply wanted to join in the celebration and not be the only house on the street without Christmas lights. So Dex created a zigzag pattern on the holly bushes flanking each window, strung lights from the eves, and added a nice border to the front door—all in multicolored lights, which Emma had said she preferred. Another little something they had in common.

"They're absolutely gorgeous."

"Are you sure? I can set them up to run with music if you want."

"No. They're perfect just like this." Emma turned and gave her a soft kiss. "I can see why your boss keeps you on. You do excellent work, Ms. Putnam."

"I hold my own." She smiled, savoring the reward she'd just received. Dex wasn't used to not being asked to change something or do more.

"Well, you are now my official Christmas light hanger-upper. If there is such a thing."

"Oh, there's definitely a thing." She smiled, enjoying Emma's warmth.

"Come on. Let's go inside and get something warm to drink."

Emma took her hand and pulled her along with her to the house. "I have hot chocolate."

"Packaged or homemade?"

"Homemade, of course." Emma shot her a wild-eyed stare.

"I'm in." She stopped on the porch to show Emma the light timer hidden just behind the holly bush. "This is all set, so the lights will go on at dusk and off at sunrise automatically." She turned the knob and opened the door for Emma.

"You're awesome, Dex." Emma stopped and stared into her eyes. "I really mean that."

The rush that flooded Dex was like a one-hundred-mile-an-hour wind gust. She'd never expected to have these emotions ever again. Dex took Emma into her arms and kicked the door shut with her foot. She let her hands roam up under Emma's jacket to the warm, soft skin of her waist.

"Oh my God." Emma grabbed her arms, yanked them from her waist, and held them firmly. "You need to warm those hands up."

"That's what I'm trying to do." Dex broke loose, took Emma into her arms again, and slid her hands up the back of Emma's shirt and jacket.

"Ack! *Before* you touch me." Emma squealed and tried to wrestle out of her arms.

"Don't I get some kind of reward for putting up your lights?" She bounced her eyebrows at Emma playfully.

"Absolutely not." Emma arched an eyebrow and blew out a breath. "I didn't ask you to. You lost that bet."

"What if I let you win?" She hadn't, and she would've put up the lights, win or lose.

"You'd better not've."

Dex laughed. "You're sounding a little like that teenage girl at the bowling alley."

"I am not." Emma's voice rose. "You didn't let me win, did you?"

Dex shook her head. "No. You kicked my butt fair and square, champ." She let her smile drop to her best sad-puppy-dog face. "But doesn't the loser deserve some sort of consolation prize?" She glanced up at the sprig of mistletoe she'd hung from the entryway light above them earlier.

Emma snaked her arms around Dex's neck and grinned. "Yes."

She sighed. "You definitely earned something." She gave her a long, lingering kiss that made Dex wish she'd actually won the bet. The stakes would've been much higher and included definite heat after dinner.

"That and hot chocolate." She gave her another quick kiss before bolting out of her arms and leading her into the kitchen.

Dex glanced around the room, which felt oddly familiar. She noticed the pink notepad with the faded rose border on the counter with something scribbled on it.

"I've been here before."

Emma rolled her lips in but didn't speak. She just leaned against the counter.

A memory flitted through Dex's head, but she couldn't quite place it. A sinking feeling hit her stomach. *The morning after the wedding.* She glanced back to Emma. "You took me home after the wedding?" Pieces of that morning flashed through her thoughts. The note she'd found on the counter, the hangover cure beside it, the advice about Grace. Dex's cheeks warmed. "What a schmuck I am. I didn't even recognize you."

"You were in a bit of a state that night."

"That's being polite." She shook her head. "I was a fucking mess."

Emma laughed as she smiled and nodded. "A total mess."

"Did we…"

Emma laughed abruptly. "Definitely not. I don't think you could've even if I'd tried. Which I didn't." She stared at her hands. "I'm really not into that kind of thing. One-night stands, I mean. Especially with plastered women."

Dex moved closer and kissed her. "How about this kind of thing we're doing here?" She moved a stray strand of hair from Emma's forehead before she took her face into her hands and searched her eyes. This news made things different somehow, and Dex wanted permission to move further. When she felt Emma's hands on her waist, she took in a breath and went for it.

"Definitely this kind of thing." Emma clasped Dex's hand and led her to the bedroom.

She stopped in the doorway, remembering the muted beige and sage-green colors before she entered the room. It appeared different but the same, most likely due to her state of mind the last time she'd been there.

"Are you okay?" Emma's soft, silvery eyes morphed to steel blue as she gazed at Dex, and the memory of her face that night became clear.

"I guess I need to get that Northwestern T-shirt back to you."

Emma grinned. "I'm surprised you haven't torched it by now."

"The thought had crossed my mind." She laughed and then took a deep breath. "Thank you," she said as she tugged Emma into her arms and ran her thumb across her soft, full bottom lip. When she gazed into her eyes again, they had darkened to an almost cobalt blue. Dex took Emma's face in her hands and kissed her softly at first and then more urgently when Emma slipped her tongue into Dex's mouth, slowly touching and baiting as it deepened. It was the most perfectly arousing kiss, one that she could continue forever if her body hadn't been commanding more.

Emma broke away and pressed her forehead to Dex's. "I'd do it a thousand more times for a thank-you like that." She turned and led her to the bed.

There would be no need for that—her drunken self-pitying days were over. Dex would willingly kiss her that way every day for the rest of her life. From that point on, neither of them uttered a word. Emma just made tiny sounds as Dex explored her body, slowly savoring it like this was their first time. In essence it was a new experience again, now that Dex knew the depths of how wonderful Emma truly was. A ragged moan escaped Emma's lips as Dex pushed her fingers into her and stroked her thumb between her folds. Dex watched as her eyes fluttered closed and then open again. Such a beautiful sight. How could she have forgotten those eyes, those lips, that face? She stroked faster, and Emma grabbed hold of her shoulders, bringing her closer, kissing her until she tore her lips away and let out a cry as the orgasm ripped through her. It was the most wonderful sound in the world to Dex.

They stayed tangled in each other, kissing and caressing, enjoying the heat between them for what seemed like hours until a loud growl came from Emma's stomach. A huge laugh erupted from her mouth immediately.

Dex widened her eyes and laughed. "Hungry?"

"Oh my God, yes. I'm starving." She rolled into Dex. "Breakfast or dinner?"

"Pancakes?"

"Definitely pancakes, and eggs, and hash browns. I need some carbs. I haven't had this much exercise in years." Emma kissed her. "Maybe even toast."

"Ooh. Do you have any of that ginger jam?" Dex remembered its zippy flavor.

Emma smiled. "You liked that, did ya?"

"It was the absolute best jam I've ever had."

"Did it work for the hangover?" Emma seemed nervous all of a sudden, like she was embarrassed about the entire exchange, even though Dex should be the one worried.

"It did." She smiled and kissed her again.

Emma touched Dex's chin with her fingertips. "I wasn't sure if it would."

"Was I your guinea pig?"

"No." She chuckled and shook her head. "It works for me, but I've never been quite that drunk."

"I've never been quite that drunk before either." Nor had she been since she'd decided to move on. Dex took in a deep breath to purge the night from her mind. She didn't want to think about Grace. Not now, while she was lying next to this sweet, beautiful woman. Each time she was with Emma, it became clearer that they fit each other more perfectly than Dex had ever fit with anyone else.

She'd never experienced such feelings before. This felt genuine, emotional, and deep. She wanted to swim in Emma's essence, stay there with her forever, drowning in the warmth surrounding her. All she'd ever known before was longing for something she couldn't have. Now she had something real.

❖

Emma lay in the dark staring at Dex. She appeared sweet and relaxed, like her dreams were filled with rainbows and unicorns. The expression of pure passion Emma had seen on her face earlier made the sight all the more beautiful. They'd made love again after their late-night breakfast, and Emma had satisfied Dex completely, at least it seemed so from the way her body trembled beneath her. She'd been worried how the night would go when Dex recognized her kitchen and realized she'd been there before. She couldn't have been more embarrassed and had apologized more than enough times. The blush that covered her face had made her green eyes sparkle, the golden sunbursts in them becoming brighter.

Emma was thankful she hadn't recalled any of it before last night. If Dex had remembered, she might not be in this very spot right now, lying in her arms, loving her. *Loving her?* She moved a swatch of hair from Dex's face and took in a deep breath. These feelings were much deeper than she'd ever experienced before, even with Amy, whom Emma had once thought she'd be with forever. She wanted to stop time and stay right here, in this very moment, indefinitely. *She could be the one.*

Dex slid her hand across Emma's stomach. "You're awake."

"Uh-huh," she said and kissed her softly.

"You should sleep. You have work tomorrow." Dex slid her hand lower.

"I should." She tried to think of what she had going tomorrow, but her thoughts scattered as Dex's fingers skimmed her center. *Holiday client lunch.*

"Fuck," she said as she halted Dex's fingers from going any farther.

"Not the response I was hoping for." Dex twisted her face into a comical frown.

She laughed. "I need to make a cheesecake for work, and I have no idea how to do it."

"You volunteered to make a cheesecake, and you've never done it before?"

"I was actually voluntold to make it."

"Ah, last one to sign up, eh?"

She nodded, hoping Dex would be willing to help.

"Well, let's see what we can do about that." Dex seemed thoughtful for a moment. "Do you have cream cheese?"

"Yes."

Dex flicked a nipple with her tongue. "Eggs?"

"Always."

Dex took Emma's other nipple into her mouth and sucked it slowly before letting it pop back out. "Sour cream?"

She moaned. "Uh-huh."

Dex trailed her tongue across her stomach. "Vanilla?"

"Oh my God. Yes."

She dipped her tongue into her belly button. "Sugar?"

"Yes…yes. I have everything you need."

Dex hovered just above her center. "Graham crackers?"

"Fuck. I forgot those," she said with a growl and pushed her fingers into Dex's hair. "But I bought a special pan."

"Good enough." Dex slipped her tongue between Emma's folds.

Emma jolted as the sensation rolled through her. Dex had barely touched her, and she was immediately ready to come. She concentrated hard to feel the wonderful warmth of Dex's tongue as it stroked her, but when she slipped a finger inside and matched the rhythm of her tongue, the orgasm crashed through her and sent her spiraling into the warm, wonderful abyss. She'd never worshipped God so loudly before in her life. Dex seemed to know everything that pleased her and how to do it well.

She reached for Dex and coaxed her up next to her. "How do you do that?"

"What?"

"Take me there so quickly."

Dex's lip tugged up into a half smile. "You inspire me."

"And I will forever remember the ingredients for cheesecake." Emma chuckled.

"My special cheesecake." Dex bounced her eyebrows. "Which we must make." She reached for her phone and checked the time. "Now."

Emma took the phone from her and tossed it to the bottom of the bed. "But it's my turn."

Dex pulled her eyebrows together. "There are no turns in this bed." A smile came over her face before she kissed Emma softly and threw the covers back. "Cheesecake first. Then we discuss turns." She found her T-shirt on the floor and pulled it over her head before she tossed Emma her robe, and then they raced into the kitchen.

"Do you have any Oreos?"

"Oreos don't last long here." She smiled sheepishly and then lifted her eyebrows. "Oh, but I do have fortune cookies. Will those work?"

"Absolutely."

She opened the pantry door and took out a huge container full of them.

"I take it you like Chinese food." Dex scanned the pantry and took the food processor and mixer from the bottom shelf.

"It's easy and close." She grinned. "When you come back for dinner this week, I'll buy."

"An offer I can't refuse." Dex unwrapped a couple of cookies and dropped them into the food processor before she tossed a handful of them in front of Emma. "Unwrap. I'll help, but you're baking, so you can own it at work."

"You're really taking a chance on me."

Dex took in a deep breath and seemed to contemplate her next words. "Yes, I am." She dropped the fortune cookies, put her arms around Emma's waist, and kissed her in such a way that Emma lost all sense of time and place. When they parted, Dex smiled and handed her another handful of fortune cookies.

So many thoughts flew through Emma's mind at that point that she had a hard time focusing on baking. She was ready to forget the cheesecake and take Dex right back to bed. She didn't want to go to work in the morning. She didn't want to leave the house ever again.

Once the cheesecake was in the oven, Emma couldn't keep her hands off Dex. She'd somehow gotten covered with cheesecake batter, but the expression in Dex's eyes when she'd let her robe drop to the floor made it perfectly clear she was up for another round. They'd made love on the couch this time, and Emma had taken her turn. She couldn't get enough of the woman who seemed to anticipate her every need. She wouldn't sleep tonight, not with Dex in her arms. Her taste and her scent lingered on Emma's lips, and she knew she'd never grow tired of this woman. She'd just dozed off when the oven timer startled her awake.

"I'll get it." Dex rolled from her side and off the couch, and Emma followed her.

Dex took the cheesecake from the oven and set it on a trivet.

Emma stood in awe at the delicacy in front of her. "This is so beautiful. I'm not sure I want to take it to work."

Dex reached into the oven and took out another cheesecake half the size of the first. "The reason I made this one."

Emma hadn't seen her slip that one into the oven. "I could kiss you right now."

"I'll accept that reward." Dex took her into her arms, and Emma kissed her deeply.

"Let's go back upstairs."

Dex smiled. "First, we taste."

Emma pulled open a drawer, plucked out a spoon, and handed it to Dex. She scooped out a tiny spoonful of cheesecake, slid it into Emma's mouth, and kissed her again. The sweet taste of cream cheese, sugar, and vanilla lingered between them. It was by far the most erotic kiss Emma had ever experienced. She took the spoon from Dex's hand, dropped it onto the counter, and pulled her back upstairs.

CHAPTER SIXTEEN

Dex thought about the night before with Emma, which had been both give and take. She and Emma didn't fight for control. Well, maybe a little, but they definitely didn't do battle. A natural exchange existed between them. They were so in sync it was spectacular, and oddly enough, Dex felt energized this morning. Of course, the four cups of coffee hadn't hurt.

She knocked lightly on Juni's front door before she slid her key into the slot and unlocked the deadbolt. Juni and Dex had exchanged keys long ago to prevent lockouts and accommodate emergency cat feedings. Sometimes Dex worked long hours to complete a landscaping job, and Juni had come to the rescue with feeding Panda more than once.

"Hey, sis," she shouted as she moved through the living room to the kitchen. Four cups of coffee weren't enough. She was going to need more to keep her from sleeping on her feet today. She took the decanter from the coffeemaker and noted that the coffee hadn't been made.

Where was Juni? She went back to the bottom of the stairs. "You okay?"

"Yes. Be right down," Juni shouted from upstairs.

She checked her watch. Nine o'clock. That was odd. Juni was usually up and dressed by eight.

Juni came hustling down the stairs and into the kitchen. "You making the coffee?"

She nodded. "I'm going to need a gallon of it this morning."

"Me too. Throw a couple extra cups in there today." Juni reached into the refrigerator, took out the orange juice, and poured herself a glass.

Dex stopped what she was doing and turned around. "For you?"

A huge grin spread across Juni's face as she slid the juice back into the fridge. "Josh is here."

"Oh my God." Dex widened her eyes. "He's here?" She dropped the bag of coffee onto the counter. "I should go. You two have morning-after things to do."

"It's okay." She smiled as she took a drink of juice. "We've been doing that all morning."

Dex picked up the coffee and continued to scoop it into the maker. After she flipped the switch on, she picked up the frying pan from the stove. "You want some eggs?"

"I already had breakfast." Juni peered over her glass at her.

She scanned the kitchen. She hadn't noticed the dirty dishes strewn haphazardly across the counter. "You had sex in the kitchen?"

Juni nodded. "Breakfast was delightful."

Dex dropped the frying pan back onto the stove and held up her hands in front of her. "Now I really need to go."

"Oh, stop," Juni said with a chuckle. "He's in the shower. He'll be down in a sec, so you can at least say hi."

"Uh, not sure I want to."

Juni tilted her head and frowned. "*Dex*, I really like him."

"Apparently so." She pointed to the dishes. "I am not cleaning up your after-sex breakfast dishes."

"During…" Juni lifted her shoulders and smiled.

She rolled her eyes. "Oh my God."

The dishes rattled as Juni gathered and slid them into the sink. "I'll fix you some eggs if you're hungry."

"No need. I had cheesecake." She shrugged and raised an eyebrow.

"For breakfast?" Juni's voice rose as she leaned against the counter, crossed her arms, and waited for Dex to elaborate.

"Emma had to take something to work for a holiday lunch today." Trying to avoid eye contact, Dex turned and took three cups from the cabinet.

"And you made it for her?"

"We made it together." Dex filled two of the cups with coffee.

"This morning?" Juni moved next to her and stared at her. "You're blushing." She took the decanter from her and slid it into the coffeemaker. "What aren't you telling me?"

"We made it at three a.m." Dex's cheeks warmed. It wasn't like they'd never discussed her sexual partners before. She'd had plenty of one-nighters. But this felt weird because Emma was different.

Juni's face split into a huge smile. "That's awesome." She pulled her into a hug.

"It was awesome." She smiled, thinking of the note she'd found on the counter after Emma had left.

> *Help yourself to anything. Call me today...please. I need to see you again soon.*
> *xoxo*
> *Em*

She'd already had the best-tasting item in the house, and she wasn't talking about the cheesecake.

"You remember the morning after Grace's wedding when I woke up to those awesome notes from that awesome girl?"

"She can't be."

Dex raised her eyebrows and nodded. "She is." The exhilaration of the whole situation washed over her, and she was sure the grin on her face was totally goofy.

Quickly crossing the kitchen, Juni slapped her on the shoulder. "Get out."

"I know. Serendipitous, right?"

"Wow. Just wow." Juni blinked a couple of times. "That's truly awesome. Now you can stop catering to Grace." Juni picked up the last empty mug and moved it from hand to hand.

"Yeah, well, she doesn't know how I feel yet, and she probably won't be happy about it." Breaking it to her would be difficult, but Dex felt something different with Emma than she ever had with Grace.

"Didn't she and Brent set you two up in the first place?"

"Come to find out, it was *all* Brent's idea. Grace was totally against it. She doesn't really like Emma."

"Fuck her." Juni shook her head as she spouted her usual response when it came to Grace. "She needs to stay out of your love life." She reached up into the cabinet, traded the empty cup for a thermal mug, and headed to the coffeepot. "Don't give her any details. She'll just try to make you feel bad about the whole thing." She swung back around. "But I'll need the full rundown, of course."

Dex smiled and went into the living room. "Of course." Juni would expect the play-by-play, but Dex wasn't completely comfortable giving it.

Josh came rushing into the kitchen and planted a kiss on Juni's lips. Dex was a little embarrassed at first, but that feeling faded quickly when Josh turned and threw her a wave. She couldn't hear the conversation from where she was sitting on the couch, but it seemed like he was in a rush. Juni poured coffee into the thermal mug and handed it to him. She was rewarded with another peck on the lips.

"Good to see you, Dex," he said as he rushed through the living room. "Come by the shop anytime, and I'll fix you and your crew up with coffee."

"Good to see you too." She gave him a wave as he went out the door. "And thanks."

Juni came back with the coffee carafe and set it on a trivet in the middle of the table. "Now where were we?"

"I think you were going to tell me about your spectacular night with Josh."

Juni filled her in on her evening and subsequent night with Josh, and then Dex told Juni about her overnighter with Emma and the familiarity of Emma's house she'd realized when she'd arrived there the night before.

"Wow. She's the one who took care of you after Grace's wedding." Juni took a big gulp of coffee and remained silent for a moment. "And she's okay with that?" She scrunched up her face.

"Seems to be. It was pretty embarrassing, but only for a minute or two. She didn't make me feel awkward at all."

"Are you all right with that? I mean, what are you going to do about those feelings?"

"I don't know, but I haven't thought about Grace much in the past few weeks."

"Sounds like you're moving in the right direction." Juni squeezed her knee. "I'm really happy for you." She plucked the cup from Dex's hand and went into the kitchen. "Now go on, get out of here. You have work to do, and I have books to shelve."

"What a life." She gave her sister one last hug and headed out to finish her day, hoping it would end as wonderfully as it had started.

❖

On her drive in to the office, Emma had stopped to get coffee, successfully avoiding Brent when she'd arrived this morning by immediately closing all the blinds facing internally and shutting the door to her office. She hadn't cracked either of them since, except to sneak out and go to the bathroom. She'd tried to work, but she couldn't keep her thoughts from wandering to the blissful time she'd had the night before. Dex was a unique find, an uncapped well of beauty and compassion. And the sex was mind-blowingly spectacular. This was uncharted territory for Emma.

She glanced at her watch and saw it was almost lunchtime. She took the cheesecake from the mini-fridge in her office and finally came out of her sanctuary to carry it to the main conference room, where they were setting up for the holiday luncheon. Fall colors decorated the room, and cornucopias and paper turkeys centered the table. Thanksgiving was just around the corner, and Emma had no idea how November had gotten here so fast. Possibly because she'd spent practically every moment enjoying the days with Dex.

Brent spotted her and attached to her like metal to a magnet as she walked. "Where have *you* been?"

"In my office working." She set the cheesecake with the other assorted items on the dessert table and cut a small slice.

"I didn't even know you were here." He lowered his voice to a whisper. "Why are you hiding out?"

This conversation was so not going to happen right now. She took a fork, sliced it through the cake, and shoved a bite into his mouth.

"It's good, isn't it?" She spoke softly with a slight lilt.

His eyebrows rose. "You made this?"

She nodded and waited for his reaction. Not that she needed Brent's approval, but it was always nice when he gave it.

"This is awesome."

There it was, the atta-girl she was hoping for. She spread her lips into a satisfied smile. "And *I* actually made it."

"Seriously?"

"Well, I had a little help from Dex. That woman can really cook." In more ways than one. Her body heated at the thought of seeing her again.

"So you were with Dex last night." She could see it wasn't a question. The man could read her like no other.

She shook her head. "Busted." She wondered just how red her cheeks were at this point. They felt like they were on fire.

"From the circles under your eyes, she can do other things as well." He took another bite. "How was it?"

"Phenomenal." She took in a breath. "Monumentally phenomenal."

"Sounds impressive. Maybe she can give me some tips."

Emma slapped him on the shoulder. "Shut up. You are bound by the cone of silence, remember?"

"Oh, yeah, that." He shrugged. "I didn't think that counted once you were a couple."

"Whoa. You're getting way ahead of me here." He was, wasn't he? They *had* been kind of inseparable since the party, but they hadn't really discussed a relationship status. "We're just having fun." She had a sinking feeling when she spoke the words. It wasn't at all how she was feeling.

"Are you sure?" He gave her a half-grin. "What was last night, your third date? Doesn't that make it one make-out session and two-plus rounds of sex?"

"Sounds about right."

"Pretty close to being a couple in a woman's eyes."

"Fuck. How are you always so spot-on for a dude?"

He raised his eyebrows. "It's a gift."

From that moment forward, any intention Emma had of doing the work she'd planned on had gone out the window. All she could think about was Dex and how she perceived what was happening between them. She'd sat at her desk staring at her computer. Had she made a mistake? Were they moving too fast? These past few weeks had been so wonderful. Being with someone who actually got her was exciting. She'd been so wrapped up in being blissfully happy, she hadn't even thought about what came next.

CHAPTER SEVENTEEN

The reflection Dex was seeing in the full-length mirror was not the one she wanted. Too much black. She flopped onto the bed and pulled off the black pants she'd just put on, then reached for the dark-blue pair she'd taken off a few minutes ago. The long-sleeved black T-shirt would go better with the jeans.

When the phone rang, Dex checked the display and cringed. *Grace.* It had been almost a week since Dex had talked to her. She'd been responding to Grace's texts but hadn't done more than respond with *I'm super busy at work.* Dex knew she wanted all the details from her dates with Emma. But Dex wasn't ready to tell her. Keeping them to herself made them seem all the more special, and Grace would find a way to spoil that feeling. She'd find fault with something Emma did.

The phone stopped ringing and a text came through.

WTF? Are you avoiding me?

She'd barely had time to read it when the phone immediately rang again. She picked it up on the way to her closet, took in a deep breath, and pressed the green button.

"Hey. What's up?" Dex grabbed a handful of hangers holding sweaters and hoodies from her closet and dropped them onto her bed as she steeled herself for what she knew was coming next.

"Seriously. Are you avoiding me?" Grace spaced the words out phonetically, but her voice was urgent and on the verge of angry.

"No. Of course not. It's the holiday season, so I'm just super busy hanging lights." She wasn't lying, but she'd been spending all her spare time with Emma. She picked up one of the sweaters, examined it, and tossed it to the *why haven't I gotten rid of this* pile. She really needed to do some winter shopping.

"As you've said so many times in your texts." Grace blew out a breath, and Dex could hear it clearly through the phone. "Are you too busy to see me today?"

Dex dropped down on the bed. She'd planned to spend the day with Emma. "Well, Emma and I are planning to hang out today."

"Oh." Her voice lilted up, and then there was silence for a moment. "Just at the house? Maybe I could come over and hang out too."

Dex closed her eyes. Grace and Emma alone with her in the same room together would be a colossal clusterfuck. Besides, she was hoping to spend time alone with Emma. "We're going to Christkindlmarket and then hit the tree-lighting in Millennium Park."

"But we always do that together." Grace's voice sounded soft and deflated.

Dex's excitement for the whole day fell. "I thought you'd be going with Brent this year."

"He's watching football."

She was trapped. They *had* always gone together, and she didn't want to hurt Grace's feelings by telling her she'd rather go alone with Emma. "I think the game's almost over." She'd been watching it in the background as she'd dressed. "Why don't you two meet us there?" she said, half hoping she'd say no.

"That's an awesome idea." The excitement in Grace's voice came through loud and clear. Had she really missed Dex that much?

"Great." She tried to make sure she matched Grace's excitement. "How's the food booth closest to the front entrance at two o'clock?" She used to love it when she made Grace that happy, but today would be laced with trepidation.

"Which booth?" Grace's voice rose.

"Helmut's Strudel. You know. The pastries you love?"

"Okay. Gotcha. Make sure you have your phone. I'll text you when we get there."

Dex let out a breath as she ended the call. *And the boss is back.* She picked up the next charcoal hoodie in the pile and slipped it over her head before she put on her fur-lined, lace-up boots. Now she just had to break the news to Emma.

❖

When Dex called Emma and told her they were meeting Grace and Brent at the market, Emma immediately sent Brent a text asking him not to come. His response, *Too late, already told her yes*, was disappointing. Emma was looking forward to spending a fun day with Dex, but Grace would make that a challenge. Experience told her that Grace would be needy enough to keep both Brent and Dex on a leash catering to her wants. Maybe this was the test she needed to see if Dex really was over Grace and truly wanted to be in a relationship with her, or if she was just a passing distraction.

They waited at the strudel stand by the entrance. Grace and Brent were late, as usual. Emma took in a deep breath, trying to hide her irritation. Grace would never put up with this if the situation were reversed.

"Do you want something to eat while we wait?" Dex pointed to the line at the pretzel booth that had dramatically shortened while they'd been standing there.

"That sounds good," she said. It might improve her mood a little as well if she got some food into her stomach. She'd been so worried about what to wear that she hadn't eaten this morning. She'd settled on blue skinny jeans and a long-sleeved navy T-shirt, layered with a purple cable-knit sweater. She'd finally left the house prepared for the cold weather in her mid-length black wool coat and Ugg boots, topped off with a gray slouch beanie.

Dex came back with the food, and the two of them settled in on a bench. Emma's mood lightened as they shared a pretzel and watched people enter. They were all so happy, a signal that the holiday season was beginning. She'd always loved the holidays, the way the air changed, aromas that brought her senses alive, and a briskness that tickled her skin. Soon Christmas lights would blanket the neighborhoods and all would be bright. Dex wrapped her arm around Emma's shoulder in a kind of possessiveness that Emma thoroughly enjoyed, and she warmed inside. Life was good.

"We finally found you."

Emma jumped when Grace's voice raked across her. She'd never get used to that imitation sweetener she doled out. "We've only been waiting for, what, an hour?"

Grace narrowed her eyes. "Well, if someone had given me the right information, we would've been here sooner." She sliced a glance at Dex.

"I told you the Helmut's Strudel booth by the east entrance."

"That explains it. We went to the Dinkel's booth," Brent said.

They wandered up and down the booths with Emma gripping Dex's hand as they trudged through the crowd. She'd only ever been there early in the day and hadn't realized how busy it got in the afternoon. It was becoming exhausting. They'd barely been able to snag a table when they'd stopped for beer and pretzels in the beer garden. The brass band was fantastic, playing waltzes, polkas, and foxtrots. Emma could've sat there for the rest of the evening listening and watching people dressed in authentic German clothing dance throughout the tent. But that was short-lived, because Grace wanted to see more of the market and insisted she and Dex go with them.

"Hey, look at this guy over here." Brent pointed to the guy carving one-of-a-kind nutcrackers, and he and Grace stopped to watch.

"Have you ever had the mulled wine here?" Dex asked Emma.

Emma smiled. "Yes. It's awesome."

"Great. I'll get us some." Dex sprinted to the booth while the three of them watched the wood-carver.

When Dex came back with the wine, Grace glanced at her and then the mugs in her hands. "You didn't bring me one?"

"Oh, sorry." Dex started back toward the drink stand.

"Can't Brent get it for her?" Emma nudged Brent in the shoulder. "Grace wants some mulled wine."

"Okay. Hang on. I want to watch this guy finish making this. He's almost done." He pointed to the wood-carver. "Isn't this nutcracker awesome?"

Dex waved him off. "I got it."

Emma tilted her head and widened her eyes. "Seriously?"

"I'll be right back." Dex gave Emma's arm a quick squeeze.

"I'll come with you," Grace said as she reached for Dex's hand and clasped it. After what appeared to be an awkward moment, Dex released it. Grace took it again and bolted to a stop, halting Dex along with her. Emma couldn't tell what they were saying, but Grace had the usual scowl on her face, and Dex's face was blank.

Emma spun around to Brent. "You suck."

"What?" He veered his gaze from the carving for a moment. "Why?"

"My date is taking care of your wife."

"She was going there anyway." He shrugged and pointed at the three-foot-tall nutcracker for sale. "I'm going to buy one of these for Grace."

"Don't you think that's a tad big?" Grace would probably never allow the monstrosity in her house.

He lifted the lever embedded in the back of it. "It actually cracks nuts."

"They all do. Hence the name nutcracker."

"Whatever. I'm buying it, and she's going to love it." He took out his wallet. "You'll see."

Emma watched Dex as she moved through the crowd coming toward her. She was absolutely beautiful, with pink cheeks and reddened lips. The army-green parka, which she wore zipped only halfway up, fit her well, and something about the way the charcoal hoodie underneath clung to her made Emma want to explore the treasures hidden beneath it.

When they finally made it through the crowd, Dex quickly went to Emma's side and traded cups with her. "This one's nice and warm," she said as she lowered her chin and stared into her eyes.

The fact that Dex had thought enough to bring her a warm cup took the edge off Emma's irritation. The softness in Dex's deep-green eyes calmed her even more. The jolt Emma couldn't deny zapped all her senses to life. She slipped her arm around Dex's waist and let the feeling wash through her. Grace watched them, her eyes dark through slitted openings, but Emma didn't care. Nothing could temper the electricity flowing between them. She wanted to be out of this place, away from all other distractions. She gave Dex a smoldering kiss, hoping she got the message. When she opened her eyes, Grace was still staring, shooting live grenades directly at her.

Brent appeared holding the huge nutcracker propped up against him. "Look what I bought you, baby." He puffed his chest out as he held it proudly. "It'll go great by the fireplace."

"Or in the fireplace," Emma said under her breath. Dex caught the comment and grinned.

Grace hesitated at first. It was clear she wasn't thrilled. Then she smiled widely, stood on her tiptoes, and kissed Brent sweetly. What a ridiculous show.

Emma leaned in and whispered in Dex's ear. "You want to get something to eat? I know this quaint little Italian restaurant nearby. I think we have enough time before the tree lighting."

Dex nodded. "I'd love to."

"Love to what?" Grace asked, and Emma rolled her eyes.

"We're going to go check out some of the other booths," Dex said, covering nicely. It seemed she wanted to be alone with her as well.

"Great. I'll come along."

"Okay. The art booths are this way." She waved Grace on.

She stopped. "On second thought, how about we meet up at the German Grill?" Grace asked.

Dex took Emma by the hand and pulled her out of Grace's earshot. "Are you okay?"

"I'm fine. I just didn't expect to have to share you with Grace all afternoon." Brent had made the day a little more bearable. She would've felt like the ultimate third wheel if he hadn't been there.

"I'm really sorry. I shouldn't have answered the phone this morning when she called." She pulled her farther into the crowd.

Emma glanced back to see Grace watching them walk away. "Grace hates art."

"I know. I thought it might give us some alone time." The grin on Dex's face was charmingly devious. "I hope you don't mind looking at it."

"No. Not at all. I love art. And I would *love* some alone time with you."

"Yeah?" Dex stopped and gazed into Emma's eyes.

"Yeah." Emma kissed her softly. She was sure Dex had no idea how much alone time she was looking forward to having with her tonight. The afternoon with Grace had been a sacrifice, but one kiss from Dex was well worth it.

"We'll cut out after we get to the end of the art," Dex said, and that's exactly what they did.

❖

Grace and Brent had been waiting in front of the German Grill for over thirty minutes before the text came through from Dex.

Hey, we decided to do Italian for dinner instead.

Grace's stomach knotted when she read the text and realized Dex had left and had purposely not told her until after she was already gone.

She immediately typed back. *What the hell, Dex?*

I know how much you love German food, so I figured you'd want to stay.

Thanks for not giving me an option.

Grace didn't wait for a response. She turned her phone on silent and tossed it into her purse. *They fucking left.* "They're not coming. Emma wanted to leave." She was sure that was the reason.

Brent shrugged. "Then let's eat." He stared at the wooden menu board above the counter. "What do you want?"

"I want Italian."

"I don't think they have any Italian here, babe."

"They don't. That's where Dex and Emma went."

He turned around to face her. "Oh. Are we supposed to meet them?"

"Nope. Apparently, Emma doesn't like having us around."

"Huh? She said that?"

"Might as well have. Fucking rude to just leave like that." She shook her head and glanced back to see if she could spot an empty table.

"We've done it before." He glanced back at the menu.

She spun around. "I have never left Dex anywhere alone."

"You're not alone." His forehead creased. "Am I missing something here?"

"You're right, baby." She smiled up at him. "I'm not alone." *Just fucking hurt.* She leaned into him. "Let's get some food."

They ordered a couple of bratwurst, and Grace took the food to the closest open table in the Grand Timber Haus while Brent got them a couple of beers.

While the music played, singing and dancing continued on the stage. But Grace was deep in thought about her conversation with Dex earlier when they'd gone to get the mulled wine. It had been strained at best. First, Dex hadn't asked her if she wanted any wine, and then she'd acted like she didn't want anything to do with her on the way to get some.

When Dex had pulled her hand from Grace's she'd immediately taken it back and tugged her to a stop and said, "Where is your heart, Dex? I'm not feeling the love anymore."

Dex had seemed surprised at first when she'd called her on her behavior. "You got married, Grace." Her voice had risen as she'd stared into Grace's eyes. She'd acted absolutely ridiculous.

"What difference does that make?" Grace honestly had no idea why it mattered.

Dex had taken in a deep breath and then shook her head. "No difference. I'm just not having the best day, that's all."

She'd glanced at Emma and saw her watching them intently. "I can see why, if Emma acts like that all the time." Her possessiveness was suffocating.

"We're on a date. She didn't expect it to be a foursome."

"The more the merrier, right?" Grace had said, and Dex had agreed.

She didn't know what Emma's problem was. Grace was Dex's best friend, and that wasn't going to change as far as Grace was concerned.

When they'd come back with the wine and Emma had cozied up to Dex and kissed her, Grace had practically thrown up. Her stomach knotted again. She wasn't about to be pushed out of Dex's life so easily.

Brent sat next to her and set the beers in front of them before swiping one of the bratwursts and taking a huge bite.

"Did you see the way Emma kissed her right there in the market in front of everyone?" Grace nibbled at her food. She wasn't really hungry anymore.

"So what? No one cares," Brent said before taking a gulp of beer.

And no one did care except Grace, which was the problem. She wasn't the most important person in Dex's life anymore, and it hurt.

CHAPTER EIGHTEEN

Sneaking out of the festival was easier than Dex thought it would be, and they'd pulled it off. The last time they'd glanced back at Grace, Brent was between them, totally obstructing her view. Dex had grabbed Emma's hand and pulled her into the crowd moving toward the art area. They'd walked up one side of the aisle perusing the art and then quickly left for the quaint little Italian restaurant in the River District that Emma had suggested. It was farther away than some others Dex knew of, but well worth the extra few minutes to get there. The place was authentically Italian.

Dex was impressed by the waft of aromas that assaulted her as they entered. "This place smells wonderful."

"The recipes have been handed down for generations. Every time I come here I want to eat everything on the menu," Emma said as she linked her arm with Dex's.

"Well, then let's have at it." Dex let her move in front of her as they followed the hostess to the table.

From the moment they'd arrived at the restaurant, the evening had been nothing short of spectacular. Everything on the menu was served family style, so after a few tough decisions, they'd agreed on a couple of dishes to share and ordered a bottle of house wine.

Emma took a sip and peered over her wineglass, and a warm feeling stirred low in Dex's belly. The food hadn't even arrived and she was ready to leave.

"So tell me about your job," Dex said, trying to stay focused through dinner. Her dad, who was quite the charmer, always told her that the best way to get someone talking was to ask them about themselves.

Emma took another sip and set her glass on the table. "It's not the most interesting career in the world, but it pays well, and I seem to be good at it."

The look in Emma's eyes seemed uncertain, like maybe she undervalued what she did for a living. Dex reached across the table and took her hand. "I'd like to hear about it, just the same."

"I'm warning you, advertising is not the most stimulating dinner conversation."

"Neither is landscaping, but when I told you about it, you listened like it was better than homemade ice cream."

Emma shifted in her chair, blew out a breath, and stared at the ceiling. "I have a confession to make."

Dex raised an eyebrow and narrowed her eyes, waiting for Emma to finish her sentence.

"While landscaping can be very exciting stuff, truthfully, nothing in the world is better than homemade ice cream."

And there it was, another shot of fresh air in Dex's heart, a place that had been deprived of oxygen for far too long. Emma was breathing life into it like no one else had ever done before.

❖

Dex glanced at the clock as Emma snuggled into her. It was already three o'clock in the morning, and time was rushing past when all she wanted to do was savor each moment she had with Emma. She had fully intended to go home tonight, but as soon as they'd hit the door, Emma had kissed her with such urgency and passion she couldn't possibly leave. They'd made love and then talked for hours. It seemed they never ran out of things to say to each other. This woman did something to her, made her feel good about herself, made her feel wanted for more than just the things she could do for her.

Emma's breathing had slowed into a rhythm of contented sleep, and Dex thought about the way she'd explored Emma's body and brought her to complete satisfaction just a little while ago. And Emma had done the same to her. She could very well be happy satisfying

Emma in every way for the rest of her life. It was the first time in forever Dex found herself looking forward to life and the future.

❖

Emma wandered into the break room at work and poured herself a cup of coffee. Her day yesterday with Dex had been hijacked, but the night following had made up for it. Dinner had been wonderful, and the tree lighting they'd gone to after was always a treat, even more so since she'd shared the whole experience with Dex. She had a way of seeing things in ways Emma had never thought about before. The surface was just the beginning for her. Dex seemed to always take a deep dive into how things worked. The intricacies of Christmas lighting were much more complicated than Emma expected, and Dex was really sweet at explaining how it all came together—sometimes with a main power source, others with a computer program to control the patterns. Emma had always appreciated the time and work that went into lighting, but even more now that she knew how complicated the whole process was.

"Are you okay?" Brent's voice pulled Emma from her thoughts.

"Yeah, why?" She took the creamer from the refrigerator and splashed some into her coffee before handing the carton to him.

"I just shot you a great one-liner, and you didn't laugh."

"Oh, sorry. I'm just really deep into a proposal right now." She really should be but hadn't been able to think of much besides Dex all morning.

"So, what happened to you two yesterday?" He used the creamer and then slid it into the refrigerator. "I looked around, and all of a sudden you guys were just gone." He raised his hands before he took a drink of coffee.

"Sorry. I wanted a little alone time with Dex." She peeked over her cup at him. "You can't blame me for that, can you?"

"Not for that, but I can for the earful I got from my wife when she realized you guys had left. A heads-up would've been nice."

Emma chuckled. "Haven't you learned to tame that yet?"

He shook his head. "Never gonna happen. She likes things her way."

"That's obvious. I just thought you might be able to rein her in some by now."

"I never argue with the boss."

"Wow. What's happened to you? Is she that special?"

"You've never seen the real Grace. She's actually very sweet and compassionate when you get to know her."

"You're right. I've never seen that Grace." The way things were going, that was probably never going to happen.

Emma remembered the summer picnic last July. She'd been in charge of the events for the day. She'd arranged three-legged races, giant Jenga, a bean-bag toss tournament, and a giant ring toss, among other games. It was the water-balloon dodge ball that had gotten Emma into trouble. She'd lobbed a balloon perfectly at Brent, and when he batted it away it had landed squarely on Grace's head. She'd picked the fullest balloon in the bucket, and it had splattered all over Grace, plastering her hair to her head and completely soaking her T-shirt. The fire in her eyes was enough to send the fiercest bear running. As soon as she eyed the balloon bucket, Emma knew she was in for it. Grace had sprinted to the bucket, filled the bottom of her shirt with water balloons, and fired each one at Emma at close range until she was soaked almost to the bone.

The whole thing hadn't even been Emma's fault because Brent had been the one to hit the balloon her way. Grace had something against her, and that was just an avenue she'd used to exact her never-ending disrespect. When you were on her bad side, the woman had a temper like a rabid coyote. Emma was sure she'd ended up in that category because of her friendship with Brent. Emma had shaken the whole incident off immediately, though her clothes had remained damp until the picnic ended that day. Emma had to admit that the chafing was a small price to pay for the scowl on Grace's face when the balloon came down on her head.

"Are you listening to me?" Brent snapped his fingers in front of her face. "What's going on with you today?"

She surfaced from her thoughts again. "Yeah, sorry. Just tired from yesterday." She leaned on the counter and gave Brent her full attention. "Now what's going on with Grace?"

"We've been fighting about money again."

"Why?"

"Sometimes I think she cares more about *it* than me. Her parents use it to get her to do things for them."

"Like what?"

"There's some fund-raising event they want her to attend. She has to schmooze with people and get them to donate. I don't like them using her like that."

"Because she'll be talking to other men? Young, attractive, rich men?"

"In a nutshell, yes."

"You told her that and she's going anyway?"

He nodded. "She wants me to go with her."

Emma shrugged as she topped off her coffee. "So go with her."

"I don't like to watch my wife flirt with other men." He narrowed his eyes. "You said she didn't care about the money. She should care more about how I feel than her parents."

"Well, maybe there's more to it than money. Maybe she feels an obligation to her parents. They did raise her, you know." Emma doubted that was the case, but she threw it out there to make Brent feel better. "I certainly didn't mean you should dictate where she can and can't go or what her relationship with her parents should be." She rolled her eyes. "That's just ridiculous. She's not a child."

"I don't like the way they manipulate her."

"Sounds like you're trying to do the same thing." She popped away from the counter and glanced over her shoulder when she reached the door. "Go with her to the freaking party. She needs to be escorted, so do it." She shook her head and walked to her office.

Jesus. Am I the only one around here who has normal parents? That probably wasn't totally true. Emma's mom could be ridiculously over the top. Emma had invited Dex for Thanksgiving, and her mom had made way too big a deal out of it. She'd even suggested that her brothers wear ties. Like that would ever fly.

CHAPTER NINETEEN

Grace was frantic when Dex arrived at her house just before eleven. The kitchen was a disaster. Grace hadn't even put the turkey in the oven yet. She'd made the dressing and stuffed it in the turkey somehow, but there seemed to be more stuffing in the pan than in the bird.

"Dex, where have you been? I'm running so behind. I don't know what to do first." Grace's frazzled expression was totally out of character.

"I've been at the homeless shelter, like every Thanksgiving for as long as I can remember."

"Oh, shit. I forgot about that." Grace took in a deep breath and let it out. "I should've come with you."

"No worries. I knew you were busy." She'd planned on going straight to Emma's until she received the 911 call from Grace. "We need to get the bird in the oven. Do you have an extra apron?" Dex rolled up her sleeves and washed her hands.

Grace took one out of the pantry, slid it over Dex's neck, and reached around to tie it behind her back. She kissed Dex on the cheek and backed up. "You're a lifesaver, Dex."

Dex took in the scent of Grace's perfume and tried to settle the feelings it stirred within her. She squatted and took out as many oven-safe bowls as she could find. This was going to take some work.

"I need foil," she said as she swiped a serving spoon from the utensil holder near the stove. She spooned the extra dressing into one of the bowls and slid it over to Grace, who covered it with the foil.

"Sweet potatoes?" Dex scanned the counter.

Grace spun around and took a bowl from the refrigerator. "I baked them last night, like you told me."

"Great. They need to be peeled and cut up." She slipped the meat of the sweet potato out of the skin, cut it into chunks, and put them in another dish. "Just like this." She spun around to the pantry and took out the brown sugar. "I'll make the syrup."

"Okay." Grace nodded and started working on the remaining sweet potatoes.

The rest of the food prep went smoothly, and they had all the dishes in the oven within an hour, with the exception of the mashed potatoes.

Grace was clearly frustrated with the whole situation. "This is ridiculous. I can't believe my parents went out of town." She dropped the last of the dirty bowls into the sink. "I don't know how Brent thought I was going to prepare a complete Thanksgiving dinner for eight people, nine, including you, while he watches football."

"I can't stay."

"What? Everyone's going to be here soon. I can't do this all by myself. I need you."

"All you have to do is take everything out of the oven and uncover the dishes." She pointed to a list she'd made. "Everything you need to do is right here. I'm sure some of your guests will offer to help." Dex had purposely put everything in oven-proof serving dishes to make it easier. She'd done this many times before when she'd brought food out for her work crew and spread it out in the back of her SUV. It was the best way to serve a group.

"What about the turkey?"

"It'll take about three hours. It should come out of the oven about three o'clock. Brent can take out the turkey and carve it. He could've probably helped you with all this if you'd asked him." She took off the apron Grace had loaned her. "You've got this, Grace. Now, I gotta go. I'm already late."

"Just stay until everything comes out of the oven. Have a glass of wine with me. Juni won't care."

"I'm not going to Juni's. I'm going to Emma's parents'."

"You're meeting her parents?"

"Yeah, and I'm late." She took her coat from the back of the chair and put it on. "I really gotta go."

"Keep your phone close."

Dex gave her a thumbs-up as she took off out the door. She was already an hour late. Thankfully, Emma's family ate dinner later than most. She was super nervous, and now she was going to probably slide in just in time for dinner. She'd wanted to make a good impression, but that had gone right out the window. She should've never agreed to help Grace today, but the desperate plea she'd given her when she'd called had sucked her in.

❖

Emma rushed to the door as soon as she heard the bell ring. Dex had sent her a text letting her know she'd had to stop by Grace's on the way and would be there in twenty minutes. She'd thought Grace had backed off, but it seemed she'd only become invisible to Emma, tugging at Dex when they weren't together. She stopped for a minute and tamped down her frustration before she pulled open the door.

"Wow. Absolutely wow," Dex said as her eyes roamed Emma from head to toe before she stepped in and kissed her.

"Hey, you." She melted into her arms and instantly forgave Dex. It was hard to stay angry at the woman who made her heartbeat double at just the sight of her. She'd never had a woman gaze at her with such desire as Dex did.

"I didn't realize your folks lived so close to my house." She handed Emma the bottle of wine she'd brought and took off her coat. Emma opened the closet and took out a hanger for her. She slid her coat on it and hung it on the rod. "How long have they lived here?"

"Since I was a child."

"Nice. I love these old craftsman-style homes. This is so much bigger than mine."

"Come on. Let's get you a drink." Emma looped her arm in Dex's and pulled her from the foyer.

"I may need more than one tonight."

"Don't be nervous. They're just like your parents."

"No parents are like mine."

Emma raised an eyebrow. "That sounds intriguing."

"Let's just say they're unique and leave it at that."

"I'll take that for now." She tugged her close and led her into the living room. "Hey, everyone, this is my...Dex." She wasn't sure how to introduce her. They hadn't really discussed their status, and she didn't want to overstep.

"This is my family. My mom, Gloria. Most everyone calls her Glo." She pointed to the two guys on the couch. "My brothers Jeff and Zack. Jeff's better half, Judy, should be around here somewhere too."

She stepped out of the kitchen and waved. "Present and accounted for." Then Emma glanced toward her dad in the recliner. "And my dad, Bill."

He popped the recliner forward, got up, and held out his hand. "Bill, Emma's dad."

Dex smiled and shook his hand. "Dex." She gave Emma a sideways glance. "Emma's girlfriend. I think."

Emma couldn't hold back the huge smile that took over her face. "Yes, my girlfriend," she said softly. The feeling of joy was overwhelming. Emma couldn't wait to get Dex alone and kiss her senseless, and as soon as the introductions were finished she pulled her into the den and did just that.

"Uck, Aunt Emma." The tiny voices echoed through Emma's head. She broke the kiss and smiled. "These are my nephews, Tyler and Jake."

They peered over the sofa at them. Shoes were off and flipped sideways by the TV in front of them, and their hair and clothes were totally tousled, as though they'd been wresting for the past hour.

"They look comfortable. Can we hang out in here?"

The boys paused the video game they'd been playing and stared up at them.

"*Mario Kart*?" Dex asked.

"Yeah. You wanna play?"

"Maybe in a little while, boys." Emma answered for Dex, and they went back to playing the game. She tugged Dex closer and rested her forehead against Dex's. "I'm not done kissing you."

"What about the boys?"

"I don't care. Did you mean what you said out there about you being my girlfriend?" Emma trembled. She never thought she'd feel this way about anyone again.

"That's okay, right? I mean, I didn't just out you, did I?"

Emma chuckled. "No, you didn't out me. My parents have known since I was thirteen."

"Then I absolutely meant it." Dex kissed her again, and Emma reacted in ways she was only beginning to understand.

Emma let out a growl. "I can't wait for this dinner to be over." She took Dex's hand and led her to the kitchen, where her mother and Judy were setting out appetizers.

Dex fielded all Emma's mom's questions with humor and finesse, which had seemed to win her over quickly. As soon as the inquisition was done, Glo sent Dex into the living room to watch football with the guys, while she, Emma, and Judy, finished getting the food ready. Dex had been reluctant to go. She'd wanted to stay and help, but Emma had kissed her softly and told her it was okay. Both her mother and Judy gave Dex their stamp of approval, which made Emma happy.

After helping in the kitchen with the dinner prep, Emma found that the boys had swept Dex into the den to play *Mario Kart* and were totally kicking her ass.

"I have no idea when I lost my gaming skills, but I'm clearly not up to the competition in this household."

"It's the tiny fingers. They move faster." Emma laughed. "Come on, boys. It's turkey time."

They'd just sat down to dinner at the extended dining-room table when Dex's phone rang. Dex took it out of her pocket, and Emma could see on the screen that it was Grace.

"I'll be right back," Dex said as she got up and went into the kitchen. Emma was tempted to follow but restrained herself. It was only a few minutes before Dex came back through the door.

"Sorry about that. A friend needed marshmallow advice. It's her first Thanksgiving dinner." She pointed to the dish of sweet potatoes on the table.

"Marshmallows can be difficult," Emma's mother said as she picked them up and passed them to her left. "One minute they're perfect, and the next they're up in flames."

"I don't doubt that is happening at this very moment." Everyone at the table laughed. Then Dex's phone rang again. "Right on cue." She hopped up and went back into the kitchen.

"Sounds like she's a good friend to whoever that is on the phone."

"Yes, the best." Emma held her tongue. This wasn't the time or place to talk about Grace.

Dex slid into her chair. "My friend, Grace, again. Sorry about that." She set her phone on the table. "You have a wonderful home here, and your yard is impeccable."

"Thanks. I don't have the energy to keep it up like I used to," Bill said.

"I'd be happy to trim up the holly bushes and shape the crepe myrtles for you."

"You like to work in the yard?"

"Dex has her own landscaping business." Emma rubbed her hand across Dex's back. "I bet she'd do wonders with it."

"I don't know. I've never thought about paying someone to do yard work."

"I'd be happy to do it for free." Her phone buzzed on the table, and she glanced at it.

"Seriously? Again?" Emma rolled her eyes. "This is too much, Dex." Would there ever be a day when Grace wouldn't be front and center in Dex's life?

"Is that your friend again?" Emma's mother asked.

"I'm so sorry." Dex started to get up.

Emma's mother motioned toward her with her fingers. "Hand it to me."

Dex glanced at Emma and then reluctantly handed it over.

"Hello, Grace, sweetheart. I hear this is your first Thanksgiving dinner and you're having a hard time." She bobbed her head up and down. "Oh, that's just miserable. Tell you what. Just scrape those marshmallows off and put on a whole new batch. This time when you put them in the oven, leave the door open just a tad and watch them. As soon as they start to brown, yank them out." She listened for a minute. "Don't worry, honey. It happens to all of us." She pushed her glasses up on her nose. "Now if you have any more trouble, just call back, and I'll be happy to help." She nodded. "You too, honey." She hit the end button on the phone and held it in her hand. "She'll be fine." Instead of handing Dex the phone, she slid it onto the buffet behind her. "You relax, and let the expert field her questions."

"Okay," Dex said and gave Emma a sly smile.

Glo fielded at least three more phone calls during dinner and shooed Emma and Dex to the living room after most of the dishes had been done.

As soon as they settled in, the microwave began to beep. "Should I get that for her?"

Emma shook her head, knowing her mother had put her coffee in for a warm-up. "She'll find it."

When Dex's phone rang again, she heard Glo shout from the kitchen. "Still? Dinner should be over by now."

Dex seemed to recognize the number on the screen. "False alarm. It's my mom." She hit the button and pressed the phone to her ear. "Hey, Mom." Dex smiled, hit the speaker button, and put the phone between her and Emma.

"Happy Thanksgiving, honey." They listened as both her parents' voices came through loud and clear.

"Happy Thanksgiving. Wow, this connection is great. Are you back in the States?"

"No. We're still in Thailand rebuilding houses. Your dad finagled some internet time from his boss." Dex smiled at Emma as she spoke. "Are you with your sister?"

"No. I'm at my girlfriend's parents'."

"What? When did that happen? Is she nice? What's her name?"

"It's new, but yes, she is. Emma."

Emma gave her a sideways glance, and she winked.

"I'm glad to hear that, honey. You'll have to tell us all about her." There was silence, and she knew her parents were waiting for more information.

"I will. Soon. I promise. Hey, Mr. Anderson at the homeless shelter says hello. He misses your help and wants to know when you'll be back. Says you're a born organizer and he needs you."

"Tell him hello back, but it's going to be a few more months before we come that way again. There's still plenty to be done here. I'm teaching English now as well."

"Oh, wow. That's awesome, Mom. He thought as much but wanted me to tell you anyway. We all miss you guys."

Dex's voice deflated and Emma felt sad. She'd never thought about what it would be like not having her parents close.

"We miss you too. We'll call again tomorrow. Now you go enjoy yourself."

"Thanks, Mom. I love you."

"We love you too, honey."

She hit the End button, smiled at Emma, and said, "Mary and Craig, my mom and dad."

"I gathered." She smiled. "Are you okay?"

"I'm awesome. You?" Dex asked.

She nodded "I guess it's official now, huh?"

Dex smiled. "Totally." She gave her a soft kiss on the lips.

Bill interrupted their moment when he flopped into the recliner next to the love seat, stretched out his legs, and pointed at Emma's brothers, who were half dozing. After dinner, they'd each immediately loosened their belts a notch and taken half of the couch. "So who's going to help with the lights this weekend?"

They stared at each other and shifted in their seats, waiting each other out to see who would speak first. They always did this when they weren't delivering the news Bill wanted to hear.

"I've got my own to do," Jeff said.

"I have to work. It's Black Friday weekend," Zack chimed in.

"You can't spare a few hours to help your old dad out. You know I can't do it myself, and we can't be the only house on the block without lights."

"No, we can't have that," Glo shouted from the kitchen.

"I can probably break away on Sunday for a little while." Jeff eyed Zack. "Will that work for you?"

Zack nodded but didn't offer any information about what his Sunday was like.

"I can help. It'll get done a lot faster with more hands," Dex said. "I hang lights in the winter to supplement," she added when they all gawked at her.

Bill's eyebrows rose. "Look at that, boys. She hangs lights." He glanced over at Emma. "I think you've got yourself a prize this time, Em. Don't scare her away."

"Dad. You've had too much wine."

"Nope. Just enough." He winked. "Right, Dex?"

"Right."

The microwave must have beeped a hundred times before Emma heard her mother shout, "Where the hell is my coffee?"

"In the microwave, Mom. You put it in there about a half hour ago." Emma glanced at Dex, who was grinning widely.

"Jesus. If my head wasn't screwed on…What would I do without you?" Glo's voice rang through the house when she joined them in the living room and picked up her book. Within fifteen minutes she was asleep in her chair.

Everyone else was focused on the football game when Emma grazed her hand across Dex's thigh to pull her attention from the TV. "Take me home?" They'd been there way past the obligatory hour after dinner.

Dex nodded. "Whenever you're ready."

Emma stared into her eyes, trying to convey how she wanted this night to end. "I've been ready since you got here."

Dex's lips curved up to one side as she got up, took Emma's hand, and led her out the door.

❖

Dex had been awake for close to an hour watching Emma sleep. They'd made love again last night. When she'd woken this morning with Emma in her arms, she'd immediately wanted to do it again, but she'd looked so peaceful, almost smiling in her sleep. Was she dreaming about the same things she had—of a life filled with love instead of heartache? She didn't know how, but Emma was slowly pushing Grace out of her heart. Not replacing her so much as making a whole new place that seemed to encapsulate all of her. It wasn't a feeling she could ever explain to anyone. She just knew Emma was special and destined to be in her life.

When Emma opened her eyes and caught Dex staring, she blushed and became more beautiful, if that was possible.

"How long?" She rubbed her eyes.

"Have I been awake?"

"Have you been watching me?"

"Maybe an hour." She smiled. "You're easy to watch."

Emma rolled her eyes before she reached up, hooked her hand behind Dex's neck, and tugged her in for a scorching kiss.

"You should've woken me. A whole hour has gone to waste while we could've been doing something else."

Dex chuckled. "Like breakfast?"

"That too." Emma made tiny circles with her finger across Dex's collarbone and seemed to go somewhere else for a moment. "Thanks for offering to help my dad with the yard and the lights. He's not as young as he used to be, and I worry about him taking on all that by himself. My brothers are busy with their own lives. They'll show up between games and put in an hour, but that won't be enough."

"It's my pleasure. I love the house, and your dad takes great care of the lawn."

"Yeah?"

"Yeah. The grass looks like it's been fertilized well, and I could do a lot with the landscaping." Dex had noticed the overgrown holly bushes and unshaped crepe myrtles. She'd also seen a couple of nice-sized flower beds in the front, flanking the steps to the porch, that needed to be cleaned out.

She stared across the room to nowhere in particular. "So, this whole girlfriend thing." They hadn't really gotten to discuss it earlier. It had just happened in front of everyone. "I may not be very good at it. I mean I haven't been in the past." She returned her gaze to Emma. "But I'd like to give it a go if you do."

Emma pulled her brows together and rolled her lips in. Dex's heart raced. Maybe she'd made a mistake putting it out there since Emma seemed to be reluctant to introduce her that way to her parents. Then Emma reached up and caressed Dex's cheek with the back of her fingers.

Emma took in a deep breath as she hooked her hand behind Dex's neck and brought her closer. "I do," she whispered across her lips and then kissed her.

CHAPTER TWENTY

G race came in hot as she pushed her way through Dex's front door. "I can't believe you just abandoned me like that."

"I didn't abandon you. I was only a phone call away."

"That's a bunch of shit." She dropped her purse on the end table. "You let that woman answer your phone all night."

"She insisted." Dex closed the door and followed her into the living room. "She helped you better than I would've. She's a great cook."

"You don't have control of your own phone now?"

"Of course I do."

"So, why did you let her? She was condescending and bossy."

Dex frowned. "Really? I heard the calls, Grace. I thought she was kind of sweet, considering you *were* interrupting dinner. You got through it, didn't you?"

"Next time you're coming to my house." She flopped down onto the couch. "You're going to come over and help me decorate the tree tonight, right?"

"Isn't Brent going to help you?"

"He's going out with his buddies and won't be home until late." Brent was becoming absolutely useless around the house. It seemed he was getting comfortable now that they were married.

"I can come over for a little while, but I actually have plans later this evening."

"Dex, this is ridiculous. Do I have to do everything alone because you're going out with *her*?"

"*Her?*" She stared at Grace. "You mean Emma. My girlfriend?"

"Great." Grace rolled her eyes and made no attempt to hide her irritation. "Now she's your *girlfriend*?" She should've never listened to Brent's stupid idea to fix them up.

"Wasn't that the plan? Why you set me up with her in the first place?"

She took in a deep breath. "I'm sorry. It just seems like you don't have any time for me."

"That's not true. I'm here with you now, aren't I?"

"For an hour or two." She wrapped her arms around her neck. "I miss you."

She put her hands on Grace's waist and kept a small distance between them. "Okay. I'll help you for a little while this afternoon."

Grace's mood perked up immediately. "Yeah! We can have hot chocolate and listen to Christmas music. It'll be such fun." She squealed with excitement.

"Okay, then. Let me get some warm clothes for later, and I'll follow you to your place." Dex ran up the stairs to the bedroom.

"Where are you two going tonight?" Grace shouted.

"Ice-skating," Dex said as she sprinted down the stairs to the living room.

The tiny hairs on the back of Grace's neck stood up. "At Millennium Park?" Another something they always did together.

"Yeah. Can you believe Emma's never been before?"

"But we always do that."

"What's the deal, Grace? Why isn't Brent taking you?"

"I told you he's going out with his buddies." She frowned.

"Emma hasn't skated in years, and she might need some help getting the hang of it again. So it wouldn't be much fun for you. I'm sure Brent will take you another night. Just ask him." She took her jacket from the closet. "Come on, let's go. I only have a few hours."

Grace picked up her bag from the end table and went to her car. She didn't like being second in line for anyone, including Dex.

Emma had been quiet the whole walk to the rink. Dex had tried to explain why she'd been late when Emma had picked her up, but having to wait in the car for a half hour until she got home had made the situation even worse. It seemed as though Grace had gotten between them again. She had no idea how she was going to resolve this conflict between Emma and her best friend.

"Hey! Fancy meeting you here."

Dex closed her eyes when she heard the voice. *Fuck.* Grace had followed them here even though she hadn't invited her.

She turned around, tilted her head, and stared. "Fancy that." She let the words roll from her lips slowly. Grace glanced away quickly. She knew Dex was pissed.

Emma peered around her. "Is Brent here?"

"No. He's not an ice-skater."

"You came alone?" The surprise in Emma's voice was clear.

"Sure. I do it all the time."

Emma turned to Dex. "And she just happened to be here on the same night as us?"

Dex let Grace move ahead of them as they walked into the rink area and fell back to talk to Emma. "I'm sorry. I told her we were coming, but I didn't invite her. I didn't think she'd just show up."

"Really?" Emma shook her head. "Even I know she'd show up. When has Grace ever needed an invitation?"

"Are you okay?"

"I'm fine. I just didn't expect to have to share you with Grace all evening."

"I'm really sorry. I swear I didn't invite her. She's probably here because we've always done this holiday stuff together, and Brent's not into it."

Grace slowed up. "It's tradition," she said, apparently catching part of their conversation.

"We need skates," Dex said, and started toward the skate rental.

"I'll get them." Grace took some money from her pocket and rushed to the counter.

"This is the second time she's horned in on one of our dates," Emma said as she found a place for them to sit and change into their skates.

"I'm sorry." She shrugged. "I don't know what else to say."

"Tell her to go home."

"That would be rude."

"And you don't think she's being rude right now?" She glanced over to see Grace walking toward them with a pair of skates dangling from each hand. "Do you see three pairs of skates there?"

"She just doesn't know your size."

"She didn't even ask." Emma shook her head. "She sure didn't have to ask for yours, did she?"

Grace held up the skates. "All set."

"Did you leave Emma's at the counter?"

"Oh, sorry. I forgot." She smiled at Emma. "You can get your own, can't you?"

"Seriously?" Emma slipped her boots back on. "I'm gonna go."

"So it will just be the two of us?" Grace asked, seeming ridiculously happy now.

"No, it will not." Dex took Emma by the hand and moved her away from Grace. "Please don't go."

Emma closed her eyes and took in a breath. "This isn't going to work tonight. Just go have fun with Grace."

"I don't want to skate without you." Dex's voice rose.

"Then you should tell her to go home." Emma didn't sound angry now. She seemed more disappointed.

"Come on, Em. It's just a few hours." Dex knew she sounded needy, but she really wanted her to stay.

"You have no idea, do you?"

"Come on, Dex," Grace shouted from the ice, and Dex turned momentarily.

Emma pulled out of her grasp.

"What? Wait." She reached for her again.

"Stop." Emma put her hands up in front of her. "You need to think about who you want to continue your Christmas traditions with. This cozy threesome isn't working for me." She searched her pocket for her keys. "Let me know when you've figured that out. I'm sure you can get a ride home with Grace." She took off quickly through the crowd.

Dex stood there watching Emma leave and wondering how her night had gone to shit without her even doing anything wrong. When they'd run into Grace in the ice-rink parking lot, all talking had stopped, and the only conversation Dex had been able to get from Emma was one-word answers. Dex had been totally stunned. She couldn't believe Grace would blatantly horn in on her date with Emma. On second thought, it was typical of Grace to get what she wanted, even if it made Emma and Dex uncomfortable. Dex just didn't think it would be such a huge deal.

She spun around to Grace, who was now at the edge of the rink watching with rapt attention. "Why the hell did you do that?"

"Do what?"

"You know exactly what I'm talking about. You showed up here uninvited, and then you didn't get Emma any skates."

"I didn't know her size."

"That's bullshit and you know it. You should've asked."

"It not like she was having a good time. Did you see the scowl on her face? She was going to ruin it for us."

"We're not twelve anymore, Grace. You can't do that to people. Especially people who are important to me."

Grace gave her a strange look. "You just started dating a month ago. How can she be more important to you than me?" She clomped off the ice. "Who was it that hung out in jail with you after that protest because your parents weren't there to bail you out...or planned and threw your college-graduation party...or kept you sane when Ranny had that car accident?" Her voice trailed off. She sank onto the bench.

Dex took in a deep breath, knowing the last one had been hard for Grace as well. "You've always been there." Grace might be rich and spoiled, but she *had* always been there for Dex. Even in the most difficult times.

"You're damn right I have. I'll always be here to take care of you, Dex. You'll never be as close to her as you are to me."

"I don't have to choose, do I, Grace?" Grace didn't respond. "I really like her. Aren't you closer to Brent now than you are to me?"

Grace shook her head. "No. You don't have to choose." She closed her eyes momentarily. "But honestly? I think I'm closer to you than anyone, including Brent. I mean I'm intimate with Brent, but that's different from our friendship." She sat on the bench. "He's not very emotional, doesn't always care what I want to do. He would never come here with me. He'd rather hang out with his buddies."

Dex sat next to her. "Did you know that before you got married?"

"Pretty much, but I'm working on him."

Dex blew out a breath. "That's a big fucking problem to be working on."

"Don't worry about it. I'll be fine." Grace bolted up. "Worry about your own problem."

"What's that?"

Grace handed Dex her skates and then slipped out onto the ice. "If your *girlfriend* can't take a little shit from me, she's certainly not going to hang around for the hard stuff."

"You need to be nicer to her, Grace."

"Okay. Got it. I promise to be nicer," she shouted as she turned around and skated backward away from her. "Now, hurry up." Whether she would or not was yet to be seen.

Dex had done something she knew she shouldn't have. She'd let Emma leave and hadn't followed her. But Emma was really pissed, and she wanted to let her calm down before talking to her. So, instead of leaving and following her home, Dex put on the skates and went out onto the ice. If Emma couldn't get past her friendship with Grace, it wasn't going to get any easier.

Chapter Twenty-One

Dex sat across from Juni at her kitchen table telling her what a mess the night had turned into. She and Grace had skated for over an hour before she'd gotten off the ice and changed into her boots. It hadn't been fun this year. She'd fallen a number of times because all she could think about was Emma. When they were done skating, Grace had bought them each a cup of hot chocolate and sat down next to her to watch the better skaters, like they usually did. The hot chocolate even tasted bad, and she loved the hot chocolate at the rink. She'd made the wrong decision letting Emma leave without her. Not that she'd really had a choice. And when they'd arrived at Grace's house, she'd flashed her a sweet smile and asked Dex to come in for another cup of hot chocolate, and she'd done it. Another stupid decision.

"What did I do wrong?"

"You let Grace hijack your date again, and you didn't do anything to stop it."

"The first time wasn't really my fault. We were going to the market, and Grace and I always did that together. I felt bad, so I invited her and Brent to come along. Brent was kind of doing his own thing, and Grace was kind of lost, so she pretty much clung to us the whole time."

"You really think that's how it all played out?" Juni raised an eyebrow. "I've never seen Grace lost in my life. She knew exactly what she was doing. You've grown up together, and she has no respect for you, at least not the kind you deserve."

Dex closed her eyes and shook her head. "I hate to think that, but she did kind of enjoy pissing off Emma."

"There you go. And yesterday, she just showed up and guilted you into staying and skating."

She got up and paced the room. "Why is she doing it?"

"Oh, Dex." Juni shook her head. "It's obvious to anyone who's ever known you how in love you are with her."

"That's changed since I met Emma." But had it really? Dex wasn't sure. She still had lingering feelings deep in her heart, and she sure as hell wasn't going to tell her sister that.

"Then stop letting Grace control you." The irritation in Juni's voice surprised Dex. "Last night was certainly intentional on her part, and you *stayed with Grace* instead of leaving with Emma. *Your girlfriend.* Damn it, Dex. Don't you see the problem here?"

She flopped into the couch. "What should I do?"

"Stop being so fucking nice to Grace." Juni's voice softened. "You have to make the break, or she's going to continue to ruin whatever chance you have at anything with Emma. You're on the ledge, Dex. You just need to let go. Take the leap into the unknown. Have faith that life will be good with Emma." Juni rubbed her back. "You've been playing it safe, waiting for someone you know you can't have."

"You want me to let go of the only woman I've ever loved. Let go of my dreams."

"They're not her dreams, honey. You need to make new ones with someone else. And I think we both know that someone is Emma."

Even though Juni was right, Dex was petrified to move on. Grace might be rich and spoiled, but she'd always been there when Dex needed her.

Juni went into the kitchen and came back with the coffee decanter. "Grace will never stop unless you make it clear to her you're in love with someone else now." She filled their cups and went back into the kitchen. "You should've gone after Emma last night."

At this point Dex was so confused, she didn't know what to do. She really liked Emma, but Grace had been in her life for a long time. She wasn't ready to cut her completely out of it. Dex had never thought she'd have two women jealous over her time. All she knew for sure was that she had to get to work. The Christmas lights weren't going to hang themselves, and she was paying her crew time and a half to work the holiday weekend.

❖

"Let me know when you're done with these, and I'll bring in some more," Bill said as he and Emma carried two huge stacks of boxes in from the garage. Glo directed them to put them next to the tree with the rest of the decorations. It was the Saturday after Thanksgiving, and Emma had always spent the day with her mother decorating the tree and making the inside of the house beautiful in holiday style.

"When did you get here?" Glo pulled Emma into a hug. "I expected that you'd be off doing something with Dex." She crossed the room to the boxes. "Or at least have brought her with you. She seems like a really sweet girl, offering to help your dad with the outside lights and all."

"Right. That's happening tomorrow." Bill swung around toward the door to the garage. "I'll get the lights down. You two have fun."

"Don't go back up in the attic without Emma out there with you."

He waved her off. "I'll be fine."

"Dex is sweet. Sometimes too sweet, I think." Emma headed into the kitchen to get something to drink.

"There's champagne and orange juice in the fridge for mimosas."

"Good. I need that today." She mixed the mimosas and brought out two champagne flutes full to the brim.

"What's going on with you?"

Emma flopped onto the couch. "Dex and I had a date to go ice-skating last night, and her friend, Grace, showed up."

"Oh, the needy one from Thanksgiving." There was no question in her mother's voice as to whom she was talking about.

"Mom, I don't know if I can do this again." She honestly thought she'd be happily married by now. Instead she was dealing with the same situation she was in with her last relationship. She had no idea how she'd gotten here once more. Women should come with hugely visible warning labels, especially ones with best friends.

"Emma, honey." She sat down on the arm of the couch next to her. "Just because she's close with her friend doesn't mean she's in love with her." She put her arm around Emma and kissed the top of her head. "Every relationship isn't going to end like yours and Amy's.

Maybe you should call Amy and talk to her about it. I'm sure she has some insight she can share."

She stiffened at the mention of Amy's name. "No. That's not happening." The wound was as fresh as the day they'd split. She took in a deep breath. "Asking my ex-fiancée why she chose Tammy over me isn't on the top of my list, Mom."

"It really has nothing to do with you. It's about the feelings she had for her best friend."

"Feelings that apparently I couldn't erase." And didn't see until Amy and Tammy were well on their way to a blissful life together.

"Do you still avoid your favorite Italian restaurant downtown because of her?"

She nodded. "The food there is overrated." It was the place where Emma had proposed to Amy. She'd said yes and had made Emma the happiest she'd been in her life. But that was short-lived. It seemed as though that proposal had been the catalyst for Tammy to profess her love to Amy. Their last conversation flashed through her head in vivid color, and her stomach knotted.

"You can't blame yourself for Amy and whatshername. It wasn't obvious with her."

"Looking back, I think there were signs."

"Signs, I'm assuming, you've seen with Dex as well." Glo tilted her head. "So with all that in your past, why were you so drawn to Dex?"

"You should've seen her at Brent and Grace's wedding. She was totally devastated." Emma let out a huge sigh as she remembered the night. She'd been so sweet and funny. The banter had just poured out of her even though she was totally plastered. Only once or twice did she seem solemn, and that was when Grace had appeared in her vision. If she hadn't been so fucking drunk, Emma would've slept with her that night and probably never seen her again. Then she wouldn't be in this mess.

"Yet you still took her home and cared for her." Glo tilted her head and flattened her lips. "And then went out on a date with her."

"I did take care of her." She'd brought this all on herself. "She's just so perfect, Mom. If I weren't already gay, I'd probably turn just for her." Emma was sure that if Grace liked women at all and had ever kissed Dex, she would never have let her go. "Grace must be crazy."

"Or just straight," Glo said as she got up, opened one of the boxes, and took out a box of ornaments. "Have they ever…?"

"I don't know, and I don't want to know." She'd thought about asking Dex a few times if she and Grace had ever had any kind of relationship other than friendship, but was afraid of what the answer might be. Despite being high maintenance, Grace was gorgeous and insanely sexy.

Glo took out another box of ornaments and handed it to Emma. "After what you've been through with Amy, it's only natural to be guarded about their friendship. Try not to let it get in the way."

"Too late." Her voice rose into a fuck-me tone. "I left last night." She took a gulp of her mimosa. "So I'm sure Grace had a wonderful time skating with Dex all by herself."

"What about Dex? Do you think she had a good time?" Glo gathered a few strands of garland and went across the room.

"I don't know." She stood up and hung a couple of ornaments on the higher branches that her mother couldn't reach. She seemed to be getting shorter in recent years. "She asked me to stay, but I just couldn't. Not with Grace there. It was too much this time."

"Letting your pride get in the way again?"

"If you want to call it that." She let out a heavy breath. "This isn't me, Mom. I don't get so caught up in a woman that I can barely think, but I am with Dex. I'm flying into the curve with no brakes. I'd run away with her right now if she asked, and that would eventually be very bad for me. I was never like this with Amy."

"It sounds like you need to stand up for yourself and fight for her," Glo said. She was good about making not-so-subtle suggestions.

Her mother was probably right, but Grace fought dirty, and Emma had no idea how to go up against her. She'd been more than patient with the whole situation, and it hurt to know she wasn't, and might never be, the most important person in Dex's life.

"Maybe so, but I shouldn't have to beg her to want to be alone with me."

"I'm sure that's not the case." She hung scattered strings of garland across the tree. "She seemed genuinely happy to be here with you on Thanksgiving."

"That's only because you took her phone and ran interference with Grace."

"Maybe she just needs time to let Grace go."

"I certainly hope so. If not, we're done."

"Why don't you go out with some of your friends or something to get your mind off her?"

"Can't. Amy took all my friends."

"What about work friends? You must have some of those."

"I have a few, but my best friend there is married to the problem."

"Oh, my. This is more complicated than I thought."

"Exactly." Emma wished she could talk to Brent about it, but that might put a giant wedge between them. No one ever liked hearing the truth about their spouse, until it was too late.

They hung the rest of the ornaments and decorated the living room with garland and lights. Glo had multiple Santa and angel statues, as well as a vintage manger scene they'd arranged throughout the main rooms of the house. The place appeared very festive, but Emma wasn't feeling the spirit. The holiday season would be long and lonesome this year.

CHAPTER TWENTY-TWO

Dex chugged the last bit of coffee she'd picked up at McDonald's on her way over to Emma's parents'. She parked in front of the house and killed the engine. The holiday music that had been blaring through the speakers stopped, and the words to "Happy Holidays" rang in her head. She noted the lack of Emma's car anywhere on the street. *Happy fucking holidays.* The sinking feeling in her chest didn't improve her mood, and the silence was suddenly deafening.

She'd sent Emma a text yesterday, apologizing for the situation at the skating rink, but all she'd received in response were two words. *I know.* Dex's day had been more than full yesterday, and she hadn't had time to dwell on what Emma had meant. Everyone wanted their lights up now. Her workload was this way every holiday season, and Dex usually loved it, but so far this year she wasn't feeling the Christmas cheer.

Colored lights were flickering on and off in front of Bill as he sat on a stool in the garage behind his workbench. He seemed to be checking an enormous pile of light strings for dead bulbs, a task she never enjoyed. Dex glanced into the back seat of her SUV at the boxes she'd loaded this morning. She'd brought everything needed to decorate the house, including new LED lights, in case Emma's dad wanted to update his display. She unfastened the ladder from the top of her SUV and carried it up the driveway, then leaned it against the house before stepping into the garage. The space was nice and toasty, thanks to the gas heater mounted on the outside wall. She noted the flat-screen TV and was sure this was Bill's manctuary.

As Dex entered the garage, she couldn't help but admire how impeccably organized everything was. Screwdrivers hung on pegboard, in size order, wrenches just above them, and various power tools were slid into what appeared to be a handmade charging station on the wall above the bench.

Bill turned around and stood up. "Hey there, young lady." He reached out and shook her hand. The buzz cut he sported had been cut even shorter since she'd seen him last. The wild white hairs sprouting from his eyebrows caused her to wonder if he'd rolled out of bed just ten minutes before.

"Good morning," she said, still staring at the charging station. "Did you make that?"

He grinned and puffed his chest out slightly. "I did. In fact, I just hung it this morning." He brushed a stray curl of wood shaving from the bench.

Dex slid her hand across the smooth wood finish. "It's awesome."

"Thank you. It keeps the tools off the bench." He seemed to watch her for a moment before he said, "Let's go inside, say hello to Glo, and get you something warm to drink." He opened the door and motioned her to go ahead of him.

"Thanks." Dex stepped inside, and the comfort hit her immediately, just as it had a few days before on Thanksgiving. The house was decorated beautifully, yet it was warm and inviting, just what she'd expected from a house that seemed so full of love.

"You're here." Glo rushed in from the living room and swept her into a hug. "Are you hungry? I have eggs, or I can make pancakes." She twisted her wrist to check the time. "Maybe a sandwich instead." She automatically started taking lunchmeat and other sandwich makings out of the refrigerator. "You can't work out in the cold without something in your stomach."

Dex smiled at her smothering, something she'd really never experienced as a child. Her parents were always on the go, working to help some good cause for someone else. "Thanks, but I already ate." She'd scarfed down an Egg McMuffin on the way over.

Glo loaded everything back into the refrigerator. "Okay, then. You'll stay for dinner. I'm going to fix a nice pot roast, unless you don't eat red meat. Then I can roast a chicken."

"I'd love to." Dex smiled and nodded. "Pot roast sounds great."

Emma had told her about her mother's scrumptious Sunday meals. The thought of seeing her later at dinner swam through her head, and her heartbeat quickened.

By the time Dex went back outside, the two crew members she'd been able to round up to assist had arrived and were already wrapping the two trees in the yard with LED lights. She wasn't sure if they'd gotten approval from Bill, but he was still smiling, which was a plus.

Once the trees were done, they started on the house. They'd slid the hooks under the shingles and were halfway done hanging the lights when they hit a snag. Bill had plugged in the old-style bulb lights he'd given them and decided they didn't match the new LEDs on the trees. He wanted to go with the new lights all around. Dex grinned at her crew of two and then started taking the old ones down while they went to the SUV and got the LEDs. This wasn't the first time a client had changed their mind midstream. Dex would owe her guys a nice dinner out sometime since they were doing this for free as a favor to her. She wouldn't make any money off Emma's parents like some other companies probably would have. That wasn't the way she did business with her friends and family.

Emma's brothers showed up between football games, just as Emma had said they would, but Dex and her crew had everything under control, and they left soon after. They were impressed by the lights and the design on the trees and mentioned they'd be happy if Emma kept her around, so she could do this every year. Emma still hadn't shown, and Dex was left having dinner, alone, with her parents.

When Dex and Bill came into the house they were met with the delicious scent of comfort food. She took off her gloves and knit hat and stuffed them both inside the sleeve of her jacket before she hung it on the oak hall tree by the door. An open bottle of red wine and a bowl of rolls sat on the table, and Dex was surprised at how disappointed she was to see only three place settings. She wasn't going to get the chance to see Emma today.

"Come in and sit down," Glo said as she filled three bowls with pot roast and vegetables. She slid them across the counter before rounding it and moving them to the table. Dex jumped up to help, but Glo put her hand on her shoulder and pushed her into her seat.

"Are you sure your crew can't stay for dinner? I have plenty."

"They said thanks, but they needed to get home to their wives."

"Must be nice to have someone to go home to, right?" Glo was obviously feeling her out. "Do your parents live around here?"

Dex took a bite and chewed before she answered. "They have a house nearby, but they're rarely there." She'd been living in Mary and Craig's house since she was a child. As soon as she'd become an adult, she'd become the caretaker of sorts for the place. She'd renovated, repainted, and made it her own, finally moving into the master bedroom a few years ago when her parents made it clear they didn't call any one particular place home anymore. Now, when her parents happened to be in town for a day or two, they took the guest room downstairs. Her brother Ranny had chosen the same life track, and on the off times when he showed up at the same time, he got the basement.

Glo lifted her eyebrows, prompting Dex to continue.

"They do a lot of voluntourism." She swiped her mouth with the napkin. "You know, volunteer, see-the-world kind of stuff. My brother as well."

"Oh. That must be hard on you, especially during the holidays."

"Not anymore. My sister and I have gotten used to being orphans during the holidays." She took a sip of wine. "Sometimes we get together with others we've worked with on charitable events around town, and we make new friends."

"So you volunteer here in Chicago?"

She nodded. "The Food Bank, Habitat for Humanity. I keep it local."

"That's very altruistic."

"I do what I can." She pushed a carrot around in her bowl. "I don't have a lot of money, but time is sometimes just as valuable."

Glo smiled softly. "Well, I'm happy Emma has you for a friend."

"Thanks, I appreciate that. Since she may not be at this moment." She set down her spoon, her stomach lingering somewhere between shaky and starved.

"Why do you say that?" She looked across the table at Bill and saw him glance at Glo and pull his brows together. "You two seemed to be getting along famously at Thanksgiving."

"Oh yeah. We had a great time at Thanksgiving. Thanks again for inviting me."

Glo picked up a roll, buttered it, handed it to Bill, and then did the same for Dex as she seemed to wait for Dex to explain more.

"You remember my friend, Grace? The one you helped through dinner?"

She nodded. "Smart girl. Seemed to get the hang of it pretty quickly." She took a bite of her dinner.

"Well, she's been my best friend since we were kids, and she's not very self-sufficient." Dex broke off a piece of the roll. "She can be a little needy." She popped the piece into her mouth and waited to see which way her stomach was going to go. It seemed to settle for now.

"I saw." Glo picked up her wine and relaxed in her chair. "So what does this have to do with Emma?"

Dex took another bite of roll and then a gulp of wine to wash it down. This wasn't the way she'd expected her night to turn out. "We had plans to go ice-skating, which is something Grace and I have always done together in the past. Anyway, long story short, Grace ended up going with us." She took another sip of wine.

"So, you invited her?" Glo took another bite of her dinner.

"Actually, no." She hesitated. "I told her we were going and she showed up."

"And when she did, you included her." Glo took another drink of wine and seemed to process the information. It probably wasn't the first time she'd heard this story. "That was nice of you."

Dex blew out a breath. "I thought so, but Emma wasn't happy about it, and Grace wasn't very nice to her." She stared down at her bowl and pushed some of the vegetables around. "Grace means well, but she can be pretty selfish sometimes."

"Sounds like you may need to set some boundaries with Grace."

"I know. It's just hard with someone who…"

"Who has a special place in your heart?" Glo asked, seeming to know what Dex was talking about.

Dex nodded. "Yes." She didn't know why, but it felt good to talk this out with Glo.

"Can I offer you a little advice?"

"Glo." Bill's voice was firm. "Maybe you should stop meddling and let the girls figure this out themselves."

"It's okay. I don't mind." Dex ate the few carrots left in her bowl and pushed her dish away. "I was hoping Emma would be here today, so I could talk to her."

"I'm going to give you a little insight into Emma." Glo finished her glass of wine and refilled it. "She had a bad experience with her last girlfriend."

Dex sat forward and put her arms on the table. "She hasn't said anything about that."

"And she probably won't." She glanced across the table at Bill, and he shrugged. "She found out that friends don't always have your best interests in mind." She let out a heavy breath and stood up. "I'm going to leave it at that." She started gathering the dirty dishes, and Dex hopped up to help.

That was an open-ended bit of advice if she'd ever heard it. "What am I supposed to do with that?"

Glo patted her on the cheek lightly. "Set your boundaries, Dex. And do it soon."

They had the dishes done quickly, and Dex was out the door soon after. She hadn't had much to say after hearing about Emma's previous relationship. Her mind had been on Emma and her heartbreak. It actually pained Dex to know she'd been hurt by someone, a friend, someone she'd trusted. Now she understood her actions at the skating rink. Dex had been thoughtless by letting Grace insert herself into their date and then not leaving with Emma. It seemed that Dex's situation might be a little too similar. Apparently, she wasn't the only one who had relationship fears.

Once her SUV had warmed up, Dex glanced up at the house and waved at Bill and Glo, who were standing in the doorway before she pulled away. The lights had turned out beautifully, and her talk with Glo had lifted the weight in her chest some. Maybe she *could* make this work with Emma.

The week had trudged by slowly. With no contact from Emma, Dex had let work occupy her time by working ten- and twelve-hour days to complete all the light-hanging jobs on her schedule for the week and keep her clients happy. Staying busy had kept her mind occupied, and she'd caught herself thinking about Emma only after the sun went down. Sleep hadn't come easy, but keeping herself exhausted usually helped. The edge of that knife hurt more than she'd thought it would right now. She missed the sparkle in Emma's eyes whenever she'd caught her watching her, the sweetness in her voice when she'd whispered in her ear, the gentle possessiveness she'd shown when they'd made love. Emma did things to Dex no one else ever had.

Thankfully it had been an unseasonably warm week for early December in Chicago. The week's schedule had been full, with Friday being the heaviest of all. It had taken her full crew and thousands of lights to cover the two-story Italian-renaissance-revival mansion she'd scheduled. At fifteen thousand square feet, the modern architectural landmark was nestled in the midst of several other elite mansions in River Forest. She'd yet to get but a few of the neighbors on her customer list but hoped this light display would win them over. Dex just hoped the weather held out because her schedule was fully booked until mid-December.

"I don't know how you do it, Dex. The place looks awesome."

"We aim to please."

"You've certainly done that." Emilio handed her a check. "I put a little extra in there for all of you. You know, a little Christmas bonus."

"Thanks. The team will appreciate that." Dex never accepted tips from her customers. She always paid them forward to her crew.

"Don't forget about the Christmas party tomorrow night. I'll expect to see you there." He gave her a fist bump.

"The best party of the year. Wouldn't miss it."

"You're bringing your girl, right?"

"I would if I had one."

He put his arm around her shoulder. "Plenty of single ladies will be there."

"Yeah?"

"Bring your best game." He winked and went back into the house.

She would definitely bring her best game. This party could be a new beginning.

CHAPTER TWENTY-THREE

Emma checked her coat at the door and took in the checkerboard-tiled entryway. The wrought-iron banister held a wide staircase that led to a landing above. She'd read somewhere in a magazine that Emilio's house had fifteen rooms, six of which were bedrooms and seven were bathrooms. It also included a fitness center and waterfall by the pool, which was ridiculous for a confirmed bachelor who used only one of the bedrooms the majority of the time. The rest were here for out-of-town relatives and guests. And this was only one of his homes. He had them in New York, LA, and Tampa as well. Wouldn't it be nice to be rich? At this point Emma would settle for a little happiness in her life.

As soon as she entered the party, she was offered a flute of champagne by one of the many servers working the room. She drank it in two gulps, then switched it out for a full one as another server came by. She needed something to improve her mood. Hopefully she'd be able to put in her obligatory hour or two and get the hell out of there.

This party was not on her fun-things-to-do list. Well, it might have been a month ago, but now it was just making her sad and uncomfortable. She hadn't brought a date because she didn't want to worry about someone else tonight. She'd even Ubered here in case she drank too much, which was entirely possible at this point. She'd come only because Emilio was one of the company's largest clients, and she couldn't think of any way to avoid being here unless she was on her deathbed. Even though she'd felt like it this past week, she wasn't actually sick.

She caught a glimpse of Brent at the bar, which meant Grace was close by. Her stomach twisted. She'd wanted to avoid seeing Grace as long as possible. Emma hadn't heard from Dex since the apology text she'd received after she'd left Dex at the ice-skating rink, and she wasn't up for seeing Grace's smug, self-satisfied face. Before she could slip out of view, Brent swung around and caught sight of her. *Fuck!*

He threw up a hand and waved her over. She'd guessed it would happen sooner or later during the night, but she'd planned for later.

He took her empty glass. "What are you drinking?"

"Champagne."

He motioned to the bartender and handed her a fresh glass. She drank it down quickly.

"What are you trying to do, get fucked up within the first hour?"

"That's my plan." She ignored his concern and glanced around the room. "Where's your wife?"

"Bathroom. She heard they have fancy giveaway soaps."

"How did you get her to come along? Doesn't she hate these things?"

"I told her Emilio was going to perform."

"Is he really? At his own Christmas party?"

"Of course not, but she doesn't know that yet. So don't blow it for me, okay?"

"Your secret's safe with me." She put her fingers to her lips and twisted her fingers. She would be spending the least amount of time possible talking to Grace this evening.

His eyes brightened, and Emma knew she was coming their way. She set her empty champagne flute on the bar and signaled the bartender for another.

Grace squeezed up under Brent's arm, peeked up, and waited for him to kiss her, which he did.

He handed her a drink. "Look who I ran into."

"I didn't think you'd come tonight." Grace pressed her lips together.

"Same." She lifted her glass and took a drink. The room swayed momentarily, so she set the glass on the bar and leaned against it. She was going a little too fast with the champagne. She hadn't eaten anything except a piece of cheese today.

Brent glanced at the dance floor and then at Grace. "How about we take a stroll on the dance floor?"

Grace gave him a strange stare as he took her drink, set it on the bar, and pulled her across the room. Freedom for at least a few minutes.

"You're beautiful, you know that?" Dex's voice was low and sultry.

A jolt zapped through Emma. It was uncanny. She'd felt Dex before she even spoke. She took in a deep breath to calm herself before she turned around. "Hey, you."

"I was hoping to see you tonight."

"I wasn't expecting to see you." Emma was uncertain about the whole thing and avoided eye contact.

"Emilio's a client."

"Oh," she said as she glanced around the room. "The lights are beautiful." She reached for her champagne.

Before she could take a drink, Dex stole the glass from her. "Dance with me?" She didn't wait for an answer. Dex moved her in front of her and guided her through the crowd.

This was a bad idea, but the pull Dex created in her was too much for Emma to resist. When they reached the dance floor, Dex spun her around, and she melted into her. They didn't speak. They just took in the essence of each other. Emma couldn't believe how good it felt to be in Dex's arms again.

When the music came to a lull, Dex brushed her thumb across Emma's face. "I've missed you."

Although they were nice, they weren't the words Emma needed to hear. She broke free from her arms and headed for the door. She couldn't stay any longer, not with Dex here.

"Emma, wait." Dex took her hand and pulled her into another room off the foyer. "I came here tonight because I knew you'd be here."

"You did?" The familiar tingle captured her. She forced herself to ignore it. "I don't know what you want from me, Dex."

"I'm sorry I hurt you."

Emma stared into her eyes, waiting for more.

"I shouldn't have let Grace come between us, and I won't let it happen again."

There they were. That's what she needed to hear. She melted into

Dex and wrapped her arms around her. "I've missed you too." Much more than she'd wanted to admit. She'd never felt the way she did when she was in Dex's arms. Safe, cherished, loved.

Emma gazed into Dex's eyes and kissed her, slowly, softly, and sweetly. They held each other and moved to the faint sound of the music from the party until it faded.

"We should probably get back out there."

"Yeah." Dex kissed her softly again before letting Emma lead her to the door. She opened it just a smidge to make sure the coast was clear before they went out. All Emma needed was for everyone at work to think she'd had sex in Emilio's study.

Everyone had gathered in the main room, where Emilio was standing on the band platform. "Thank you all for coming to celebrate the holidays with us tonight. The band is happy to take requests, and both the bar and the buffet are open." Everyone clapped. "Please enjoy your evening," he said and hopped off the stage.

"Come on. You probably need some food." Dex moved Emma to the buffet table.

"How do you know these things?"

"I watched you come in." She scrunched up her face. "Was it two or three glasses before you reached the bar?"

"Three."

"Did you eat today?"

Emma shook her head. "Wasn't hungry. Haven't been hungry in days."

She took her to a table instead and pulled out a chair for her. "I'll be right back."

The room was filled with people drinking, eating, and laughing. Emma felt a little foolish now. She hadn't expected to drink so much, so quickly. And she definitely hadn't expected to run into Dex.

She glanced over at the buffet table where Dex was filling a couple of plates with food. Dex caught her watching and gave her a wink. God, she was cute. Dressed in flowy black pants and a red silk blouse, she was the picture of everything Emma had ever dreamed of in a woman. The perfect Christmas present.

❖

The food and dancing had sobered Emma up quickly, and she really hadn't minded when Grace swept Dex off to the stage to talk with Emilio. Everyone seemed to be having a good time until Grace spun around, her eyes narrowed and fixed on Brent.

He took a gulp of his drink and set it on the table. "Oh, shit. She's coming in hot. You'd better scatter."

"Reinforcements?" Emma asked as she watched liquid spill across a nearby table when Grace slapped her glass onto it. She marched across the room with Dex following close behind, visibly talking to her.

"Uh, I don't think that will help."

Emma intercepted Dex on the way and led her away from the impending explosion while Grace gained speed on her way to the miserable train wreck she was about to stage. She was about to either shock or entertain over half of the semi-drunken partygoers, and she didn't seem to care who was taking in the show.

"How did you know she was going to freak?" Dex asked.

"This isn't my first work event with them. Grace hates these parties. Only comes for the shows or the perks, and there will be neither of those tonight."

Dex watched Grace as she lit into Brent. "Wow. Hadn't seen this before."

"I guess you're lucky that way." Emma smiled. "Dessert?"

Dex continued to watch, appearing thoughtful. Perhaps she hadn't really meant what she'd said earlier about removing Grace from the equation. But then she turned to Emma and said, "I'm in."

The two of them picked out an assortment of desserts, sat at an empty table, and watched the rest of the messy scene unfold. Brent seemed to listen passively as Grace shot into his space and raised her voice. People at the surrounding tables glanced their way. Some went back to their conversations, and others remained glued to the scene. The vein in Grace's neck throbbed as she blasted him. There was no way to turn the volume down on this explosion. It wasn't until she stabbed a finger into Brent's chest that Emma saw any reaction. He balled his fists but kept them at his sides. His jaw was so tight she could see the muscle in his cheek pop back and forth as he clenched his teeth. He was clearly holding back. Too many people he worked with were at the party, so he couldn't go off on his wife in front of them. Even if she deserved it.

Brent finally brushed past her and went to the bar, and Grace retrieved her drink from the table where she'd left it. She immediately downed it and didn't stop there. Next, she grabbed the first eligible male and pulled him to the dance floor. This was more entertainment than Emma had expected tonight, much more so than any performance from Emilio.

It was close to an hour later when Grace rushed to the bar and slammed into Dex, practically knocking her off her feet.

Dex steadied her. "Are you okay?"

"I'm fine."

Dex blinked and moved back a few steps. "How much have you had to drink?"

"Just a few of those special Christmas cocktails."

Emma held Grace up as she wedged herself between them and swayed backward. "Jesus, those things are lethal. At least I had the sense to stick with champagne."

Grace gave Emma a sluggish glance and then focused on Dex. "Listen, Dex. Here's the deal. I wanna go home, and Brent won't take me." The words were slurred, but Emma caught the gist of the conversation.

"I got this." Emma searched the room, found Brent drinking at a table with his buddies, and darted that way "Your wife wants to go home."

Brent shrugged. "I'm not ready to leave yet."

"She's asking Dex to take her."

"That's fine. Whatever." He shrugged and turned to the conversation he was having with the group of guys.

"You're a *shitty* husband, you know that?" The words came out harsher than she'd intended, but Brent was royally pissing her off.

That seemed to get his attention, and he swung back around. "What? Why?"

"You need to pay attention to your wife before someone else does it for you."

"Just plant her at a table with someone. She'll be fine."

"So you're not going to take her home?"

"Fuck, no." His voice rose. "She's acting like a spoiled princess."

"Hell of a night for you to grow some balls." Emma spun around and raced across the room to Dex and Grace.

"What'd he say?" Dex asked.

"He's being an ass."

Grace nodded. "Exactly." She swayed, and Dex steadied her.

"Come on. Let's go." Emma put her arm around Grace.

Grace twisted and peered at her through half-mast lashes. "I have to pee."

Fuck, can this night get any worse?

Dex slipped under Grace's shoulder. "I'll take her." She reached in her pocket and took out a valet slip. "Can you get my SUV, and we'll meet you at the door?"

By the time Dex came out with Grace, Emma had pulled the SUV forward to give the valet room to retrieve other cars. Dex was practically carrying Grace, who was in worse shape than Emma had thought. She jumped out to open the door, and Dex buckled Grace into the back seat behind her. She immediately fell asleep. Emma started to round the car to the passenger seat, and Dex waved her off.

"I'll get in the back with her."

They were almost to the house when Grace bolted forward in the seat and slapped her hand to the headrest. "I'm going to be sick."

Emma jerked the wheel to pull the car over quickly, jumped out, and yanked the door open. Grace spewed all over Emma's feet. She raised her head and gave her a glassy-eyed stare. "Whoops."

When Dex rounded the car her face went white. "Well, that's just fucking fantastic."

Emma couldn't stop the laugh that erupted from her lips. "At least she didn't get my dress."

"Yet." Dex moved Emma back before she settled Grace against the seat. She rummaged around on the floorboard and held up a shopping bag filled with spare Christmas lights. Dex emptied the bag, handed it to Grace, and shut the door. "Hang on a minute, and I'll get something to put your shoes in."

Dex headed to the back of the SUV. "Stay there. I have some trash bags. I always keep them to line the back whenever I'm transporting plants."

Dex opened the back of the SUV, took out a bag, went back to Emma, and squatted down in front of her. "Step into this." Emma did as she said and put her hand on Dex's shoulder as Dex slid her hand down each of Emma's calves to her heels and slipped off her shoes. Emma couldn't stop the jolt that shot up her legs and hit square in her midsection. If the situation wasn't so disgusting, the whole act would've been totally erotic.

"Okay, now step out." She picked up the bag and tied it shut before she tossed it into the back and closed the hatch.

"If you want to take shotgun, I'll drive the rest of the way." Dex glanced through the window. "Grace seems to be out again."

"Sure." Emma was surprised when Dex swept her up in her arms and carried her around to the passenger seat. She was even more perfect than Emma thought she was before.

They didn't talk much, and even if they had, they wouldn't have been able to hear much. Grace was snoring loudly in excellent rhythm by the time they reached the house.

Dex gripped the steering wheel and took in a deep breath. "I'm so sorry. This is not *at all* the way I thought this night would play out."

Emma shook her head and chuckled. "Totally not what I expected either." But Emma saw more good in it than bad. Dex was sitting in the seat next to her smiling. Even Grace couldn't spoil how she felt right now.

"We'll leave earlier next time." Dex glanced back at Grace. "Much earlier." She reached into the back seat, retrieved Grace's clutch, and fished out her keys. "I'll get her in the house, and then I'll be right back."

Dex seemed to be struggling as she tried to open the door. Given the state Grace was in, she was bound to be dead weight. Emma got out of the car, sprinted up the walkway, took the keys, and unlocked the door. Emma slipped in ahead of Dex and went toward where she remembered the bedrooms were.

"Last one on the right," Dex said as she followed her.

Emma reluctantly pushed through the bedroom door, almost afraid of what she might find, and then quickly pulled the blanket back so Dex could pour Grace into bed. Emma unfastened one of Grace's strappy stilettos while Dex took off the other. No way were they getting her dress off, so they pulled the blanket up and left her to sleep it off. She was going to have a helluva hangover tomorrow.

"Maybe you should fix her some of your ginger concoction."

"Or maybe I just want her to feel like shit tomorrow for ruining our night."

Dex smiled. "I can go with that." She glanced over her shoulder into the bedroom before she pulled the door partly closed. "You can take my SUV. I think I'll stay here tonight. Who knows if Brent's coming home."

"Do you mind if I stay with you?"

"I'd love that. I just didn't think you'd want to. I mean with Grace here and all."

"She's harmless enough now." She hesitated. "And to be honest, I'm not quite ready to leave you yet."

"Do want to go talk in the other room?" Dex asked.

"I'm too tired to talk." She remembered the guest bedroom from the tour Dex had given her at the housewarming party. She pushed open the door across the hall, which was furnished with a queen-size bed. "Can we just lie down?"

"Sure."

Emma climbed into the bed and waited for Dex to take off her shoes and crawl in next to her.

Dex slipped her arm around her. "Are you okay?" she asked as her fingers floated across Emma's shoulder.

"I'm fine." She snuggled in close and put her head on Dex's shoulder. "But we're not having sex in Grace's guest room." Even though she wanted to be more than close to Dex, the weirdness of it all was too much.

Dex laughed. "Uh, no. That would be totally creepy."

"Thank you for putting the lights up at my parents' house."

"I was glad to do it. I mean, your dad can be a bit of a control freak, but I like him." That earned Dex a pinch to the belly, and she squirmed.

"If you think my dad's bad, wait until you get to know my mom better."

"I got a pretty good glimpse of your mom's power at dinner. It was surprising how quickly your dad stopped talking when your mom shot him that glare."

"Oh, you saw the look."

"More than once," Dex said with a chuckle.

"That's pretty powerful stuff." She sat up and tried to mimic her mother's glare.

Dex shook her head. "Not even close."

"What?" Her voice rose as she pushed up on her elbow and narrowed her eyes.

Dex smiled. "You're in the vicinity now."

She flattened her lips and raised an eyebrow.

"Oh yeah, that's it. Totally terrifying." Dex blinked a few times. "Where did that sweet girl who was just here go?"

"Right here." Emma gave her a soft kiss. "Now get some sleep before I rethink that no-sex thing and we end up with a creepy memory to deal with." She snuggled into Dex and let the happiness wash through her. She was ridiculously glad to be close to her again.

Emma had just started to doze off when she heard the front door slam shut. Multiple thuds in the hallway meant Brent was home and stinking drunk. She glanced up at Dex to see if she'd heard him too. Her eyes were wide open.

When the headboard thumping and low groaning started, Emma immediately bolted from the warm, cozy spot in Dex's arms. "Oh, my God." She floundered to get out of bed. "We have to leave." The wild stories Brent had told her about Grace and their sex life were true.

"Yep." Dex launched from the bed, picked up her shoes, and peeked out the doorway. She took Emma's hand and quietly led her down the hallway. After stopping only to slip on her shoes, she opened the door, picked up Emma, and carried her to the SUV.

Emma had no words to deal with what they'd just experienced, and she guessed Dex was pretty tongue-tied about it as well. The vehicle was exceptionally quiet as Dex drove. When the Bluetooth from her phone connected to the sound system, Dex had immediately hit the power button on the console and turned it off. It was late and there was minimal traffic, with no road sounds except the tire whine on the pavement. Emma wasn't quite sure what to say. The whole disturbing scene had completely freaked her out, and she was sure it had had the same effect, if not worse, on Dex.

She reached over and touched Dex's arm. "Are you okay?"

Dex shook her head before she glanced over at Emma and grimaced. "Now that was disturbingly creepy." They both burst out laughing.

CHAPTER TWENTY-FOUR

Emma watched Dex as she slept. It had been close to three by the time they'd arrived at Emma's house. When Dex had walked her to the door, she'd seemed uncertain. Emma was as well, but she'd asked her to stay just the same. If nothing else, they needed to talk. Of course that didn't happen. Emma had gotten in the shower to clean up, and Dex had slipped in to join her soon after.

Soft, slick hands had taken her from behind. She could still feel Dex's lips as they grazed her shoulder, and she shuddered. Then the deliciousness of her soapy palms circling her breasts had been almost unbearable. When she'd trailed her fingers in tiny circles down her sides to reach her center, Emma's knees had buckled. Dex had clamped her arm around her, holding her steady. Emma had slapped her hands to the shower wall, bracing herself for the inevitable orgasm, and Dex had somehow made her come three times before Emma had pushed her hand away. They hadn't taken time to dry themselves before tumbling into bed, where Emma took over and touched every part of Dex, reveling in her scent, her taste, her everything. God, she'd missed that body. She stretched her arm above her head and groaned. She hadn't been this sore in weeks, and she'd missed it.

Everything would be perfect if Grace would just back off and leave them alone. She didn't know what to do about this situation. It was becoming more apparent that a conversation between the two of them was necessary.

Dex rolled over and slid her arm across Emma's stomach. "Good morning."

"Morning." She brushed a strand of hair from Dex's eyes.

"Last night sure was a mess."

"In more ways than one." Emma laughed. "I don't think my shoes are salvageable."

Dex raised her eyebrows. "But it wasn't a total loss, right?"

"No, not total." She kissed her and was immediately ready for Dex again. "Why do you have to be so damn sexy?"

"You think I'm sexy?"

"Ridiculously, unbelievably, steamingly hot sexy." She slid her hand between Dex's legs and groaned. "Do you have to work today?"

"Uh-huh. But I have time."

Emma crawled on top of her. She found this position, gazing down at Dex's gorgeous body beneath her, stimulating, to say the least. Dex had the capability of making Emma come right now with only one finger, if she'd let her. But this was about pleasing Dex. She wedged a knee between Dex's legs and pressed it ever so lightly against her center. Emma groaned when Dex bucked into her, and her wetness coated her thigh. Emma moved Dex's smooth, white thighs apart, settled her hips between them, and began rocking back and forth.

She took one of Dex's breasts, kneading the nipple with her fingers while she circled her tongue around the other, making it stand at attention before she sucked it into her mouth. Emma would never tire of this pleasure. Dex's breasts were soft and firm all at once, and holding them in her hands and mouth totally turned her on. But as Dex raised her hips, it became apparent that more parts of Dex needed attention. She moved slowly down Dex's body, breathing, hovering just above her stomach. She gave it a quick lick, and Dex responded with a quiver, prompting her to continue downward. She fit her shoulders between Dex's widely spread thighs and took in the view of her swollen center. She'd never enjoyed someone quite so much as she was enjoying Dex at this moment.

Dex lifted her hips again and said, "Em, I need you to do something…" She growled. "Now."

Emma laughed softly and lightly trailed her tongue through the length of her. Dex squirmed beneath her, pressing hard against Emma for more. Emma sank her mouth into Dex's center and happily sucked and licked until the noises coming from Dex were no longer comprehensible, and then she slowed. Dex grabbed Emma's hair and forced her closer. As Emma continued with long, slow strokes, she slipped two fingers inside, angled them upward, and curled them against the perfect spot, creating a pulse of tremors from Dex.

"Oh my God, yes." The words rumbled out of Dex's mouth, and Emma pressed harder until she felt Dex tighten around her fingers and launch into orgasm. Emma watched the beautiful sight unfold. Pleasing Dex was the most intoxicating feeling in the world.

Dex reached for her. "How do you do that?"

"What?" She took another swipe at her center with her tongue and watched Dex's belly bounce.

Dex growled. "You have no idea where you take me."

Emma crawled up her body and kissed her. When Dex reached between Emma's legs, she gasped at the unexpected pleasure. Dex smiled. Apparently this wasn't going to be a one-woman show this morning. Her center throbbed and she ached to be touched. It wouldn't take much to make the finale happen. Dex watched with rapt attention as she circled her hand above Emma's nipple. Each slight touch sent a ripple of pleasure through her, and the feathery strokes almost made her come right then. She'd been so concentrated on the sensations, she hadn't noticed when Dex had rolled on top of her and taken complete control.

She crept down Emma's body, leaving a wet, hot trail with her tongue that sizzled in its wake. The ripples Dex was creating were long and slow. Emma needed them to peak soon, or she was going to crash into oblivion. When she felt the flat of Dex's tongue glide across her, she grabbed a fistful of sheet and clasped it. Not yet. She wanted more time to enjoy this feeling of ecstasy. When Dex pushed her fingers inside simultaneously with a long stroke of her tongue, Emma tumbled into a shattering climax. Shards of light flickered behind her eyelids as she rode it out. Dex continued to stroke her, taking her back up again and never letting her come completely down from one spasm before pushing her into another. Emma reached for her to stop. She was so sensitive now, if she let Dex continue she'd never be able to walk again.

Dex moved up next to her and kissed her. "I could do this all day."

"If I could take it all day, I'd let you." She shuddered as one last jolt hit her. *I love you.* She stopped herself from saying those all-important three words.

The lovemaking had been slow and methodical this time. Dex had left every one of Emma's senses sated. The woman anticipated her every want and need. No other partner in Emma's life had satisfied her so completely. And she had a few champions to compete with, including her last, who'd left a gaping hole in her heart, which had now begun to fill.

Dex took in a deep breath and let it out. "As much as I'd love to stay here with you all day, I need to get going."

"Do you really have to?"

"Unfortunately, I have lights to hang."

"If I haven't already told you, my parents' house looks awesome, by the way." That miserable weekend flashed through her mind.

Dex chuckled. "I have a one-hundred-dollar bill I need to return to your dad. He slipped it into my jacket pocket when I wasn't watching."

"Thanks for taking care of that for him."

"Anything for you." Dex smiled.

Emma smiled. "Really?"

Dex nodded. "Emma, I really—" Dex's phone chimed. "Ugh." She reached over and picked it up from the nightstand.

Emma caught a glimpse of the screen. *Grace again.* Up popped the confusing messages teetering between her brain and her heart. Intense as her feelings were for Dex, they were also complicated. There would always be something between Dex and Grace.

"You should send Grace a bill for your shoes."

"I should."

"I'll deliver it personally."

She'll deliver it personally. The sinking feeling returned, but Emma shrugged it off. She didn't want to think or talk about Grace right now. It would crush the whole wonderful experience she'd just had.

"How many houses are you doing today?"

"One, possibly two." She glanced at the time on her phone. "In fact, I'd better get going. I've got a big two-story on South Grove booked this morning. My crew will be there soon." She got up and pulled on the pair of jeans, T-shirt, and hoodie she'd brought in from her SUV the night before. Dex always kept a spare set of clothes in case weather hit while she was working.

"Okay. Can I fix you something to eat?"

"Nope. You just stay right there looking beautiful. I'll grab something on the way." She gave her a quick kiss. "I'll call you later, okay?"

"Sure."

Emma had something to do today as well. She planned to let Grace know there were boundaries with Dex now.

Emma waited down the street, watching as Brent pulled out of the driveway and drove in the opposite direction toward work. She didn't want this scene to play out while he was around. In fact, Emma didn't want him involved at all. Hurting him was something she wanted to avoid at all costs, and if this happened the way she thought it might, he and Emma could both end up the losers in this whole mess.

She knocked on the door and waited. No answer. She knocked again. After a few minutes she heard Grace's sickeningly sweet voice say, "Did you forget your key, baby?" The door flew open, and she was met with the stunning image of Grace dressed in only a bathrobe. The woman knew how to train a dick.

Her smile dropped. "I thought you were—"

"Brent? Dex? Or some other unsuspecting soul you've captured with your magic?"

"What do you want, Emma?" She closed the door slightly, and Emma pushed through it. "I'm really not up for this. I have a huge headache."

"I know. Who do you think brought you home and poured you into bed?" She didn't take off her coat because she wouldn't be staying long. "You need to stop. You can't tease Dex all night and then go home and fuck Brent like a savage." She'd heard plenty of Brent's stories about his wild wife, and last night had confirmed them all.

Grace's eyes narrowed. "What the hell are you talking about?"

"We were here last night when Brent got home. We caught the beginning of the show."

"Jealous of what you don't have?" One of Grace's eyebrows popped up, and she gave Emma a smirk that she wanted to smack right off her face.

"Oh, Dex and I have plenty of that." Emma saw something cross

Grace's face—anger, sadness, surprise. She didn't know what, but the news she'd just delivered had made the intended impact. "Stop enticing her with something you're never going to give her."

Grace slammed the door as she spun around and narrowed her eyes. "You need to mind your own business."

"She is my business. I love her." *I love her? I love her.*

"You could never love her like I do."

"You don't love her. You just want her to pine after you. Just like everyone else in your life. Don't think I didn't notice the way you bent over and whispered in Dex's ear last night. Your boobs were practically in her face." Emma had also noticed how Dex had closed her eyes momentarily, taken in a breath, and then focused her attention on Emma as though she were trying to resist the temptation Grace had set before her.

"That's what you want, isn't it? For Dex to pine after you instead of me?" Grace's face was crimson.

"I would never manipulate her like you do. That's not normal, Grace. I give her what she wants."

"You only say that because she still wants to spend time with *me*."

"You don't really want her to be happy. If you did you'd leave her alone."

"I'm her best friend, Emma. I'll always be in her life. Deal with it."

"I wish you would just disappear."

Grace laughed. "So you want me dead now." She picked up her phone. "Should I call Dex? Tell her that's what you want?" She pressed a button, then held up the phone to show a call going through to Dex.

"You are really fucked up." She swiped the phone from Grace's hand and tossed it to the couch. "Why don't I go find Brent and tell him just how close the two of you are?" She spun around to leave.

Grace caught her by the arm. "No. I don't love her like that." When Emma focused on Grace's hand clasped around her arm, she let it drop. "We were involved once, but that was over a long time ago."

Emma's neck heated, and the room immediately felt smaller. This was information she hadn't heard before or expected. "So you just flash those tail feathers of yours in front of her whenever you need to feel good about yourself."

"She'll never love you like she loves me." Grace opened the front door. "You need to either accept that or get out of her life."

The pathway became sketchy as Emma scrambled to her car. She fumbled with the key fob, hitting every button until she finally heard the familiar chirp. Once she was in the driver's seat, she fought to take in a breath. No wonder Dex couldn't get over her. She pressed her forehead to the steering wheel. It would be Emma's own fault if she went any further with this relationship.

Had she misread the whole situation? Were Dex's feelings for Grace purely platonic? She shook her head. No, she remembered the state Dex was in at the wedding. She was clearly in love with Grace. A huge rock had formed in Emma's stomach. Carrying a torch from a schoolgirl crush was one thing, but knowing Dex had actually had sex with Grace was a whole different story. She had to know if Dex felt the same for Emma as she felt for Dex, or she had to break this off now. If she didn't, this would only end badly for Emma. The thought of losing Dex had already created a massive explosion in her heart.

She pulled up in front of the house where Dex was hanging lights and honked. She hadn't known the exact address, so she'd started at the beginning of South Grove and driven until she'd found her.

Dex ran to the car. "Hey, this is a nice surprise," Dex said as she leaned through the window opening and kissed her.

Emma plucked a cup out of the holder in the console and handed it to her. "I thought you might need some coffee."

"Awesome." She took it from her and glanced over her shoulder. "If you have a few minutes, I can probably take a break."

"Sure." She reached into the back and set a jug of coffee on the console. "I brought some for your team too."

"Oh, man, you're spoiling us." Dex ran around the car and hopped into the passenger seat.

"It's pretty cold out there." She tapped the temperature reading on her dashboard, which showed twenty-six degrees.

"Are you okay?" Dex seemed to notice Emma's mood.

"I'm not sure." She stared at the steering wheel, out the windshield, at the coffee on the console between them. Everywhere but at Dex. The internal battle of what she should do and what she wanted to do was raging inside her.

"Talk to me." Dex reached over and took her hand.

She blew out a breath and summoned her courage. "I went to talk to Grace this morning."

"Why?" Confusion seemed to set in with Dex.

"It seems like she's always in the middle of everything we do. Even when she's not physically between us, she's calling."

Dex's phone chimed right on cue. She ignored it.

"I can't continue"—she glanced at the ceiling and slowly shook her head—"whatever this is I have with you, if you're still in love with Grace."

The pink hue starting to return to Dex's cheeks disappeared. "What did she tell you?"

Not the reaction Emma wanted. Just one word of protest to let her know it wasn't true would've given her hope, but there was none. The rock in her stomach doubled in size. "I don't know what I was thinking. I can't compete with her."

"I'm not asking you to compete with her, Em."

"Oh, but you are. Every time you bring her into the conversation, tell her where we're going, or talk to her about me."

"I don't talk to her about you."

"Because she doesn't want to hear it, right?"

Dex nodded.

"Well, there's one good thing."

"What are you so scared of, Em?"

She gripped the steering wheel. "I'm scared that you'll never love me as much as you love her." She stared up at the ceiling, took in a deep breath, and let it out. "When I saw you at the wedding, I was off-the-charts smitten." She closed her eyes as the vision filled her head. "I thought, how can she still be single? Then I saw your face after Grace and Brent said their vows. And then you caught the bouquet and got so fucking drunk. I knew you were in love with her."

"I can't deny that." She shook her head. "But you've become very important in my life."

"But you're not completely over her."

"I'm trying."

"Sometimes I feel like this thing that I *think* we have"—she motioned with her hand between them—"is one-sided. I need you to be all in with me." She let her hands fall from the steering wheel. "I'm right here. I've stripped away all my walls. I've let you in. I need that from you too."

"Then please stop making this about Grace."

"I can't. She's right here in the middle of us all the time."

"You're making it more complicated than it is."

"Then help me uncomplicate it. Just tell me what you want, Dex, even if it's Grace. If that's the case, I'll just go away, and you won't have to deal with me anymore." Dex's silence was more than an answer. Emma closed her eyes and tamped down the pain inside. "I thought maybe you'd gotten over her, but it's pretty apparent that you haven't."

"I have. I am, but it's not that simple, Em. We have a lot of history together. She's been my family since I was twelve. We've been through things together that I just can't forget."

"I'm not asking you to forget your history with Grace, Dex. Hell, I'm not even asking you to cut her out of your life. Most women would insist on that. But I can't share your heart with her or compete for your attention. I won't." She shook her head. "So I'll leave you to whatever you need to do until you decide what you want."

Dex reached over and swiped a tear from Emma's cheek with her thumb. "But—"

"Don't do that." Emma reached up and removed Dex's hand. "Please." She squeezed her eyes shut. "The thing is…there's this girl that I love, that I'm not sure I can live without." She paused a moment to keep from sobbing. "But I can't live with her if she's in love with someone else." Emma picked up the jug of coffee and handed to her. "I want to be the one, Dex. I really do. But I need all of your heart, half of it won't work, and I just don't know if I can hang around and wait for you to get over her. Take some time. Figure it out. I can't be second choice, and I'm afraid you'll end up hating *me* for hating *her*."

Dex got out of the car and just stood there staring through the window at her. Emma ignored the tears streaming down Dex's face as she put the car in gear and sped away. She let out a huge sob as she glanced up at the rearview mirror to see Dex still standing in the middle of the street when she turned the corner.

CHAPTER TWENTY-FIVE

Dex sat on the couch at home in the dark with Panda on her lap. She'd been successful at keeping Emma out of her thoughts while she was working, but all her distractions were gone now. She glanced out the plate-glass windows spread across the front of the house. The glow of Christmas lights had begun to light the room. She stared at the magical hues she'd loved since childhood and thought about how the day had played out. She'd already replayed it too many times in her head, and she didn't know how their relationship had disintegrated in so little time. Panda purred as Dex rubbed under her ears.

Everything had been wonderful Sunday morning when she'd left Emma's house. She'd been so happy to see her when she'd showed up at the job site, then totally stunned at the emotional bombshell Emma had dumped on her. And she'd been even more surprised at herself for not having the courage to tell Emma how she felt about her. The more she thought about watching her drive away, the more it hurt.

Knowing how much Emma was hurting and that she'd caused it magnified the pain in her heart a thousand times. She'd watched the emotions play out in Emma's face as she'd gone from thoughtful, to curious, to intensely sober, and then, in a flash, detached—all in the span of ten minutes. Seeing the tears flow down her cheeks had sliced right through Dex, and she couldn't do anything to fix the situation. She couldn't think of any way to ease her pain until she fully purged her feelings for Grace and put the loyalty she held for her in its proper place.

Emma was right. Dex hadn't given her heart to her completely because she was terrified of being hurt again. She'd created a wall to prevent her heart from being smashed to pieces like it had been when she'd given it to Grace so long ago. Any smart girl would've distanced herself from Grace right then.

She took her phone out of her pocket and stared at the voice mail she'd received from Grace during the middle of her conversation with Emma. Her fucking timing was ridiculous. She still hadn't listened to it and slid it onto the side table. She was going to have to deal with her, but she couldn't do it right now.

The front door flew open and Panda scattered. "Dex, are you home?" Juni asked as she hustled inside. "I brought pizza."

"I'm here," she said softly from her place on the couch.

"Why is it so dark in here?" Juni flipped on the lights, and Dex blinked to adjust to the brightness. "Have you just been sitting there since you called me?"

"Yeah." She hadn't known what else to do.

Juni dropped the pizza box on the kitchen counter, took her coat off, and hung it on the back of the kitchen chair before she came into the living room. "Fuck, Dex. You haven't even changed your clothes yet."

"Didn't feel like it. No reason to."

"Oh, honey. It can't be that bad. What happened?"

"Emma told me yesterday that she doesn't want to see me anymore."

"What? Just like that? She didn't give you a chance to talk?"

She shook her head.

Juni flopped on the couch next to her. "Then why don't you march right back over there and tell her how you feel?"

"Because I don't know how I feel. Maybe she's right."

"Jesus, Dex. Don't you think you should've thought about that before you made her fall in love with you?"

"Thanks, Captain Obvious. That makes me feel a whole lot better." She launched off the couch. "What kind of pizza did you bring?"

"Hold on a minute." Juni launched off the couch as well and followed her. "I need more details."

Dex took a couple of beers from the refrigerator, opened them, and handed one to Juni. She leaned against the counter and took a long pull before she told Juni what Emma had said to her, fighting to keep her emotions under control as she recited the events. When she lost the battle, Juni rounded the counter and took her in her arms.

"I've never encouraged Grace's neediness. Have I?"

"You haven't encouraged it, but you haven't rejected it either."

She swiped at her tears. "Explain."

Juni backed out of Dex's personal space and propped herself against the adjacent counter. "Here's the thing, Dex. If I were Emma and you were a guy, I would've left you in the dust a long time ago." Juni had her attention now. "You can't be in love with Emma and still jump every time Grace calls."

"I don't do that."

"Yes, you do. Enough so that it came between you and Emma." Juni paced across the room. "Grace has you so fucked up, you may be permanently damaged. Too damaged for any other woman. I have to give Emma credit. She tried."

"That fucking blunt gene you have that comes along with the sister gene sucks."

"I know it does. But you need it right now. Everyone at Grace's wedding saw how devastated you were, including Emma. Yet she took care of you, left you sweet little notes in the morning. Remember?"

Dex closed her eyes. "I do."

"Has Grace *ever* done anything like that for you?"

"Not like that, but she's always been there when I needed her."

"You have to know by now that she's never going to be that person for you." Juni poked a finger into Dex's chest. "That person is Emma. You know you've made a big fucking mistake by letting Grace interfere. I can see it in your eyes right now."

She lifted her shoulders and let them drop. "So what do I do?"

"You wait a few days. Emma's going to miss you." She ripped a few paper towels from the rack and snagged a slice of pizza from the box. "In the meantime, you have to tell Grace that Emma comes first. Set the boundaries, Dex, or she won't ever stop." She held the slice in front of Dex, and she waved her off. "You work out in the cold all day. You have to eat." She took Dex's hand and put the slice in her palm.

She blew out a breath and took another pull on her beer. "That'll be a challenge."

Juni chuckled. "At best. But you can't beg forgiveness from Emma until you've taken care of the problem." She grabbed another slice of pizza from the box and settled into a stool at the counter.

"And Grace is the problem."

Juni shook her head. "Not just her. You're in this one up to your eyeballs."

"I'll call Grace tomorrow and take care of it." Dex took a bite of the pizza and her stomach rolled. She tossed it back into the box.

Grace rushed through the front door at Dex's house. "Sorry I'm late. I didn't get your message right away, couldn't find my phone." She held it up before she dropped it into her purse, which she set on the end table. "Damn thing slid between the cushions on the couch."

Thinking maybe there was something to what Emma and Juni had said, Dex had called Grace. She needed to prove to herself that nothing was there, that she'd let go of her feelings for Grace. She also needed to set boundaries.

"I thought you were seeing Emma tonight."

"I thought I was too. She wants to take a break."

"Oh? Why?" Grace's voice rose. She was putting on a very good show.

"It just feels like we're going too fast, that's all." She didn't want to go into the whole reason with Grace because Grace *was* the reason.

"Sounds like she's having commitment issues."

She flopped onto the couch and put her feet on the coffee table. "Maybe." *One of us certainly is.*

Grace pushed Dex's feet from the coffee table and sat next to her. "You know I hate that."

"Sorry. I forgot." It wasn't like it was her house.

"You're going to miss her, aren't you?" Grace's voice was soft and comforting as she sat on the couch next to Dex and rubbed her back.

"Actually, I am." It had only been a few days, and she'd already wanted to call her a hundred times. "You don't have to make it sound so permanent."

"Sorry. I wasn't trying to. You've just been spending so much time with her." She took her hand away. "Sometimes things can get overwhelming. Maybe a break is the best thing." She dropped against the couch cushions. "I could certainly use one from Brent right now."

"What?" Dex snapped her head around. "You've only been married for, what, three months?"

"Almost four, and it's not like we weren't together before the wedding. Now that he's moved in with me, he's turned out to be a totally different person." She sighed. "He's kind of a slob, and since I only work part-time, he expects me to do everything around the house. And he's totally obsessed with money all of a sudden. Save, save, save, that's all he talks about. I like having the things I have and buying things when I want."

It appeared the conversation was going to be about Grace again, as usual. "This isn't new. You told me this before. Have you talked to him about it?"

"I tried, but somehow he always makes me forget what I'm trying to say."

"You mean, you have sex, and then everything's great."

She nodded. "I don't know why that happens. It's not like *that's* perfect. I don't even think about him when I masturbate."

"Wow." That was a whole lot of too much information.

She shifted toward Dex. "Is that weird?"

Dex shifted in her seat. "Kinda."

"What do *you* think about?" Grace asked the question with such nonchalance, Dex was caught off guard.

"Um, I think about getting off." Until recently, she used to think about Grace, but she'd pushed those thoughts out of her mind the moment she'd started seeing Emma. *Emma.* She took in a deep breath, and that thought rang in her head.

"You don't think about Emma?"

The lump in her throat that had just begun to subside returned. *I think about Emma all the time.* "No. I don't think about her or anyone else." Not anymore. That would only make it take longer. "What do you think about?" It was a bad idea to ask, but Grace was going to tell her anyway. Because Grace shared everything with Dex.

"Sometimes Brent. Sometimes the guy who works out across

from me at the gym. Sometimes you." Her voice rose at the end of her sentence like it was a delightful afterthought.

What the fuck? "Me? Seriously?" She'd never shared that nugget with Dex before.

Grace looked at her hands before she glanced up at Dex. "Sure. Haven't you ever thought about it? With me?"

She was way too close for this conversation. "Uh...not lately." Dex slid farther into the couch. "You're married now."

"But you have thought about it, right?" Grace stared at Dex, clearly waiting for an answer.

"What the hell is going on with you, Grace?" She twisted sideways and pulled her leg onto the couch between them. "Aren't you happy with Brent?"

Grace dropped her head against the couch and stared at the ceiling. "I am happy for the most part. But I miss hanging out with you."

"So you want to sleep with me and fuck up your life?"

"*No.*" Grace shook her head. "I didn't say that, but I really have thought about you." She sighed. "If it were only possible to have your personality in Brent's body."

Dex threw a hand up in front of her. "Stop. *Now.*" She bolted from the couch and crossed the room. "There will be no more of this kind of talk." She went into the kitchen, took a beer out of the refrigerator, eyed it, put it back, and grabbed a soda. No alcohol tonight, not after that bombshell conversation. This was not at all the way she'd seen this night going. It was supposed to be the exact opposite. She busied herself in the kitchen making a salad and trying to settle her thoughts back to normal. The doorbell rang, and she thanked God that he'd created pizza-delivery guys. When the evening had started, Dex hadn't expected anything like this, not in a long shot.

When Grace got home, Brent was on the couch, filthy feet on the coffee table, watching the game. Forget the fact that she'd asked him a gazillion times not to do it. She ignored him and went upstairs. Other thoughts were circling in her head at the moment that she had to deal with.

She undressed, put on her nightshirt, and crawled into bed. Maybe Emma was right. Maybe she was fucked up. She had definitely stepped over the line tonight by purposely making Dex think she'd fantasized of her in ways other than friendship, that there might be something more between them, but there couldn't be. The shock on Dex's face was unmistakable. Her stomach churned. The whole conversation had undermined her relationship with Brent and her friendship with Dex. She blew out a breath. She didn't understand her own actions and apparently couldn't control them either.

Emma. The name rang in her head. Why did Grace dislike her so much? She was, in fact, a great match for Dex. But Grace just couldn't buy into the whole relationship between the two of them. She remembered the first time she'd seen Dex gazing at Emma the way she used to gaze at her. It had hurt more than she'd thought it possibly could. It was at the Christmas market. Brent was off doing his own thing as usual, and when she'd turned to talk to Dex, she'd spotted the electricity between them. Grace had suddenly felt like an outsider, which sent an inexplicable bolt of anger through her.

She'd thought Emma was gone for good after the ice-skating incident, but when she and Dex had both shown up at Emilio's Christmas party, Emma had taken center stage again. At the time Grace hadn't wanted to analyze why. She'd just known she needed Dex's attention. So she'd immediately captured it from Emma by leaning in and whispering in Dex's ear, showing some cleavage as she always did. She'd gotten the response she'd wanted. Dex had closed her eyes momentarily and taken in a breath. But then Dex had focused her attention on Emma, not Grace. From that point on Emma had become the enemy, and Grace couldn't stop the wrath she'd rained upon her.

She'd been so nervous tonight with Dex, and with good reason. Even though she'd known her practically since the beginning of time, she'd never led her to believe they were anything but friends before now. Tonight she had done just that. It was selfish, but she'd pushed Dex to tell her if she'd ever thought about her sexually, an intimate question to which she already knew the answer. Normal conversation had ceased at that point, and the whole evening became a gigantic pile of awkward.

Grace was going to have to apologize for being such an ass and make it right, or things between them would never be the same again. Dex knew how insecure Grace was, didn't she? She'd understand why she'd acted the way she had. Wouldn't she? "Fuck," she whispered. She'd made a huge mess of everything.

Chapter Twenty-Six

To keep her mind off Dex, Emma had been throwing herself into her work for the past few days. It seemed to help for a while, but then her mind would get tired and wander back to Dex. She'd been drinking excessive amounts of coffee to keep going, because sleeping only brought reality full force into her dreams. She gazed out the window at downtown Chicago. It was a beautiful city when the sky was clear. And it was even more gorgeous during the holiday season with all the hues of reds, blues, and greens streaming from designs on the tall buildings.

Lights immediately brought her thoughts to Dex again and all the feelings for her she couldn't suppress. Emma had never been able to master the art of compartmentalizing her emotions. Trying to figure out how to make her heart stop aching for the second time in her life was going to be a challenge. The first had been with Amy, her last substantial relationship. It had taken Emma the better part of a year to get over her. Until recently, she'd still avoided certain restaurants and parts of town because she didn't want to chance running into her. Now there would be new places she wouldn't frequent in the future because of Dex.

A light knock on the door brought her out of her thoughts. "Hey, what's going on with you?" She heard Brent's voice and spun around in her chair. By that time, he'd already crossed the room and taken a seat in the chair in front of her desk.

She flipped her glasses from her head to her nose and straightened a few documents before setting them in a neat pile to the right of the phone on her desk. "Nothing. I'm good." Brent had been her sounding board since they'd started working together. He wasn't always right, but he'd given her some sage advice in the past when she'd had relationship issues. She didn't know how he'd react to this particular problem.

"Come on. I can tell something's wrong. You haven't come out of your office in three days, except to get coffee."

She blew out a breath and rolled her lips in. "I know I'm really fucking bad at love, but I thought this time was different."

He pushed forward in the chair. "What? I thought things were good with Dex." Apparently Grace hadn't relayed the news yet.

She plucked off her glasses and dropped them onto the desk. "No. Not at all. I can't believe I did this again. When I saw her at your wedding, I should've known better. What's wrong with me?" She dropped her head to her desk. "Fuck me."

"What are you talking about? Don't go all crazy on me."

She shook her head. "How do I always pick the wrong girls?"

"I picked Dex."

"Grace didn't have anything to do with it?" she asked.

"No. She didn't want to put the two of you together. But I could tell that you and Dex would be perfect for each other."

The whole situation made sense now. She bolted out of her chair and paced the office. "This is *your* fault." She stopped and pointed at Brent. "You knew what happened with Amy, and you still set me up with Dex."

"What the fuck, Em? Amy was in love with her best friend."

"So is Dex." She was so riled up, the words were out of her mouth before she could stop them.

Brent pulled his brows together. "But Grace is her best friend, *and* she's straight." The poor guy honestly seemed confused. He had no idea.

"You are *so fucking* blind. They're *always* together." She continued to pace. "Grace is like a drug that Dex can't purge from her system."

"I know they spend a lot of time together and they talk all the time, but…" He hesitated, seeming to be lost in thought, and then he appeared to absorb what she was saying. "You don't think they're…"

Emma rubbed her forehead. "I don't know. Anything's possible." She shrugged. "All I know is that Grace is in the middle of my relationship with Dex." She went behind her desk and dropped into her chair. "Grace keeps Dex on a leash. Whenever she gets a little distance,

Grace injects her with her pathetic neediness, hits the recoil button, and snaps her back."

Brent launched out of the chair. "I take exception to that. She's not needy at all with me."

"*Because* she has Dex to take care of everything for her!" The sentence came out louder than Emma had intended, but Brent really needed to answer this wake-up call.

Brent raked a hand across the back of his neck. "Do you really think something's going on between them?"

"I hope not, but I honestly don't know."

Brent left her office in a rush, and Emma knew where he was going. She shouldn't have said the things she had to him. But Emma genuinely didn't know why Grace had such control over Dex, why she needed to have such an influence in Dex's life, which Emma was now a part of whether she wanted to be or not. All she knew was that she couldn't be happy the way things were, and she still had a glimmer of hope that Brent could fix it from his end.

Dex retrieved the lights from the shelf in Grace's garage where she'd placed them after she'd taken them down last year. She wasn't looking forward to going back out into the frigidly cold temperature. Her feet had just begun to thaw from trudging through the snow on the previous job she'd completed. This was her last house of the day, and she would be inside eating a nice warm dinner soon. Grace's usual payment. She wiped the sweat from her forehead, a remnant of the sauna she'd created in her SUV on the way over, she thought. She shook off the chill that ran down her spine and plodded to the front yard. She was definitely clammy. It wasn't a huge job, but she needed to get moving. The sun would be down soon, and once it was gone the temperature would plummet.

She and Grace had engaged in minimal conversation when she'd arrived. Grace had actually seemed surprised to see her. But she'd already had Grace on her schedule for today and wasn't about to cancel, especially after what had happened last week.

Grace had sent her a text apologizing for the whole weirded-out conversation, said she'd been having issues with Brent. But Dex still wasn't happy with the way they'd left things. She hadn't actually had a chance to talk to her about Emma. Considering last week and after mulling it over the past few days, Dex was unsure as to whether she should discuss any of her private feelings for Emma with Grace.

All the lights were laid out in the snow below each area where Dex planned to hang them. She'd just taken the ladder off the SUV and propped it against the house at her starting point when Grace hurried out the front door carrying a travel mug. She raised the mug and stood at the end of the walkway, waiting for Dex to come to her. She'd managed to put on her jacket, but her feet were covered only in fluffy pink slippers. Dex did as expected and slogged through the snow to see her.

"It's hot chocolate." She handed it to her. "I thought you might need something warm." She smiled like everything was normal between them. Maybe it was, in *her* mind. "You're staying for dinner, right? I have a chicken in the oven roasting. I'm getting pretty good at this cooking thing."

"I'm not sure. It's been a long day, and I'm not feeling so hot."

"All the more reason why you should stay."

"I'll see. When I'm done here, I may just go home and crash." Dex coughed.

"Then I'll fix you a plate to go."

"Sure. That'd be nice." She glanced at Grace's feet. "Now get back inside before your feet freeze."

Dex had turned to go back to the ladder when she heard Grace call her name. She turned around to catch a solemn smile on Grace's face. "You're the best," she said before disappearing into the house.

Business as usual.

Grace had already put the chicken in the oven to roast, and the potatoes were cooking on the stove. She really wasn't all that bad at this domestic stuff. When she heard the door open, she rushed into the living room to see Brent and tell him all about it, but he didn't give her the chance.

"What the hell is Dex doing out there putting up our lights?" He took off his wool coat. "I told you I'd do it this weekend." His voice was firm.

Grace's heart pounded, and she came to a complete stop. "She offered, so I thought it would help you out."

"It's twenty degrees outside." He slid his coat on a hanger and slammed the closet door. "Fucking freezing."

"It doesn't look that cold. The sun's shining."

"You take way too much advantage of her."

"She just showed up like she does every year." She didn't want to tell him about their last awkward conversation.

"She just showed up?"

"Yeah. She comes by all the time and helps me out with things around the house."

"Things you should be asking me to do?" He headed into the hallway toward the bedroom.

"I like spending time with her."

He stopped and turned around. "If I didn't know better, I'd think you were in love with her, not me."

Grace was stunned. Why would he even think that? Had Dex said something to Emma?

"Are you?" He tilted his head. "In love? With Dex?" He said the words individually, making them sound all the worse.

Grace hesitated, not knowing quite how to explain what she had with Dex. It was definitely love, but a different kind of love than she had for Brent.

"Oh, shit. You are?"

"No. I'm not in love with her." She shook her head. "Well, maybe I am in a way." The expression on Brent's face told her she had to clarify what she'd just said. "I'm in love with you. I want to spend the rest of my life as your wife. The love I feel for Dex is different, but it's just as strong." She dropped down onto the couch. "I mean, I don't want to sleep with her or anything like that, but she's been in my life since we were kids. We have a connection that I just can't break. I don't want to."

"You need to start making some choices, Grace."

"Why do I have to make a choice?"

"Emma told me what you've been doing to Dex."

"Emma needs to mind her own business."

"It is her business. She's in love with Dex."

"She couldn't possibly be in love with her. They haven't known each other long enough." She spun around. "Besides, Dex isn't in love with her."

"How do you know that? Have you even asked her?"

"No, but she would tell me if she was."

"You're so self-absorbed you can't even see it."

"I am *not* self-absorbed."

"Yes, you are. Always have been." He went into the bedroom and pulled some clothes from the dresser. "Look at the poor girl out there hanging lights for you when she's sick. And she's doing it for free."

"You said I had to cut back on spending."

"I also said I'd do the lights."

"Christmas is only twelve days away, and you haven't done them yet."

"I was waiting for a warmer day." He took off his suit and tugged on his jeans and a long-sleeved, waffled Henley shirt.

"What are you doing?"

"I'm going out to help her."

"Then you might get sick."

He stopped and stared at her. "The exact thought you should've had when Dex showed up here today." He pulled a Chicago Bulls hoodie over his head. "Emma is my friend, and Dex is yours. You're messing with all our lives, and if you keep it up, it's not going to turn out well." He rushed down the hallway, yanked open the closet door, and plucked a beanie from the top shelf.

"You're like a pimple on her ass, Grace. Leave her alone." He went out the door and pulled it closed behind him.

CHAPTER TWENTY-SEVEN

The constant buzzing of the phone brought Dex out of her cold-medicine-induced sleep. She checked the screen—four missed calls from Grace. She'd called John, her crew supervisor, last night and told him she'd be out today and then put her phone on silent when she'd gone to bed. The congestion in her sinuses was so thick, her head felt like it was about to explode. She plugged in her unlock code and hit the button for Grace, who answered immediately.

"Hey," she said, her voice gravelly.

"Thank God you finally called me back. You had me so worried. I was just getting ready to come over there." Grace rattled the sentences off so quickly, Dex's head hurt worse than it already did.

"I'm fine, just trying to get some rest. I've got a head cold."

"I'm so sorry about yesterday. I didn't realize you were sick. You shouldn't have been out in the weather like that putting up lights."

"It's okay. We got them done." Dex coughed.

"Are you okay? Can I bring you something?"

"No. I'm just going to take a day and sleep. I have to whip this fast. My schedule this year is full, and I can't afford to miss another day."

"Can't your crew handle it without you?"

"They probably can, but I need to be there. The customers made the contract with me. Plus, it gets done a lot faster with more hands." She coughed again. "I'm going back to sleep. Talk to you later."

When Dex woke up later that afternoon, Grace was sitting on the side of the bed watching her.

"I brought you a cup of tea."

Dex glanced at the nightstand to see a whole pharmacy of drugs.

"And some ibuprofen, decongestant, and cough medicine." Grace picked up each bottle and set it down again as she named them. "I didn't know what you had."

"Thanks, Mom." Dex let out a laugh that quickly morphed into a cough. She launched out of bed and went into the bathroom.

Grace followed her to the door. "Are you okay?"

"I've been better, but I have to pee." She blew her nose before she came out of the bathroom, which didn't help the ringing in her ears one bit. When she got back to the bed, Grace had doses of all the medications ready for her. She really was acting like her mom.

"Here." Grace handed them to her one at a time with a glass of water to chase them down. "Now drink some tea, and then you can lie back down."

She took a few sips of tea and handed it back to Grace before crawling into the bed fully clothed in her sweatpants and hoodie. Grace handed her the remote to the TV and put a fresh box of tissues on the bed next to her.

"Get some rest. I'll be back to check on you in a little while." She patted her on the leg and then went to the door.

"Hey, Grace."

Grace stuck her head back through the doorway. "What do you need, honey?"

"There are some lights by the couch. They're for my neighbor. He's supposed to come by and get them later."

"Got it." She crossed the room and pulled the blanket up around Dex. "Just text me if you need something."

"Thanks." She hadn't expected Grace to show up and take care of her, but it was nice that she had.

The door to Brent's office had been closed all morning. Emma hadn't seen him in the break room or in the hallway at all. It was clear he was avoiding her. He was one of her best friends, and she had to fix this wall she'd created between them. She hadn't meant to make him think Grace was unfaithful. Well, maybe she had, but blaming him for her own mistake was way out of line.

She knocked lightly on the door before she heard him say, "Come in."

"Can we talk for a minute?" She pushed the door open slowly, trying to gauge his mood before entering.

"Sure. Have a seat." He glanced up briefly before he flipped his hand to one of the chairs in front of his desk.

Extreme politeness, not the best greeting. Emma crossed the room and sat on the edge of the seat. "Listen. I'm sorry I said all that stuff about Grace and Dex yesterday."

He dropped his pen onto the desk and laced his hands in front of him. "You're right. She leads Dex around like a puppy dog."

"But she loves you."

"Sometimes I wonder if I'm enough without the money."

"You really suck at reading women."

Brent's eyebrows rose. The comment seemed to have shocked him. "It's not like there's a manual or anything."

She threw her hands out in front of herself. "You have me."

"Well, then tell me, oh master of women."

She squinted and gave him a cheeky grin. "Ha ha. Very funny."

"I'm serious. Tell me."

She shook her head. "She doesn't care about your money. She's uber-rich on her own. If she cared about that, she sure as hell wouldn't have married you. She would've found some other trust-fund yuppie to punish."

He leaned in closer. "I'm listening."

"She cares about how you treat her. Open the door for her, pull out her chair, and protect her from the bad shit—even if it's her parents. But do it gently. Forget about the money. She can buy whatever she wants. Your wife is beautiful. If you don't pay attention to her, soon enough, someone else will come along who will."

"I'm trying, but I have no idea how her mind works. What she did to you and Dex is fucked up."

He was right about that. If Grace hadn't come between them, she'd be happy and in love with her right now. She pushed the thought from her mind. Then she cleared her throat and blinked to hold back the tears brimming in her eyes. "How is Dex?"

"She's sick."

Emma leaned forward in the chair. "Oh." Her first thought was to go to her, take care of her, and tell her she'd always be there for her. But she couldn't do that until Dex made up her mind.

"Yeah. I came home last night, and she was putting up the lights at my house."

"By herself?"

"Yeah. I went out and helped her finish. She couldn't stop coughing."

"Does she have the flu?"

"She said it's just a head cold."

Emma got up, walked to the window, and stared out at the falling snowflakes. "I hope she's not working today. It's miserable out there."

"Knowing Dex, she probably is. You know what she always says, 'The lights have to be strung.' She's got a helluva work ethic." Brent stood at the window next to her. "It does seem pretty bad out there. Maybe you should go see her."

"Maybe." She continued to watch the snow blow across the sky. "Anyway, I just wanted to say I'm sorry."

"It's cool, Em." He bumped her shoulder with his, and she knew things between them were good.

"Well. I'm going to head home. I don't want to get stuck here all night." It wasn't like she had anything better to do.

"Okay. Be safe. Call me if you get stuck."

"Will do." She smiled as she left Brent's office. Outside of her family, he was the most dependable person she knew and also a really good friend.

The forecast this morning had said the snow should stop in a few hours, but you never knew how accurate that was. They'd given only a 20 percent chance of precipitation today, and it was currently falling thick. Emma went into her office and gathered a couple of files she could work on at home if the snow got too heavy. She'd stop at the store on her way home to pick up provisions just in case. A big pot of soup sounded really good.

Emma pulled up in front of Dex's house and sat for a moment watching the snow flurries. She was thankful it had slowed some since she'd left. Driving in these conditions was stressful and exhausting.

Dex's SUV was in the driveway, which meant she was probably sicker than she'd let on. She rarely took a day off.

The flurries waned as the knot in her stomach grew. Emma wasn't sure if she was ready to see Dex again. It had sounded like a good idea when she was at the store. She'd gone home and made soup with chicken-bone broth and vegetables. She'd also made a small pan of cayenne brownies and tucked a note in with them in case Dex didn't feel like eating them right away.

Now that she was here, her insecurities were taking hold like Gorilla Glue. She drew in a deep breath and blew it out. From what Brent had told her earlier, Dex probably needed some comfort food. So Emma just needed to get over herself and get out of the car. Bringing Dex something warm to eat and checking on her was the right thing to do, even if they weren't seeing each other anymore.

She gathered the bag containing the soup and brownies from the front seat, maneuvered through the freshly fallen snow, and knocked on the door lightly. She didn't want to wake her if she was asleep, although she hadn't thought about what she'd do with the food if Dex didn't answer. She was caught off guard when the door swung open and Grace was standing in the entryway.

Grace put her hand on her hip in her usual irritated fashion. "What are you doing here?"

"I could ask you the same thing."

"Dex is sick, and I'm taking care of her."

"Don't you have a husband at home to take care of?"

"I take plenty good care of my husband. Not that it's any of your business."

Emma shook her head. "Listen, Grace. I didn't come here to spar with you. I brought some soup for Dex." She peered around Grace. "Is she up and about?"

"No. She's upstairs sleeping. I'll take it." Grace reached out and took the soup from Emma's hands before she could protest. "It's not vegetable, is it? I'm not a fan of that."

"It's chicken vegetable, and the soup is for Dex, not you. Has she been to see the doctor? Are you making sure she has lots of fluids?"

"You don't worry about Dex. I can take care of her." She started to close the door, but Emma put her hand up and stopped it.

"You know, you may be able to take care of her, and you may also be her best friend, but you'll never be her soul mate, Grace. You lost that opportunity when you married Brent."

"Nothing has changed between Dex and me just because I got married."

"Maybe not for you, but it has for Dex. Don't you think she deserves a chance at happiness? Or do you want her to be alone the rest of her life?"

"Well, *you* certainly didn't make her happy. If you had, you'd be on this side of the door right now." She nudged the door closed with her shoulder and left Emma standing on the porch in the snow.

Emma wanted to charge right through the door and demand to see Dex. She closed her eyes and took in a breath. No. She wouldn't do that. She had no right. She was the one who'd broken off the relationship. It was a mistake to have come. If she wanted Dex to figure out what she wanted, she needed to leave her alone. Emma just wished Grace would do the same.

CHAPTER TWENTY-EIGHT

Grace couldn't believe that woman had the nerve to show her face here after the crap she said to Brent, making him think something was going on between her and Dex and pushing Dex to think there could be something more. She hadn't expected anything more from Dex than she always had, and if that was an issue for Emma, too bad. Dex needed a girlfriend who supported her, and that included supporting her friendship with Grace.

After rummaging through the pantry, she found some crackers and bottled water and put them in a shopping bag. She took a tray from the living room before she dipped out a bowl of the chicken soup Emma had made and a cup of only broth for herself. She added a placemat to the tray and set the soup on top before she reached into the silverware drawer for a spoon.

When she got upstairs, she was surprised to see Dex sitting up in bed flipping through the TV channels. She must be feeling better.

"Who was at the door?" Dex asked when she came into the room.

"Your neighbor, picking up the lights." She sure wasn't going to tell her it was Emma. That would only make Dex feel worse.

"Oh, good." Dex pulled the blanket up around her waist and flattened it.

"I brought you some soup." Grace slid the tray across Dex's lap.

"Homemade? This looks awesome."

Grace nodded. "I thought it might make you feel better."

The spoon was in the soup before Grace crossed the room to the door. "This is delicious. Thanks, Grace."

"You're welcome." Grace was more than happy to take credit for the soup.

Dex stared at the soup and scrunched her brows together.

"What's wrong?" Emma had better not have put anything weird in the soup.

The vegetables splashed back into the bowl as Dex held up her spoon and tilted it. "Since when do you like vegetable soup?"

"I don't. But I know you do, and the soup is for you."

Dex smiled. "Now it tastes even better." She took another bite.

While they ate their soup, they watched some comedy show that Grace had no clue about. Dex laughed a few times, which threw her into a coughing fit each time. Once Dex was finished, Grace took the empty bowls downstairs and put the leftover soup in the refrigerator. She hadn't checked the bag for anything else until just now. It contained a small batch of brownies with a note. Grace read it and grimaced at the smiley face that punctuated the sentence. She crumpled it up and tossed it back in the bag. *Ridiculous.* These were going home with her. Panda hopped up onto the stool and stared at her.

"I guess you want to be fed too." She found the bag of cat food in the pantry and poured some into the bowl on the floor. "I suppose you need water too." She picked up the bowl, filled it, and set it next to the other bowl. "Hey, get out of there." She swiped the bag of brownies from near Panda's head, then picked her up and dropped her to the floor. Then she rolled up the top of the bag and stuffed it into her purse.

When Grace went back upstairs, Dex was covered up to her neck with the blanket.

"Can you turn up the heat?" Her voice wavered as she shivered. "I'm really cold."

"On it." Grace went into the hall and checked the thermostat, which was set to seventy-two, plenty warm. Dex probably had a fever. She took another blanket from the hall cabinet and spread it across the bed before she crawled in under the blankets next to Dex and wrapped herself around her. "I've got you." Dex closed her eyes and was immediately asleep again.

Grace's body shook along with Dex's as the chills vibrated through her. She held her tight, warming her with her own body heat. She had to get this fever to break.

Dex thrashed back and forth in bed, calling out Emma's name

numerous times during the night. Sometime during that time, Dex's fever had broken. Suddenly her clothes had been drenched, and Grace had helped her change. After that, Dex turned onto her side and slept calmly for the rest of the night. Grace had mixed feelings about the fact it wasn't her name Dex had called out instead of Emma's. After all, she was the one here taking care of her.

Grace had gotten up and left early. She'd said she needed to get to the grocery store. Brent had invited friends over to watch the game again, and they needed snacks, which was fine with Dex. She wasn't up to having the conversation she needed to with her this morning. It was sweet of Grace to make the chicken soup, and she didn't know if she would've made it through the night without her. But when Dex had woken this morning with Grace wrapped around her, the proximity had been too intimate. She'd actually thought it was Emma until she'd turned over. Wishful thinking. She'd known it was a long shot, but she'd hoped that Emma would've at least sent her a text to check on her. That was a silly thought, though. Emma probably had no idea she was even sick.

When she entered the kitchen, Panda was flipping something around on the floor, and it wasn't one of her toys. The cat had a habit of stealing things from the counter, the dresser, or wherever she perched. Dex tried to get it, but the little bugger was going to fight her for it. She finally wrestled it away and flattened the crumpled piece of note paper on the counter.

They're probably not as good as yours, but I tried.

It was from Emma. The pink paper with the faded rose border, the handwriting, the sweet smiley face punctuating the sentence was all her. *What the fuck?* What wasn't as good as mine?

Panda yelled at her with a ferocious meow. "Okay, I'm working on it," she said as she folded up the note and slipped it into her pocket. She filled the cat's dish, freshened her water, and rubbed the top of her head.

Dex was headed out the door when she spotted the stack of

Christmas lights she'd left for her neighbor next to the couch. Maybe Grace had given him the wrong ones. She glanced at another stack she had piled by the entryway.

She gathered them up, headed next door, and knocked on the door. The door swung open almost immediately. "Hey, Chevy. How's it going?" he asked.

Her neighbor had a thing for cars, and when he didn't know someone's name or couldn't remember, he called them by the make or model of their car. Dex had stopped telling him her name a long time ago.

"Good." She held the boxes out in front of her. "I think my friend may have given you the wrong lights last night when you came by."

He seemed confused. "Um, no. I hadn't made it over there yet." He took them from her.

"Oh. I must've misunderstood."

"Maybe it was the hot girl who came to see you. The Ford, not the Beemer."

Ford? Had Emma come by and Grace hadn't told her? "Oh. Well, you have them now. You need any help putting them up?"

"Nope. I got it. Dodge, the new guy across the street is gonna help me after the game." He set the boxes just inside the door. "Thanks for picking them up for me. It saved me a whole lot of money."

"Sure, no problem. Merry Christmas," she said as she turned to go.

"Merry Christmas to you too, Chevy."

She sprinted back to her house, climbed into her SUV, and headed to Grace's house. If Emma had come by, Grace should've told her no matter how sick she was.

The door into the house from the garage was open when Dex got there, so she stopped in the doorway when she heard Grace and Brent arguing. Their voices were muffled at first, but then Brent raised his voice, and she clearly heard him say, "Emma told me she went to see Dex, and you told her she didn't want to see her and sent her away."

"Dex wouldn't have wanted Emma to see her like that. Besides, I was already there and Dex was sleeping. I didn't want Emma to catch whatever Dex has."

"Did you ask her? Did you even tell her she came by?"

Dex stepped through the doorway. "No. She didn't. I had no idea."

Grace spun around and smiled. "Dex, you look so much better. Don't tell me you're going to work today." She dropped the bag of groceries onto the counter and moved toward her. "Your fever hasn't come back, has it?" She tried to touch her forehead, and Dex batted her hand away.

"Why didn't you tell me Emma was there?"

"I told you. Your fever was high. You just don't remember. I was going to remind you today. It just slipped my mind."

Dex reached into her pocket, took out the note, and handed it to Grace. "Did she make the soup?"

Grace closed her eyes and let out a heavy breath. "Yes."

"Yet you told me you'd made it."

"No, I didn't. You assumed."

"Well, *that* makes a huge difference. I can't trust you at all, can I?"

"Of course you can. I just left a few details out about yesterday. I didn't lie to you."

"I don't believe you."

"Why wouldn't you believe me?"

"Over the past two months, you've done everything in your power to come between me and Emma."

"That's not fair, Dex. If Emma had really wanted to stay last night, she would have."

"Seriously?" She glanced at Brent, whose face was blank. "Even Brent thinks it's weird that you didn't tell me." She turned and went out the door.

"Dex, wait!" Grace raced out after her. "I just—"

She spun around, and Grace ran into her. "You just what, Grace?" Dex hauled her into her arms. "Is this what you want from me? To know that I imagine it's *me* holding your hand, kissing you senseless, and making you squirm until you come every night?" They were so close, Dex could feel Grace's rapid breath on her lips. "Do you imagine that with me?"

She took her face in her hands and pressed her lips to Grace's, expecting the fireworks she'd imagined for all those years to explode inside her. But there were none. The face that flashed in her mind at that moment wasn't Grace's. It was Emma's. *I'm in love with Emma.* She closed her eyes as the warmth rushed over her. Yes, she was absolutely, wholly in love with Emma. "Oh my God. I've made a horrible mistake."

Grace stood there looking dazed before she backed up and rolled her lips in. "I'm so sorry, Dex. I know I messed up. I don't know what I was thinking." She raked her hand through her hair. "Strike that, I do know. I was jealous. I should've been happy you've found someone who can love you in the ways I can't. I *am* honestly happy for you, but sad because I want to be part of your happiness and I'm not."

"I have to go." Dex spun around to leave.

Grace caught her by the arm, and Dex swung back to her. "Let me fix this. I really do want you to be happy."

"No. You stay away from Emma. You'll fuck it up. You can't help yourself. Go back inside to your husband." She jerked out of her grasp.

"But—"

"I mean it, Grace. Stop fucking with me and *let* me be happy." Emma had been right about Grace all along. She hoped she hadn't blown any chance she'd had at being with her. She had to find a way back into her heart.

Grace could feel Brent standing right behind her now. "What the fuck was that?" His voice echoed in the garage.

"It was nothing." That was a lie. It was a huge something, just not what Brent thought it was.

"She just fucking kissed you."

Her stomach churned. "It meant nothing, Brent. I swear. She just needed to know." Grace needed to know too.

"To know what?"

"That she loves Emma." *And she doesn't love me anymore.* Grace felt like the tiniest person on the smallest planet circling the earth right now. She'd made a mess of Dex's life for her own selfish reasons.

"She had to kiss you to figure that out?"

"God, Brent. Sometimes you are so dense." She hurried past him into the house. "Dex has been in love with me since we were in seventh grade."

He rushed inside after her. "Are you in love with her too?"

Grace tried to hold her tears, but they sprang out like a leaky soaker hose.

"Oh my God." Brent raked a hand across his neck. "If she's who you want, you need to tell me right now."

Grace's mind swam as she threw herself into him and pressed her face to his chest. *No, no, no. She is not at all who I want.* She sucked in a deep breath as the tears streamed down her face. "I don't want her. I want you."

He took her by the shoulders and created some distance between them. "Anyone looking at this picture would never get that."

"Brent, please. She's my best friend. That's all. I've never wanted anyone but you." She didn't know how to explain the conflicting emotions inside her head or her heart. That's all Dex had ever been to her, but they were connected in a way she was with no other.

"Then why are you trying to keep them apart? Emma told me you and she had words before she broke up with Dex."

"I don't know why." She shrugged. "I thought I was trying to make sure she didn't get hurt."

"But now they've both been hurt. You're fucking with people's lives here. Don't you want Dex to be happy?"

"Of course I do."

"Then fix this clusterfuck you've created and let them be happy."

"Okay, okay. I will." She sobbed. "What did Emma tell you?"

"She said you were a bitch, as usual."

"You think I'm a bitch?"

"You know I don't think you're a bitch."

"Do I? We've been disagreeing on so many things lately."

"Is that why you've been clinging to Dex?"

She nodded. "I needed some emotional support." She paced the floor. "I'm certainly not getting any from you. Ever since you moved in here, you started making rules without even discussing anything with me."

"What are you talking about, Grace?"

"The money. The food. Everything. I should have a say in this relationship too."

"You do."

"No. I don't. We used to talk. You actually used to listen to me, and you cared about what I had to say. You don't do that anymore. What happened? Did I do something to change that?"

Brent seemed stunned. "I wasn't trying to do that. I just want us to be smart about money. You know, for when we start a family."

"A family?" Grace hadn't thought that far ahead and wasn't sure she even wanted kids. With a series of nannies and parents that were rarely present in her life, her own childhood had been sketchy at best.

"Yeah. I know we haven't really talked about it, but I think you'll be a great mom."

"You do?"

"Yes." He hauled her into his arms. "You've been taking great care of me for the past couple of months."

She chuckled against his chest. "You are a big child, aren't you?"

He squeezed her tighter. "I'm sorry, Grace. I'll try to be a better husband."

Just those words made everything in Grace's life seem better. She'd been able to say what she needed to Brent, and he hadn't left. He was still right here holding her in his arms. Her future seemed clearer now.

❖

It was clear now that what Dex thought she'd wanted for most of her life wasn't what she really wanted at all. In just a matter of weeks, Emma had captured her heart, and she'd been too stupid to realize it until now. Until Grace had tried to blow it all to smithereens.

Her phone rang, and she jabbed at the button on the steering wheel to bring the call through the car stereo. "Emma?"

"No, it's me, John. I've been trying to get ahold of you all morning. Your voice mail's full."

"Sorry. What's up?"

"We need more lights at the Lancaster place. Can you bring some?"

"How many are you short?"

"About ten strings."

She glanced over her shoulder and took a rough count of what she had loaded in the back seat of her SUV. "I think I've got enough with me. I'll be there in about ten minutes." She pushed the End button on her steering wheel and then picked up her phone to check her messages. There was only one message she hadn't listened to. It was from Grace, and she'd left it a few days ago. Dex wasn't sure she wanted to hear it after what had just happened. But she needed to clear it and free up her mailbox in case customers tried to call. It couldn't have been that important, or Grace would've mentioned it. She'd been with her all day yesterday.

She touched the voice mail button on her phone, and it played automatically through the car speakers.

"You are really fucked up. Why don't I just go find Brent and tell him just how close the two of you are?"

When Emma's voice came through the speaker, Dex picked up the phone and checked the screen to confirm the call had been from Grace.

"No. I don't love her like that. We were involved once, but that was over a long time ago."

That was Grace. What the hell? *We were never involved, not* ever *in any kind of sexual way.* If they had been, she wouldn't be in the state she was in today.

"So you just flash those tail feathers of yours in front of her whenever you need to feel good about yourself."

Emma was pissed and going hot at her.

"She'll never love you like she loves me."

Grace's voice became faint, and Dex upped the volume.

"You need to either accept that or get out of her life." She heard a door slam and then Grace's voice again. *"Crazy bitch."*

She pulled to the side of the road and listened to it again. Grace had been the reason Emma had broken it off with her. She'd lied and made Emma think they'd been together and something was possibly still going on between them. She sat staring out the windshield letting the information sink in.

It didn't make sense. Grace was her best friend, and she'd never once led her to believe there could be more between them. Why would she tell Emma there was now? She'd had something real with Emma, and for some selfish reason, Grace had destroyed it. Just one more reason she had to distance herself from Grace whether she got Emma back or not.

Chapter Twenty-Nine

When Emma pushed the door open to Brent's office, she found him standing staring out the window. That was odd. He wasn't really the contemplative type. He looked deflated somehow, slumped, shoulders hunched, head hanging low. As she crossed the room, she glanced at the picture lying flat in the middle of his desk as though he'd been studying it.

She picked it up and examined the photo of him and Grace standing on the white, sandy beach in front of clear, blue water. It was from their honeymoon in Greece. Grace seemed to be the center of everyone's misery at the moment. Emma set it upright in the spot where it usually stood and strolled over to stand next to Brent at the window.

Brent broke the silence immediately. "I never get tired of looking at this city."

"It is beautiful." He was sad about something. He'd tell her if he wanted her to know.

"I'm sorry, Em. I've been a shitty husband."

She sliced him a sideways glance. "Aren't you talking to the wrong woman?"

He shifted one foot forward as though he were smashing a bug and then slipped his hands into his pants pockets. "If I'd been paying more attention to Grace, she wouldn't have been interfering in Dex's life so much." He spoke to the window as though he couldn't say it to her face.

"You mean clinging to Dex all the time?"

"Yeah. Well, Grace and I have started seeing a counselor." He dropped his shoulders and blew out a breath.

"Really? That's a big step for newlyweds." She turned to face him, and he veered his gaze to his shoes.

"We need it. Probably should've gone before we got married." He rubbed his forehead. "I've been lazy. I let Dex take care of things for Grace."

"Wow. You really see that now?" She said it gently, trying not to throw him an "I told you so" look.

He nodded. "We talked about me being a better husband and her being more independent."

"How?" It was an honest question. "I mean, how are you going to make Grace stop calling Dex when you're not around or not quick enough?" Emma needed to know if Grace was truly going to become less dependent on Dex or if she was just going to hide it from Brent.

"I'm going to work on listening more, and when Grace needs something, she's going to work on asking me first instead of calling Dex."

"That sounds like a good start. If you can make it happen." Not that it would help Emma. Grace had pretty much torpedoed everything she'd had with Dex.

"That won't be too hard." He raked a hand across the back of his neck. "Grace took credit for the soup you brought her, and Dex is pretty pissed at her right now."

With the way Grace had greeted her the other night, Emma pretty much knew that was going to happen. "Is Dex feeling better?"

"Yep. Seems to be all well now. If it makes you feel any better, Dex pretty much told her to fuck off."

She had to conceal the smirk on her face. "She actually said that?"

"Not in so many words, but Grace tried to call her a number of times, and she wouldn't answer. So she sent her a text and invited her over tonight for Christmas Eve dinner. She came back with a big fat no."

A wave of sadness rushed Emma, and her stomach churned. She sincerely hoped Dex wasn't spending Christmas Eve alone, or Christmas either, for that fact.

"She'll probably go to her sister's. Grace said that's where she usually goes for the holidays."

That made Emma feel a little better, but her heart was still heavy.

A few weeks ago she was the happiest she'd ever been and thought she'd be with Dex during the holidays. Now they would both be alone. Well, not totally alone. They'd have their families, but that just wasn't the same.

Brent swung around to his desk and took something from the drawer. "Here. I brought you this."

"What? We never exchange gifts."

"I know, but I feel like shit for fucking up your life."

She pulled the bow from the box and opened it. Inside she found a beautiful modern-art sculpture of entwined lovers. "Lovers? Really?"

"Grace feels really bad and thought maybe it might bring you luck. We brought it back from Greece."

She chuckled and shook her head. "Or just to pass on the curse."

"Or that," Brent said as he took his coat from the hook on the back of the door and put it on. "Merry Christmas, Em. I'll see you next week." He left her standing by the window staring at the statue.

"Yeah. Merry Christmas." She inched slowly to the desk, set the statue on the corner, and turned to leave. She spun around and picked it up again, then took it into her office and slipped it into her bag. Her love life couldn't get any worse at this point, so it couldn't hurt.

❖

Emma sat in her car in front of her parents' house. A new sign in the yard read "Holiday Christmas Light Contest Winner." The lights decorating the house were beautiful as they sparkled in perfect rhythm. It was Dex's work, something she'd done for Emma out of the goodness of her heart. She was sure her dad was thrilled. She checked her phone again. No response from the text she'd sent Dex earlier asking if she was okay.

Baking cookies was so not what she thought she'd be doing this Christmas Eve. It was her own fault. She'd canceled on her mother more than once to go out with Dex, which was clearly a wrong decision on her part. She took the statue that Brent had given her out of her bag and stared at it for a few minutes before she laid it on the back seat and covered it with a stray blanket she kept in the car. The lovers were going to be left out in the cold tonight.

She let out a sigh and got out of her car. She wasn't looking forward to putting on a happy face tonight, but at least there would be wine. The chilled air immediately shocked her. She pulled her scarf around her head and sprinted up the pathway. The front door blew wide open as she went into the house. She quickly pushed it shut and leaned up against the oak door for a few moments. Coming home usually made her feel better, but right now all she could think about was Dex and how happy she'd been at Thanksgiving. It wasn't about food or family. Her happiness had been because of Dex. The woman got her in every way, and she missed her more than she wanted to admit. She closed her eyes. *Stop whining. It was your choice.*

She pushed off the door, dropped her overnight bag in the entryway, and took off her coat. "I'm here. Where is everyone?" The Christmas music was playing as usual, but she'd expected to see most of the family in the living room watching TV and playing games.

"Your dad's in the garage, and your brothers aren't here."

"They're not here?" That was odd. The family was always here for a Christmas Eve dinner of spaghetti, meatballs, and garlic bread. It was Emma's favorite, which she loved more than she loved the turkey on Christmas Day. Then after dinner everyone would open that one package under the tree that had their Christmas pajamas in it. Couples always got matching ones, and the kids' patterns came as close to their parents' as possible, although superheroes might take precedence this year. Emma would be out of the couples category for two years running now.

"Yet. Did I forget to say that?" Glo said.

Emma continued into the kitchen, kissed her mother on the cheek, and saw the mounds of cookies covered in green and red plastic wrap on the counter. *What the hell?* "Is Judy here?"

"Nope."

"You did it all yourself?" Emma was a little annoyed that her mother hadn't called her and told her the cookies were already baked before she'd gotten there. She still had gifts in her bag to wrap and would've done it at home before she came over if she'd known the cookies were done. "And where's the spaghetti?"

Before Glo could answer, the door swung open, and her dad came in from the garage.

"Judy's at home with the kids. I had to call in alternative help today."

Emma raised an eyebrow. "Dad helped you?" She found a small opening in the plastic, snagged a cookie from underneath, and took a bite.

"That would be a miracle," she said with a laugh as Bill cleared the doorway.

She stopped mid-chew when she saw Dex right behind him standing in the threshold, dressed in jeans and a green V-neck sweater and looking as beautiful as ever.

"Hey," Dex said as she stepped into the kitchen and closed the door behind her.

Emma froze as the tingle washed through her. She went from excited to happy to scared all in a matter of seconds. "You helped my mother with Christmas cookies?"

"Yeah. We had a blast." Dex put her arm around Glo and squeezed. *What the hell?*

"Don't act so stunned." Glo slipped her apron over her head. "She's a great baker."

She set the remainder of her cookie on the counter and glanced at Dex. "I didn't know you were…" She turned to her mother. "I didn't know she was coming." She narrowed her eyes. "Did I miss a text or something?"

Glo patted her on the shoulder. "Nope. I didn't tell you because I was afraid you wouldn't come."

"That was a definite possibility." Emma flattened her lips.

"Well, since I'm here, hopefully you're not leaving." Dex raised her eyebrows and gave Emma that sweet, unassuming smile she adored. "I thought maybe we could talk."

"That's my cue." Glo tossed her apron into the laundry room. "Your father and I are going to Jeff and Judy's for dinner. We're eating and opening pajama gifts over there tonight so the kids can get to bed early." She stood between the two of them and took Emma's shoulder with one hand and Dex's with the other. "I expect to see you two later. After you've talked." She nodded. "I'll save you some spaghetti." She gave each of their shoulders a squeeze before she brushed past Emma and met Bill at the door, where he stood waiting with her coat. "And bring a plate of cookies."

Emma waited until they were out the door before she turned her attention to Dex. She looked good, so good Emma couldn't take her eyes off her. "Well, this is awkward." Emma rubbed her forehead. "I don't know what my mother was thinking."

"I asked her if I could come."

"You did?" The surprise in Emma's voice slipped out involuntarily. "I mean, why?"

"I miss you, Em. Your smile, your laugh, your eyes. I've missed you every moment of every day since you left me standing in the street."

The vision of that day popped into her head, and her stomach knotted. She wanted to go to Dex, take her in her arms, and tell her she'd missed her more than she could say. Instead, she forced herself to back up and lean against the counter. They still had a huge problem to deal with. "What about Grace?" She knew what Brent had told her but still wanted to hear it from Dex.

"Grace and I are taking a break from our friendship for a while." She propped herself against the opposite counter and grasped the edge of the granite. "Turns out I need to work on my independence from her and she needs to work on her communication with Brent." Dex let out a heavy breath. "I was an idiot not to have seen it sooner."

"Oh." A surge of hope filled Emma, and she had to physically calm herself by taking hold of the counter too.

"Oh? That's it?"

Emma tilted her head. "Well, I'm not going to disagree with you. You were an idiot." She suppressed a smile.

"I'm really sorry, Em. I should've never let you drive away that day." She kneaded the counter with her fingers. "What I felt for Grace wasn't love. It was some kind of fucked-up sense of obligation. A lifelong codependence. That's done now, Em. I promise."

"Don't you say that if you don't mean it." Emma's voice trembled, emotion ready to spill out any moment.

"I meant every word." Dex pushed off the counter and crossed the kitchen, closing the distance between them. "I never knew what love really was until I met you. I've never felt for anyone the way I feel for you, and if you'll have me I'll spend the rest of my life showing you how much I love you." She took Emma's face in her hands and kissed her gently.

Each one of Emma's senses zapped to life as the kiss deepened. She felt at home again, with Dex, right here in this very moment.

She broke the kiss and let her forehead rest against Dex's. "I love you too."

Dex wrapped her arms around Emma, and she melted into her. Tears mixed with kisses as they held each other for close to an hour. Emma never wanted to leave the warmth of Dex's arms again.

"I'm such a mess." Emma laughed as she wiped the tears from her cheeks and stared into Dex's eyes. "I'm so glad you're here." In a matter of minutes her life was good again. Her bah-humbug Christmas had morphed into the most wonderful holiday ever.

Dex glanced at the counter and shrugged. "I had to come. Who would've made the cookies?"

Emma chuckled. "I've never loved Christmas cookies more in my life than I do right now."

Dex's eyes sparkled as the lights from the Christmas tree reflected in them. Emma could never forget how the sunbursts danced brightly in the emerald-green pools whenever they locked with hers. She had no idea why she'd ever let anyone take that gaze away.

The game wasn't even half over, and Dex was losing badly at *Super Mario Kart.* Emma's nephews Tyler and Jake had been taking turns showing Dex the rear ends of their cars. Now that Emma had joined the game, she'd taken the lead, and Dex was still dead last. The competitive streak definitely ran in the family. Emma huddled closely on the couch as the game ended and smiled up at Dex.

She shook her head. "Do you always win?"

Emma scrunched her nose. "Pretty much."

She leaned near and kissed Emma, tingling as she thought about the bet they'd made. Dex was getting smarter. She'd made a wager that would benefit them both later that night, and she couldn't wait to pay up.

"Come on, boys. It's time for presents." Glo stood in the threshold of the door and shooed them out. "You two as well."

Dex had brought presents for the boys as well as one for Emma's parents. She and Emma had exchanged their gifts for each other throughout the night and into the early morning. Then they'd lain in bed, wrapped up in each other, watching the sun rise through the bedroom window. Waking up with Emma was the most precious gift in the world.

They'd spent the rest of the morning working at the homeless shelter serving Christmas dinner. Emma had stood right alongside Dex dishing out food and mingling with people and was a natural. Juni and Josh had been there as well, and they'd gotten to know Emma better. Juni had told Emma she'd been rooting for her all along and was so glad to see her and Dex together. It seemed that Juni was Emma's biggest fan. After they finished and were headed to Emma's parents' house, Emma had told Dex she'd found the whole experience totally fulfilling, and they'd made a pact to do it together every year.

Dex and Emma settled in on the couch, and Bill handed everyone a present, with the largest in front of Emma's mom.

"I bet I know what this is," Glo sang out as she ripped the paper off the wooden creation. Her face dropped. "What exactly is this?"

"Oops." Bill jumped up, took it from her, and set it on Dex's lap.

"For me?" It was a cordless tool-charging station just like Bill had made for his garage.

"Yeah. You said you liked mine."

"Wow. This is…" She swallowed to keep the tears from forming in her eyes. She set it on the coffee table in front of her, then bolted up and hugged Bill.

He squeezed her and patted her on the back. "I'm glad you like it."

"I absolutely love it." She hugged him much longer than necessary before she dropped onto the couch and stared at it. She'd never had anyone make her anything so special. Emma took her hand and squeezed it. This was turning out to be the best Christmas ever.

Bill retrieved the other large present from under the tree and handed it to Glo. "This one's for you."

She opened it and squealed. "My bird feeder." She held it up for everyone to see. "It's perfect."

Dex sucked in a deep breath. She loved her mother and father, but seeing them on Christmas Day wasn't something she could ever count on. Here, she was in the midst of Emma's family, and her heart was full. The love they shared for each other was overwhelming. It was the perfect holiday with the perfect girl and her perfect family. Dex couldn't ask for anything more in her life right now.

EPILOGUE

The day couldn't have been more perfect if Dex's fairy godmother had conjured it up with her magic wand. The sun was shining, and there wasn't a cloud in the sky. The temperature had topped out at seventy-four degrees, and a mild breeze had kept the guests comfortable in their seats. The fall weather had cooperated perfectly for the outdoor ceremony. Dex and Emma had decided to keep the wedding small and spend the bulk of the money they'd saved this past year on their honeymoon, of which the destination was yet to be determined.

The day had been perfect. Dex couldn't believe how lucky she was, and the permanent grin on her face made it clear she was right where she wanted to be. Her eyes welled as she watched her lovely bride stroll onto the perfectly polished hardwood area centering the room. Dex had hit the jackpot. Emma was both captivatingly sexy and irresistibly sweet. Dressed in a simple white dress that fit her curves perfectly, Emma turned and blew her a kiss. The jolt zapped through Dex as it always did when she looked at her that way. They'd been together almost a year now, and Emma still took her breath away. Emma waved at the crowd of women who'd gathered in front of her and spun around. Dex winked at her, Emma sailed the bouquet into the air across the dance floor, and women scrambled for it. There would be no sadness today, no drunken sobbing, only tears of joy as the new chapter in their lives began.

Dex's world had shifted into a new realm of happiness, and Emma had been the cause. She guessed she should thank Grace for putting her in that pitiful, hopeless state at her wedding where Emma had found her last year. But the one she was really grateful for was Emma.

She'd put up with more than she should have, more than most women *would* have. She'd put herself on the line and waited Dex out until her heart was finally free of Grace, and it had been worth it. Dex couldn't imagine her life with anyone else.

As the band began to play, Dex took Emma into her arms and spun her around the dance floor.

"I'm not sure how, but it seems you won the bet this time." Emma's soft, silvery-blue eyes sparkled as she gazed at Dex.

"I may have had some inside information." They both glanced over at Juni, who was clutching the bouquet as she danced with Josh. "She's a scrapper, that one. Always could take me down."

"I'd like to try to take you down." Emma's eyes darkened to the steely blue hue Dex adored.

"No contest there. I surrender." Dex kissed her, and all in her world felt right.

She couldn't wait for the party to be over. They would leave for their honeymoon in the morning, a road trip. The wager between them had been their destination—West or East Coast. The sign on the back of their car would read California or Bust. Emma had never been to San Francisco, and Dex was looking forward to showing her all the sights. But tonight they would go back to the place where, without even realizing it, Dex had first come to know the essence of Emma one bleary-eyed morning last September. Soon they'd be wrapped up in each other under a wonderfully warm fleece blanket in what was now *their* home, and she planned to live happily ever after in that very spot.

About the Author

Dena Blake grew up in a small town just north of San Francisco where she learned to play softball, ride motorcycles, and grow vegetables. She eventually moved with her family to the Southwest, where she began creating vivid characters in her mind and bringing them to life on paper.

Dena currently lives in the Southwest with her partner and is constantly amazed at what she learns from her two children. She's a would-be chef, tech nerd, and occasional auto mechanic who has a weakness for dark chocolate and a good cup of coffee.

Books Available From Bold Strokes Books

A Wish Upon a Star by Jeannie Levig. Erica Cooper has learned to depend on only herself, but when her new neighbor, Leslie Raymond, befriends Erica's special needs daughter, the walls protecting Erica's heart threaten to crumble. (978-1-163555-274-4)

Answering the Call by Ali Vali. Detective Sept Savoie returns to the streets of New Orleans, as do the dead bodies from ritualistic killings, and she does everything in her power to bring their killers to justice while trying to keep her partner, Keegan Blanchard, safe. (978-1-163555-050-4)

Friends Without Benefits by Dena Blake. When Dex Putman gets the woman she thought she always wanted, she soon wonders if it's really love after all. (978-1-163555-349-9)

Invalid Evidence by Stevie Mikayne. Private Investigator Jil Kidd is called away to investigate a possible killer whale, just when her partner Jess needs her most. (978-1-163555-307-9)

Pursuit of Happiness by Carsen Taite. When attorney Stevie Palmer's client reveals a scandal that could derail Senator Meredith Mitchell's presidential bid, their chance at love may be collateral damage. (978-1-163555-044-3)

Seascape by Karis Walsh. Marine biologist Tess Hansen returns to Washington's isolated northern coast, where she struggles to adjust to small-town living while courting an endowment from Brittany James for her orca research center. (978-1-163555-079-5)

Second In Command by VK Powell. Jazz Perry's life is disrupted and her career jeopardized when she becomes personally involved with the case of an abandoned child and the child's competent but strict social worker, Emory Blake. (978-1-163555-185-3)

Taking Chances by Erin McKenzie. When Valerie Cruz and Paige Wellington clash over what's in the best interest of the children in Valerie's care, the children may be the ones who teach them it's worth taking chances for love. (978-1-163555-209-6)

Breaking Down Her Walls by Erin Zak. Could a love worth staying for be the key to breaking down Julia Finch's walls? (978-1-63555-369-7)

All of Me by Emily Smith. When chief surgical resident Galen Burgess meets her new intern, Rowan Duncan, she may finally discover that doing what you've always done will only give you what you've always had. (978-1-163555-321-5)

As the Crow Flies by Karen F. Williams. Romance seems to be blooming all around, but problems arise when a restless ghost emerges from the ether to roam the dark corners of this haunting tale. (978-1-163555-285-0)

Both Ways by Ileandra Young. SPEAR agent Danika Karson races to protect the city from a supernatural threat and must rely on the woman she's trained to despise: Rayne, an achingly beautiful vampire. (978-1-163555-298-0)

Calendar Girl by Georgia Beers. Forced to work together, Addison Fairchild and Kate Cooper discover that opposites really do attract. (978-1-163555-333-8)

Cash and the Sorority Girl by Ashley Bartlett. Cash Braddock doesn't want to deal with morality, drugs, or people. Unfortunately, she's going to have to. (978-1-163555-310-9)

Lovebirds by Lisa Moreau. Two women from different worlds collide in a small California mountain town, each with a mission that doesn't include falling in love. (978-1-163555-213-3)

Media Darling by Fiona Riley. Can Hollywood bad girl Emerson and reluctant celebrity gossip reporter Hayley work together to make each other's dreams come true? Or will Emerson's secrets ruin not one career, but two? (978-1-163555-278-2)

Stroke of Fate by Renee Roman. Can Sean Moore live up to her reputation and save Jade Rivers from the stalker determined to end Jade's career and, ultimately, her life? (978-1-163555-162-4)